praise for robert a. burton's doc-in-a-box

"Taut, blackly comic and unrelenting. This novel, like its surgeon's scalpel, cuts close to the bone."

—*The New York Times Book Review*

"Terse . . . hard-edged."

—*The Los Angeles Times*

"A compelling first novel . . . don't plan to talk to anyone for the next several hours."

—*San Francisco Chronicle*

"Wonderful—tightly written with a truly unique perspective. This book has real depth."

—*Los Angeles Reader*

Also by Robert A. Burton

Doc-in-a-Box

Final Therapy

>cellmates

>cellmates

robert a. burton

AN AUTHORS GUILD BACKINPRINT.COM EDITION

Cellmates

AN AUTHORS GUILD BACKINPRINT.COM EDITION

Published by iUniverse, Inc.

For information address:
iUniverse, Inc.
2021 Pine Lake Road, Suite 100
Lincoln, NE 68512
www.iuniverse.com

Originally published by Russian Hill Press

Book design by razor riders grp

ISBN: 0-595-32970-5

Printed in the United States of America

TO ADRIANNE

ONE

Artie singleton stood at the rear counter of Shazam, his cluttered Columbus Avenue store known for its extensive collection of old comic books and hypertext CD-ROM fiction. By afternoon the shop's three aisles would be jammed with those seeking nostalgia alongside those rooting for the demise of traditional narrative. Artie loved the balance, often provoking agitated exchanges between customers trying to move time in opposite directions.

So far it'd been a slow morning, foggy outside, dreary inside, only a handful of browsers. He missed the idle chatter, a request for a free demo at one of the half-dozen computers filling the central aisle—any opportunity to step away from his own life and move someone else's characters through an infinitude of possibilities.

A young couple, similarly androgynous in black leather and spiked pink hair, entered, headed for the *Wonder Woman* section. They wanted to be noticed; Artie ignored them.

"You got any copies of the November 1941 *War Nurse*?" the woman asked.

"Fresh out," Artie said, not wanting her to have the only copy, which was primo and went for fifty, no negotiations. He kept the one-of-a-kinds in a separate bin behind the counter.

"We're down from Petaluma. Your store's supposed to have everything." The man spoke through clenched teeth. He was sucking on a purple toothpick.

"*War Nurse* is hard to come by. Scarce as house calls."

"Come on, let's go," the woman said to her friend. But the man was thumbing through the January 1982 issue of *Scripture Man*.

"Dig this," he said, pointing to a panel where Scripture Man was reciting from the Book of Job. The man stepped onto a footstool at the end of the aisle and began reading aloud.

"'Have you got human eyes; do you see as mankind sees? You, who inquire into my faults and investigate my sins, you know very well that I am innocent.'" He thrust his clenched fist aloft in an exclamation of victory.

"Finish the quote," Artie said.

The man shook his head.

"Give me that." Artie grabbed the book and began reading, his voice booming in the high-ceilinged store. "'No one,'" he paused and looked at the couple. "'And no one can rescue me from your hand.'" Artie gave the comic back to the man.

The man stepped down from the chair. "One man's opinion. Right, hon?" The woman wasn't listening. "So how much?" he asked Artie.

"Twenty dollars."

"Only two when it was new," the man said, pointing at the price on the cover.

"The item's hot. *Scripture Man* may be advance word of the second coming."

"My friends warned me about you." The man scowled as he unzipped his jacket, pulled out a wad of ones and handed twenty to Artie.

Artie shrugged as he shoved the money in his pocket. "You want a receipt? If you're clergy, this could be deductible." But the man was through with Artie. He had his arm around his girl-friend, their hands in each other's rear pocket.

"Investigate my sins," he said to her as they left the store. "You game?"

The door closed. Artie did not hear her reply.

He picked up the original February 1940 issue of *Captain Marvel*. In the first few frames Billy Batson was selling newspapers and sleeping outside the railroad station. A whirl of old papers floated up from the gutter. The squat art deco station, as always, was ominous with loss and premonition. His father must have known he would die young, before he could share the comics with his only son. Why else would he have kept each of them separately wrapped in clear plastic, filed chronologically, thirty boxes labeled THE EXCLUSIVE PROPERTY OF ARTIE SINGLETON.

Artie was sorry that his father hadn't lived to witness the rise in the value of collectible Americana. Five boxes had covered the down payment on Shazam. The rest had been his startup inventory. The best he'd sorted into two boxes that he kept in a special case: FOR DISPLAY ONLY. NOT FOR SALE.

Holding onto Captain Marvel, he paced the aisles, seeking distraction.

His father died when he was three, his mother a month ago, though he had been expecting it for years. By the time he graduated from high school, she was asking his friends to repeat their names. Artie would cringe with embarrassment. Later, alone with his friends, he would joke that his sour personality stemmed from drinking outdated mother's milk. The accompanying look of disgust was always good for an uncomfortable laugh.

He never meant anything by it.

Mary Singleton had been a psychiatric social worker, Montessori school volunteer, Sierra Club member, weekend watercolorist, devotee of Jung until she discovered his anti-Semitism, three years each a Unitarian, Christian Scientist, Ram Dass follower, then a long final stretch of generalized ecumenical ardor. Above all else, she had been Artie's best friend, pal, and advocate. He was her sublime gift, coming to her when she had abandoned all hope of bearing children.

After his father's death, she'd raised Artie in a small North Beach flat. A sixties UC grad, her heart was hardline Berkeley, complete with a simultaneous emphasis on academics and rebellion. "I want you kicked out of Harvard, not some community college," she offered as guidance and inspiration.

Artie tried. Harvard outfoxed him. When he skipped a month of classes, was found reciting Montaigne late one night to an empty Copley Square, and made a half-dozen clinic visits convinced he was the first case of a new retrovirus, his freshman advisor nodded nonjudgmentally. "These things sometimes happen." During a telephone conference, the student health psychiatrist assured Mrs. Singleton that her boy was decent, not by nature a troublemaker.

Harvard gave him advanced placement and an independent study program. Not required to attend classes, hand in papers, or take tests, his eccentricities tolerated, even encouraged, Artie was stymied. His energy improved; his dry cough mysteriously disappeared—as did his urge to read aloud.

He considered then rejected political involvement. Student unrest was a given; Harvard Yard was pockmarked with clusters of the discontented. Drugs and booze were ubiquitous. Rebellion had lost its teeth, had been reduced to a social event.

Artie graduated *summa cum laude* in American literature.

"Perhaps you could get expelled from grad school," his mother said at the commencement exercise.

It was the last time they joked together.

Forgetfulness escalated.

"A virulent form of Alzheimer's," the neurologist had said.

"You remind me of someone I once knew," said his mother, before sentences faded into pauses.

Two years of his life were put on hold while she unraveled in a drab nursing home fronted by a cold blue wheelchair ramp and reeking of disinfectant. His only flesh and blood.

It was about time he got functional again. He could start by finishing the final draft of his hypertext disk *Clothesline*—a courtroom drama shaped by the reader's choice of apparel. Fifty outfits in the opening-chapter jury closet. *Pick the jury*, said the flashing menu. Each piece of clothing was linked to different judgments and world views. There was a wardrobe closet for the judge; he gave different jury instructions depending on whether he wore single- versus double-breasted, high boots or cordovan lace-ups. There were other menu closets for the attorneys and the defendant. The trials ranged from two days to three weeks; each morning the reader was required to dress all the participants.

Outfitting the judge with white shoes affected the sentence and terms of probation. Tassels upped the bail. A wide paisley tie increased the odds for community service. Lorgnettes made contempt of court more likely. A judge with a long ponytail was a joker, programmed for random unpredictable sentences.

A simple metaphor: appearance is outcome.

Artie couldn't get back into the groove. He'd been a jerk, insensitivity squared. After the doctor's visit—*the doctor's visit*—he'd shrugged and said, "Don't worry, Mom, in a couple days you'll forget all about this." He did remember putting his arm around her, stroking her hair while she tried not to cry. He hadn't meant it to sound that way. Honestly.

The words echoed, clung to his mind, tilted his mood.

His IQ had been clocked at over 160, but going in the wrong direction. Smug, self-centered, constantly mocking. Even his sense of humor was a dangerous weapon.

ed graduate school. By now he'd have his PHD and his own university cubicle. No, he'd told his advisor. That'd be like being assigned to the lower galley in the slave ship of letters.

"Comics and hyperfiction—now that's the ticket."

To his surprise, his store had become a magnet for the outrageous, the scorned, the academics, the trendy. Shazam was hot in the local mags; he got plenty of party invites and shots at the lovelies.

He was rolling, he told himself as he shoved the wad of dollar bills in the register and waited for the fog to lift.

TWO

Trying to ignore the pain under her ribs and along her lower spine, Sarah Woolfson pulled a cardboard box from the rear of her closet. Inside were hundreds of photos. The earliest were neatly labeled in a hand-cut leather album, the more recent ones compiled in packets and held together by rubber bands. Slowly, with her right foot, she pushed the box toward her bed. She paused twice to catch her breath.

The effort was worth it. She would go through the photos one at a time, then put them away. For good, she thought, at the same time trying to ignore the knowledge of how little time she had left.

She was glad Hank had gone first. She'd hate for him to see her like this. Barely ninety pounds, bent like a question mark, only sandy wisps of her once-wild blond hair remaining. The pain was bad enough, but she never believed she'd end up this color, her skin like old Camembert, an announcement of cancer's ripening. She tried to imagine herself as a fireball of sex and love, dancing the night away at the old Fillmore, Hank's admiring look frozen in the flickering strobe lights.

Yes, it was okay this way. She would tie together the loose ends.

Last week had been Rosh Hashana. She wasn't religious and wasn't the least bit interested in celebrating the new year. But tomorrow would be Yom Kippur, a day to clear the slate and settle old wrongs. Maybe she would fast, though the word *fast* had lost its significance. Not eating was no longer a sacrifice.

She considered. There was no reason to be apologetic for what she'd done. *In vitro* fertilizations had been standard practice for nearly twenty years. Reproductive clinics were big business, the daily newspapers filled with endorsements and advertisements that even included pricing. Some couples were choosing the procedure over natural conception. Pre-implantation genetic testing could detect a host of illnesses—suboptimal or imperfect embryos could be discarded. Talk shows debated whether *not* undergoing preimplantation diagnostics represented an unnecessary risk. Disabled children were suing their parents for allowing them to have been born.

Sarah felt that science had gone too far, the new testing giving natural conception the peculiar stigma of being unfair to the unborn.

She wasn't interested in science, had only been trying to help women who couldn't have children on their own. To have known that the technique was available and to have done nothing would have been immoral.

She and Hank had tried to anticipate the unforeseeable. Countless sleepless nights were spent debating whether or not the children should know of each other's existence. Of course that was impossible—the legal implications were too great. They tried to comprehend an immense number of *what-ifs*. What if a child wanted to meet his biological parents? His brothers? What if the biological parents claimed rights to the children? And so on.

But they hadn't imagined the extraordinary advances in the technology of organ transplantation.

Each of the children had perfect matches. To leave them in ignorance would be withholding a potentially life-saving treatment in an emergency.

Sarah had chosen to die at home. The morning nurse had opened all the windows in the house. It was a spectacular Indian summer day; blue jays and hummingbirds jockeyed for position on the feeder hanging just beyond the bedroom window.

She missed Hank. She was sorry she'd never see another fall.

She rolled on her side, feeling a fullness and dull pain. Not enough to worry her. She was beyond that. A hummingbird floated at the window, looking at her. She nodded, composing her letter.

THREE

If I knock off the whole family, then later change my mind, can I work my way backwards in the program and choose another path?" Welinda Dupré asked. She was a tall, bony woman in her late twenties, with short, frizzy, carrot-red hair and tiny Ben Franklin glasses that accentuated the narrowness of her heavily freckled face. Normally, customers sat at the computer station in the center aisle. Welinda stood, hunched over, her body in constant motion. She was playing the new hypertext *Autobiography*, a program which allowed nearly infinite constructions and revisions of a life story.

"You'd have to start over," Artie said from behind the counter. "There are specific rules against backtracking on family decisions of that magnitude."

"What if I make an act of contrition?"

"That only works for verbal insults and minor mayhem, not murder."

"I thought anything was possible in fiction."

"Some values are absolutes. If you want a program that abandons one-way time, try *Cyberwalk* or *Quantum Leap*."

"I was really looking for a domestic drama that allowed time to go in both directions."

"Aren't we all?"

"You're a smart guy—why don't you write one?"

"Narrative requires a forward impulse. And responsibility for choices."

"But disassembled time would be a perfect rebuttal to cause and effect."

"Welinda. I'm trying to do my mail and make an honest buck. Besides, your hour is up. It's another ten dollars, or the machine goes blank."

The six computers in the center of the store averaged nearly five hundred a day in rentals. Customers who would browse for hours before buying a five-dollar *Batman* reissue would gladly plunk down handfuls of bills for the opportunity to gain control over fictional characters. It was a comment on their sense of disenfranchisement that they applied body English to the imaginary. Witness Welinda plotting against her video mother.

Welinda changed two twenties for tens. A minute later she was back at the computer, trying to figure out the maximum punishment she could mete out to her fictional parents and still allow for subsequent reconciliation. It was tricky—the paths weren't obvious. A wrong turn and she might be abandoned, ignored, orphaned, or disinherited. Welinda took copious notes, moved slowly through the text. Artie figured she was good for another two hours, minimum. To cover her costs, Welinda relieved Artie some nights and the occasional weekend. Though he took the public stance, often and loudly, that man must pay for his addictions, especially the electronic, Artie often charged Welinda half-price, sometimes nothing at all. He would make a ceremony of taking her money, only to give it back as inflated wages.

Welinda—intermittently employed software designer, blues pianist, world-class game freak, second-degree black belt in karate—was his friend. They had met when she was on the rebound from a blowhard saxophonist, and had briefly flirted with romance. "You give great action, but it's starting to feel like incest,"

Welinda had said at the conclusion of their last sexual outing. To his surprise, Artie had agreed; they fit better as brother and sister. With a curious absence of embarrassment or self-consciousness, they shifted from lovers to best friends, Welinda confiding when there was something juicy to confide, but mostly just hanging out with Artie.

Artie glanced down at this week's mail forwarded from his mother's last nursing home. It was mostly junk. *Time* offering three years, eighty percent off newsstand prices. AARP sponsoring an Alaskan cruise. UC Hospital having a half-off colonoscopy week. A hundred dollars for an ounce of prevention.

Endless catalogues.

One day he would have his mom's name scratched from the various sucker mailing lists. Not yet. Somehow junk mail mitigated her death.

He looked at an envelope from Sarah Woolfson, one of his mom's oldest friends. Put it with the others, he told himself. Wait until you're less emotional. But the address was written in a feeble script that begged for a prompt reply. It was his moral obligation, the son's last rites.

Welinda was coming up the aisle. "You got a smoke? I've got Mom at the doctor's. It could be cancer, it could be a benign lump. Tough call. I miss her already."

Artie pointed to the NO SMOKING sign over the register. He offered Welinda a stick of gum. "Better for your health, especially if cancer runs in the family."

Welinda stood at the register, chewing and thinking. Artie opened the envelope and started to read.

September 23
Dear Mary,
I hope this letter finds you well and in good spirits. I know I promised not to write. Then again, maybe I should have written sooner.

There is something that you need to know. All the children came from a single embryo. Arthur has nine genetically identical brothers.

I have the names of the other mothers, though it's been a long time and I doubt that the addresses are current. I'm not sure what to do, but we should talk as soon as possible. There's more that I need to explain.

If you'd rather, I'll speak to Arthur directly. I leave that up to you.

P.S. I've just come across some great shots of us at Berkeley, including one of you with Mario Savio. Remind me to show them to you.

Love from your old friend,
Sarah

Artie grabbed the cash register.

"You okay?" Welinda asked.

"Huh?" Artie said. He stared at the letter vibrating in his hands. "Yeah, I'm fine. Just some minor illness in distant family. Go on, you better get back to your mom. She could be needing you."

"Unlikely. She's probably still filling out forms in the waiting room."

"Welinda. Please."

Artie waited until Welinda was back at the computer before he read the letter again.

It was inconceivable, a practical joke. Artie checked the envelope for clues. The handwriting looked like an old person's. The envelope was posted from the Nicasio post office. His mother had mentioned Sarah, and the good old days at Berkeley. She'd never hinted that she was a jokester.

"It's benign," Welinda hollered from the center of the store. "But we have to repeat the biopsy in two hours. Pretty clever program, if you ask me."

"I've got something important to do," Artie said. "Could you watch the store for a few minutes?"

"Minimum wage is an extra hour."

"Sure."

Alcohol gave him cluster headaches. He didn't care. He slipped next door to Valentino's where he downed three aspirin and two double shots of tequila. With his head pounding, his left eye ready to burst, he walked the three blocks to his North Beach apartment and checked his mother's address book. Sure enough, Sarah Woolfson was listed.

He dialed the number. *Yes, this is the home of Sarah Woolfson,* someone said. *But she's sleeping now. What's your name? Yes, she was expecting your call. If you'd like, you could come for a visit.*

Artie made arrangements, hung up the phone, took two more aspirin. He considered another drink, but his brain felt about to explode. He grabbed his pillow, wrapped it around his head, and concentrated on the throbbing. Better than thinking about the possibilities of the letter; at least the headache was a familiar pain that eventually would wear off.

FOUR

Sometimes Sarah hoped to die in her sleep. Sometimes she imagined the disease slowing. To be well again was beyond her imagination. But to see the springtime. The leafless fruit trees outside her window would be blossoming by mid February. Glorious whites and pinks. That was within reason, within hope and feasibility.

Today she wasn't wishing for springtime, only that the room smelled fresh and that she seemed presentable.

The photo album was on the nightstand, next to her pills, glasses of mineral water, and fresh apple and prune juice. Sarah lifted it, balanced it on her chest. It was heavier than she'd remembered, as though it were her final ledger.

She had done other things with her life. Her marriage had been a work of art, she and Hank crafting their days into a series of finely polished moments. That alone was a singular accomplishment. And she had been a hard, dedicated worker.

But the boys, that was different. A contribution.

Her hands trembled as she flipped through the pages. All of the mothers had sent photos early on. Most came in plain envelopes. Mary had sent yearly birthday snapshots. Though Arthur looked like all the others, Sarah saw a special twinkle. The most recent was of Arthur graduating from high school. He was already taller than six feet, with a narrow face, dark curly hair, and quiet brooding good looks—though in one snapshot he was mugging for the camera, his smile definitely mischievous. Sarah suspected a complex personality, a man of contradictions. And attractive.

Mary occasionally included an update, including circumspect allusion to Arthur's adjustment problems and scrapes with school authorities. She had sent a copy of his acceptance letter to Harvard. Then the letters stopped.

Sarah wanted to phone, but that wasn't part of the agreement. "I will not contact you unless there is a medical necessity," she had promised each of the mothers, including Mary. It was only fair. From the beginning she and Hank had expected that the mothers would want to distance themselves. When the photos stopped and the addresses were not updated, they told themselves that it was because of the fear of potential criminal implications. They knew better. They were tainted.

Sometimes they felt hurt. At other times their secret was a lovely stain that gave their life a quiet dignity. Still, she would have liked to have heard from them, from the mothers and the sons. Seen how they were doing, how they turned out.

She took comfort in the early photographs, looking at them over and over through the years, imagining.

Mary's son was coming to visit.

Her first impression of Arthur: kind, perhaps a little too intense, and definitely sexy in his clean white t-shirt, faded jeans, and worn leather flight jacket. She loved his fine features and his long tapered fingers, like those of a nobleman in an El Greco painting.

For the moment she forgot her pain. She felt light, buoyant, immensely relieved.

Carolyn, the day attendant, brought a wooden slat-backed chair from the kitchen, placed it near the head of Sarah's bed.

She fluffed up Sarah's pillows, made sure that she was comfortable, then left the room. Sarah motioned for Artie to sit.

One look at Sarah and Artie knew that this was not a joke. He wanted to ask all the questions at once. He also wanted to hear nothing, to get up and run from the room. If he didn't know, maybe it hadn't happened, wasn't true, was only a rumor, a vicious nightmare dragged into the light. Possibilities remained as long as he was in the dark. He had the feeling of being in a doctor's office, waiting for a biopsy result that would forever change his life. And it wasn't a game, not like Welinda and her CD-ROM mother.

Sarah was staring and smiling. "So you're Mary's son," she said. She took Artie's hand and held it lightly.

"You knew her at Berkeley?"

"I'll say. Your mom was special. I've got stories, but she'd shoot me if . . ." Sarah's voice became even softer. "She's okay?"

Artie explained about the Alzheimer's.

Sarah's eyes misted over and she looked out the window. "I wish I'd known. I figured she had her reasons for not keeping in touch. But not that." She wiped her eyes. "It's never how you imagine it. Life. Death. Anything." She turned back to Artie. "I wish I could have said goodbye."

Artie shifted in his chair.

Sarah raised her hand. "You don't have to ask. It was such a beautiful craziness. Naturally we'd have liked our own, but it wasn't in the cards. Then Henry perfected his technique. We wanted to do . . . something." Sarah shrugged, her bed jacket bunching up against her bird-thin neck.

"Technique?"

"It's so simple when you think about it. Identical twins occur when a developing embryo accidentally splits into two. Henry was a reproductive biologist. He was doing research at a fertility clinic when he developed a special wire loop and a micropipette that allowed him to artificially induce twinning. We did it once, took a half of one embryo. One time only. Once we had our own embryo, we were able to duplicate the divisions several more times. The actual parents had their child and we made ten infertile women into mothers.

"Who were they?" The phrase *real parents* popped into Artie's mind, but he quickly dismissed it. Not parents. Donors. As in kidneys, corneas, hearts. It was a matter of degree. They may have donated everything, but they were not his parents.

"Henry never said, except that one was a brilliant scientist and the other a famous novelist."

"You have no idea?"

"He felt it was wiser that they remained anonymous, even to me."

Sarah looked away. She knew. Artie was certain of it. He wanted to press the point, but didn't, uncertain how he would feel if he had names. So far there was still the possibility of some misunderstanding. Names would eliminate even that modest hope.

"So all ten were from the same embryo?" he asked.

Sarah nodded.

"The way embryos are cleaved for prenatal genetic diagnostics?" Artie had seen scientists on TV separating out a single cell; it looked like a technically difficult but simple-minded procedure, mainly a matter of hand-eye coordination.

Again Sarah nodded.

"You have any pictures?"

Sarah motioned to the album. Artie hesitated, fingering the leather-covered album tentatively as though it might explode or, worse yet, open onto an alternate universe. He took a deep breath, spread his feet, planting them firmly, as if a proper stance and good balance might soften the blow.

The album was arranged chronologically. Artie glanced at the first page, tried to turn away, but kept coming back to the frightful sameness. The only differences were in the camera angles, the lighting, the quality of the prints. The photos reverberated like an infinity of reflections in barbershop mirrors. Artie had to remind himself that each picture represented a different person.

He was surprised to see how chubby he'd been as a baby. How chubby all of them had been. How they'd all had the same growth spurt at ten—the childhood fat melting away, each of them reduced to spindly arms and legs in photo after photo, the gawkiness of adolescence emerging like the arrival of a season.

"Which one's me?" His mouth was dry, his voice uneven.

Sarah reached over and, one at a time, lifted up a free edge of several of the photos. "I tried to write your name on the back of all the pictures your mom sent. Let's see." Sarah continued looking, examining at least a dozen baby snapshots before she stopped. "There, that's you." She pointed to his name printed in red felt-tip pen.

"You sure?" He looked for some sense of himself in this early photo. But the surrounding identical faces were too distracting. And neutralizing. He could have easily seen himself in any of them. Or none of them.

"There. That one's also you," Sarah said after examining the back of several more photos. "I think you're about two in this one."

"This is definitely me?"

"You have my word."

"I'm not questioning, but it seems these photos would be so easy to mislabel."

"Henry was a perfectionist. That's you. You can count on it."

Artie flipped through the first few pages, then, on a hunch, turned to the back. There was a photograph of what appeared to be a fertilized egg viewed under a microscope. The next was of a two-celled egg. Then a four-celled egg, then two four-celled eggs.

"Henry wanted to document the very beginning. He was the scientist in the family."

"We all came from this?" Artie pointed at the picture of the single cell.

"Your mom and dad couldn't have their own. They tried everything. I told them that it was experimental, illegal, maybe immoral. But you should have seen how happy they were."

He returned to the front of the book and began to trace the faces through the years. The photos made him dizzy. It was like trying to assign significance to a row of identical numbers, cans of soup, grains of sand.

He wanted to ask, "How could you?" but realized the inanity of the question. If she hadn't, he wouldn't be here asking why. He had no moral grounds for criticism. No. He should be overwhelmed with gratitude. Better than saving his life, she had created his life. He tried to hand her the pictures, but she declined.

"You keep them. They're no use to me anymore."

"Some of the others might want to see them. I'm sure you'll be getting other calls."

Sarah shook her head. "You're the only one I've contacted. I'm not sure if any of the other addresses are current. It's been a long time since I've heard from the other mothers. I was hoping that you could—"

"I'd rather not. Just knowing is more than enough."

"You could locate the others, arrange for a meeting."

"Ten of us in a single room?" Artie picked at his cuticle. A thickness in his throat made it difficult to swallow. Ten of him wearing *Hello, my name is* nametags, milling and comparing. He coughed, trying to dislodge the feeling.

"Mary said you were a good boy. Smart and sensitive. All at once would be too much. You find them, meet them, one at a time. Explain what Henry and I did. Let them understand."

Artie looked at the night table, at the juices and vials of pills. It was a simple request.

"I'd hoped that you'd never know. Then again, I've always wanted a big family." She made a sweeping motion with her hand, her gaze wandering over the room. "Henry's been gone five years." She reached over and touched the photo album. "Sometimes, late at night, I imagine you boys . . ."

She made a small dismissive gesture. "Don't mind an old woman's ramblings." Then: "I've left a little money, care of my attorney, Bill Barrett. Use what you need." She handed Artie a business card and a single sheet of paper. On it were nine typed names. She patted Artie's hand, and the album. "Please."

Artie slipped the list and the card into the album, tucked it under his arm.

"You'll visit again? If it's not out of your way?"

Artie nodded.

"Alzheimer's. That must have been really tough on both of you."

"Is there anything I can do for you?" Artie asked as he rose from the chair. He was light-headed, and gripped the album as though it would provide support.

"You're doing it," Sarah said.

Carolyn was in the doorway. She had a syringe on a tray. Sarah held up her hand. "One last thing," she said to Artie. "I'm sure your mom was proud of you." She looked away, and said softly, "I know I am."

Artie slid into his rust-red '78 Peugeot and headed back along Lucas Valley Road, past a series of low-slung ranch houses. He entered a grove of redwoods, the fall sun filtering through the dense overhang of overlapping branches. There was a sudden drop in temperature, a coolness born of crowding. And out again into rolling hills. In the distance a single giant oak tree was outlined against the pale blue sky.

"Find the others," the dying woman had said. He should never have opened the letter. Welinda Dupré wanted a program to reverse time *and* revise the family options. Let Welinda find the others.

In movies a dying person's wish so often becomes another's obligation. But this was real life. He owed Sarah nothing.

Except his existence.

She should have considered the options, how he'd feel, how they'd all feel.

Knowing that they were ten.

What he needed was a point of view, a starter kit for how to think about his new status. Ten identical brothers reeked of cheap science fiction. The idea of a new family of ten was hokey, with its hall-of-mirrors reunions, a constant stream of cards and letters, brotherly love by the carload. Brothers coming out of the woodwork. Under the sofa. Sharing every achievement and thought.

He could see himself as an individual defrocked, reduced to a carbon copy, or he could see his future filled with the coziness of family. He knew better—either choice required an overwhelming dose of self-deceit.

Artie drove quickly, skidding around several tight corners. The sound of squealing tires reminded him that he was only inches from the rock-and-gravel shoulder and the grove of redwoods beyond. Rounding the curves, he was in control of his destiny. In this small movement he played a role.

The curves soon gave way to a long, straight stretch of road. He might as well be on autopilot, his presence at the wheel no longer necessary. Fine. There was one other option. He could drive back to the city, burn the photos and Sarah's letter. He could pray for repression to set in. Perhaps in time the others could be reduced to a forgotten nightmare.

This notion lasted a few seconds, until another wave of unreality swept over him.

He was a clone. A fucking clone.

He wanted to blame Sarah, as though he might have somehow come into existence without her. Perhaps he'd have appeared as someone else.

Nonsense. California hooey.

To make it worse, Sarah had been his mother's friend. He owed it to his mom. By getting in touch with each of the others he could make amends for his cruel comments to her. It could be an act of repentance.

Another jolt of apprehension shot down his arms.

Did the donors have their own son? Did Sarah know? Artie imagined the knock on the door, some agitated father demanding that Arthur Singleton, replicant and spare parts man, donate a lung, a piece of liver, a kidney, maybe a frontal lobe, to his son. First come, first served. Hierarchy invoked as moral precedent. He's the original, you owe it to him, the father would say, with a note of condescension. Without him you'd be nothing.

Have a heart.

The father'd drag him to his son's bedside, have Artie look down on his likeness lying in a coma—victim of mugging, auto pileup, attempted suicide. It's the least you can do, after what he did for you.

It'd be easier if we knocked him off and I took his place, Artie would answer.

He was on the road from Alpha to Gamma, he thought as he reached the on-ramp to Highway 101. He should head south, get back before Welinda gave away the store. He turned north, accelerating without destination, his foot to the floor, his mind racing in neutral.

Several times he considered calling Emily, a perfect fair-weather friend. With a spectacular body unencumbered by moral qualms, a mind the color of raw dirt, a scheme of things as superficial as icing on a puff pastry, Emily would be the optimal distraction. Artie could see her listening pseudoattentively, her hands fluttering at her hair while she waited for the conversation to swing back to her, or somebody she knew or wanted to know. Her utter indifference was what he needed. "Ten identical clones? Yeah, well, so? It's just science. You didn't think they'd stop at sheep, did you?" Emily didn't chew gum, but her attitude did.

He could bury his face in her lovely breasts. But Emily hadn't talked to him in a month. Maybe it was a mistake getting upset because she didn't want to accompany him to his mom's funeral. "I'm too young for death," she said. "Besides, Sheryl Crow is singing at Slim's. You go, take care of business, then meet me afterwards."

"It's not business," Artie had said, as though talking to himself. Not that it mattered. Emily subsequently accused Artie of being too self-absorbed, too morbid. "If I want despair, I can look up my own family." Emily's parting words.

There was no point in phoning.

He stopped fifty miles up the road, at a hamburger joint in Cloverdale. The meat was greasy, the fries clumped together. Artie scraped off the sweet pickle relish, but the hamburger was ruined, tainted with cheap Heinz.

"You got another bun?" he asked the heavyset balding counterman.

The man took the green-and-pink-stained bun and threw it in an aluminum garbage bin at the end of the counter. He gave Artie a fresh bun from a plastic bag. The motion resonated with significance. Spare parts for the hamburger.

"If I gave you back the meat, and you gave me another patty, would this still be the original hamburger?" Artie asked as he sipped on his Bud and toyed with his tasteless fries.

"No, because it'd cost double. It'd be twice the original." The man stood in front of him, his counter rag tucked into his apron. The air was suddenly thick with the smell of ammonia. "You in philosophy over at the JC?" the man asked.

"No. I'm in a quandary down in the city."

The man shrugged, still standing directly in front of Artie. The restaurant was nearly empty. Three men at the counter hunched over their coffees.

"Yes?" Artie said, feeling the man watching him.

"You didn't say thanks. For the extra bun."

"Well then, *mille fois, merci.*"

"That won't do. Not around here. And yes, if you're wondering, I'm dead serious. Everyone expects something for nothing. It's the revised American way, and it makes me sick. I've had it right up to here." The man put his hand to his throat.

"You want to hear something to make yourself sick? Imagine finding out that you're not who you think you are. That some wild scientist type has made ten of you."

"You mean as in clones?"

"Yeah. Exactly."

"Where'd you read that? *National Enquirer?*"

"Didn't read. It happened. Ten guys from one egg. You think someone not thanking you for an extra bun makes you pissed? Try that one on."

"Ten of me?" The man turned, looked in the mirror behind the counter and made a few faces at himself. He turned back to Artie, his brow furrowed with opinion. "That happened to me, I'd kill the other suckers. Kill 'em dead as old thoughts. There's enough room for one of me. Period. End of discussion."

"Pretty scary if it really happened."

"I already told you. Let's change the subject. That kind of thing is spooky, gives me the willies." The man was silent for a moment, then said, "So where'd you read it, just in case I'd like to know more?"

"Didn't read it. Heard about it. From a reliable source."

"Ten of me running around, ruining my reputation. No way. I'd shoot 'em, leave 'em right in front of the science building where they were created. So everyone could see. If they caught me, I'd plead self-defense. *Your honor, they were stealing my spirit.*"

Artie headed for Highway One and the coast, the long way back. Through the open sunroof stars clustered in a rectangle of overhead blackness. He wanted to sit by the water, hear the ocean and his thoughts clearly. When he reached the beach, he was overwhelmed by its strangeness. It was not the gentle lapping of familiar waters, but the jagged fathomless edge of the continent. How easily he could fall off, or over the palpable but invisible horizon.

He paced along the beach, trying to calm himself. The water was his friend. He was a superb swimmer, certified in scuba diving. On a dare, he'd once gone night diving off Cape Cod.

It had been fun, had reeked of romance and adventure. For a while Artie had been Harvard's underwater answer to Jack London. Artie under the waves, the others in the party remaining on the shore, fearful, mocking, envious. Artie emerging from the icy waters, stumbling up the shore, a lobster in each hand.

But if there had been ten of him, each with fistfuls of lobster and shit-eating grins?

Everything seemed cheapened. Walking the beach—as romantic recluse, thinker, jilted lover, poet—and seeing your likeness coming toward you, head down in the same manner, the same uneasy gait born of darkness and shifting sands? Would you nod or turn the other way? If, upon turning, you were to encounter another, and another? Find yourself surrounded?

"Find them," Sarah had asked him.

"Kill 'em," the counterman had said.

Only yesterday he'd been feeling sorry for himself, for his up-coming solitary Thanksgiving. Now being all alone was a superficial wound, a mere break in the skin. Preferable?

Artie felt the cold at his back, the wetness of his pants, sand in his shoes. He did not shake out the sand before sliding back behind the wheel. It made more sense to be uncomfortable, as if he might as well adjust to his new condition.

FIVE

B ig sister found little brothers," Welinda Dupré said two days later, rushing into Shazam.

Artie, standing behind the counter, put his finger to his lips. In the next aisle two teenage girls sorted through a bin of *Nightcrawler* and *Captain Future*. Artie hadn't told Welinda of his visit with Sarah Woolfson; he was afraid of being found out and becoming media fodder. He'd said the original letter was only a prank that should be checked out. Welinda said that she had friends who specialized in the DMV.

She approached the counter, holding a computer printout in her hand. "Hot off the presses. All but Mark Caputo. No need for a word of thanks," Welinda added as Artie snatched the print-out and began reading.

```
Bunker, Thomas
4 Calle Clara La Jolla, Ca. 92037
D.O.B. 3-30-63 P.O.B. Los Angeles, Ca.
Ht: 6' 2" Wt: 193 Hair: Drk Brn  Eyes: Gry
Organ Donor: No
Misdemeanors: DUI (Marijuana) 91, 93, 96.

Lafora, Paul
All Welcome Church 9 First St. Portland, Or. 97238
D.O.B. 4-3-63 P.O.B. Coos Bay, Or.
Ht: 6' 2" Wt: 191 Hair: Drk Brn  Eyes: Gry
Organ Donor: Yes
```

Ligott, Roger
P.O. Box 3213 Whidbey Island, Wa. 98277
D.O.B. 4-2-63 P.O.B. Tacoma, Wa.
Ht: 6' 2" Wt: 189 Hair: Drk Brn   Eyes: Gry
Organ Donor: Yes
Misdemeanors: Failure to Disperse, Resisting Arrest 97

Lippe, Jefferson
19 Ocean Way Montecito, Ca. 93108
D.O.B. 4-4-63 P.O.B. Newport Beach, Ca.
Ht: 6' 2" Wt: 189 Hair: Drk Brn   Eyes: Gry
Organ Donor: No
Misdemeanors: Reckless Driving 95. License suspended six months, reinstated.

Newman, Asher
11783 Highway 1 Big Sur, Ca. 93940
D.O.B. 3-27-63 P.O.B. Monterey, Ca.
Ht: 6' 2" Wt: 186 Hair: Drk Brn   Eyes: Gry
Organ Donor: Yes (to exclude heart)

Robbins, Les
c/o Bradley's P.O. Box 19, Sierra City, Ca. 96125
D.O.B. 4-2-63 P.O.B. Santa Barbara, Ca.
Ht: 6' 2" Wt: 183 Hair: Drk Brn   Eyes: Gry
Organ Donor: No
Restricted License: 91 (driving on medication)

Sadler, Bernard
123 Hidden Way Bakersfield, Ca. 93304
D.O.B. 3-29-63 P.O.B. Bakersfield, Ca.
Ht: 6' 2" Wt: 198 Hair: Drk Brn   Eyes: Gry
Organ Donor: Yes

Weinstein, Harold
32716 Scoreboard St. Las Vegas, Nevada 89130
D.O.B. 4-9-63 P.O.B. Sacramento, Ca.
Ht: 6' 2" Wt: 179 Hair: Drk Brn   Eyes: Gry
Organ Donor: No
Misdemeanors: Disorderly Conduct 89, 91, 92.

"If someone asks?" Artie said without looking up.

Welinda held up both hands. "Just rambling down the information highway, both eyes on the cursor. I swear I was watching where I was going, when up popped each guy's credit rating, genetic predisposition to Alzheimer's, alcoholism, tardiness, and insubordination, not to mention cholesterol level and HIV status." Welinda bowed her head in a mockery of contrition.

Artie copied the data onto the store laptop, then transmitted the information to his home computer.

"Thank god for small favors," Welinda said when Artie finished. "They don't include dick size."

"Some information should remain in the public domain." Artie pointed to himself, then held his hands two feet apart.

"As I recall . . ." Welinda gave Artie a shared-secret-but-don't-get-any-ideas smile.

"By the way. What if it's true? The letter."

"No chance. I looked it up. Remember, we're talking doing this nearly twenty-nine years ago. They didn't begin cloning cattle until the late '80s. All the scientists insist that human cloning has never been done. Here's an article from the Washington Post. November 23, 1993." Artie pulled a wrinkled photocopy from his jacket pocket.

Embryos Not Cloned After All
Scientists say human-cell experiment was unsuccessful

The brave new world of cloning human beings is not here—yet—George Washington University researchers insist, disclosing that a much-publicized experiment at duplicating human embryos did not work despite press reports stating otherwise.

"A lot of work needs to be done before we can learn why these cells cease developing," said Dr. Jerry L. Hall, the lead scientist on the project. "Until that's done, nobody's going to be cloning anybody.

"I think it's totally reprehensible that some of these ethicists are feeding the public the idea that these things could happen. If people would only stop and think about why people might choose to do these things, they'd see how preposterous it is."

"That's reassuring. Right from the horse's mouth," Welinda said.

"Pretty sophisticated practical joke, these computer entries. Probably some hypertext nut," Artie said, wondering if Welinda believed him. He couldn't tell. Welinda was already walking back to the video terminal, more concerned with her own never-ending family problems.

That evening after work, Artie logged onto Central Information on his home computer. Seven telephone numbers were current; Les Robbins's was outdated, though his address matched the one on Welinda's list. Mark Caputo wasn't listed.

He ran his eye over the list of available phone numbers; he chose the one who lived the furthest away—Roger Ligott, from Whidbey Island, an hour north of Seattle.

Roger was out. Artie left a message on his machine that he'd just received word that they might be relatives. Twins, actually. "Please phone. We should talk." He leaned back in his chair, told himself that he'd done all he could. He would wait to hear from Roger and see how the conversation turned out before contacting any others.

No. He had promised Sarah.

He sat down at his computer, began composing the letter. He found himself unable to type out the word *clone*, and settled on introducing himself to each of them as possibly being a twin raised apart. If interested, they could contact him for further information.

By morning the letters were in the mail.

SIX

"ello? Is this Arthur Singleton?"

"Speaking."

"You're making some kind of joke. Right?"

Exactly what he would have said. The man's voice was his—rapid, staccato, with the slightest hint of a New York accent, a trait that his mother had wondered and joked about, Artie being strictly West Coast until college. Artie sat on a stool. He began to perspire. Worse, he knew what Roger was going to say next.

"Some crank call to try to extort money. Bullshit. You've got the wrong guy. You stop phoning, or I'll call the police."

"I wish it were," Artie said softly. "I'm not any happier about this than you seem to be."

"Happy isn't the issue. I told myself not to phone back, but here we are. You've got fifteen seconds to prove yourself."

"You have a fax machine?"

"I'm not giving you the number. Then it's a lifetime of junk mail."

"Okay. You fax me your photo and I'll tell you yes or no."

"That won't help me."

"Then I'll mail mine. Of course it'll take several days."

Roger paused, then gave in. The two men exchanged their fax numbers.

"You first," Roger said.

"Together," Artie said.

He told himself that he was prepared, that he'd seen Sarah's photo album, that there shouldn't be any surprise. But the sight of himself emerging from his fax machine took his breath away. He ripped the photo from the machine and held it to the light, looking for some distinguishing difference. He walked to the bathroom and held the photo up in front of the mirror, assessing his reflection against Roger's.

The similarity was so profound it was almost mathematical, down to the same slight bump on the bridge of each nose. Artie had never been sure whether he had been hit as a kid or if he'd been born this way. Now he knew. Artie continued the conversation from the bathroom, holding the portable phone with one hand, Roger's photo with the other. He pretended he was talking to Roger in person, but he could not decide on whether to look at the photo or his own reflection in the bathroom mirror.

"Well?" Roger said.

"I think we should get together."

"Yeah."

"Let's flip. Heads I fly up, tails you come down here."

"How do I know I can trust you?" Roger asked.

"Can you trust yourself?"

Artie logged onto Travelnet and booked a same-day round-trip superdiscount fare and car rental. Welinda would be tickled to have the work. He punched up Washington, zoomed in on Seattle and Puget Sound. Within seconds he had a color map and his tickets.

He had pretended to lose the toss. He didn't want Roger on his turf—seeing his store and apartment, looking at his collection of old movie posters, sitting in his easy chair, on his couch, looking out his window at Grant Avenue.

He had no idea how he would react, and wanted the option of falling apart away from home.

Whidbey Island is a one-hour drive and a thirty-minute car ferry ride northwest from Seattle. Roger lived along the sparsely populated north coast at the far end, facing Puget Sound. The small log-and-stucco cabin was a quarter-mile from the nearest neighbors, deep within a grove of pine trees, accessible by boat or a poorly maintained dirt road. Artie was glad he was in a rental car—the potholes would have sent his Peugeot to the wreckers.

A mud-splattered jeep sat in the dirt clearing in front of the cabin. Roger was alongside, his elbow on the roof. He wore jeans, a blue work shirt, and lace-up construction boots. He looked older, his face lined and weathered from the sun. For this subtle difference Artie was grateful.

This is family, he reminded himself as he slowly set the handbrake, being double-sure the car was firmly in *PARK*. He patted his pockets as though he might have forgotten something.

Despite his stalling, the moment arrived. Roger was opening the driver's door. Artie stepped out of the car, took one look, and let out a nervous laugh.

So did Roger.

"So much for that," Artie said. The two men walked into the front room of the cabin. Roger offered Artie a seat in an easy chair facing a large stone fireplace. The warmth from the fire was reassuring. The scene was one of low-key domestic drama, not the high-tech of science fiction.

"Would you care for a drink?" Roger asked.

Artie started to say no, but Roger added, "Just half a jigger of tequila, not enough to get a headache."

"How'd you know about the headaches? You get them?"

Roger nodded as he poured two light drinks. He handed one to Artie then sat back in his chair. The angle of his body, the way he rested one knee against the armrest, the tilt of his head, the way he sipped his drink—the similarities were eerie.

"I thought that tequila was an acquired taste," Artie said, knowing differently but hoping that Roger didn't.

"Identical taste buds. According to my reading." Roger's face remained tight, the beginnings of a smile fading.

Artie took a sip of his drink. "When we're through comparing, do you think that there will be something left that's mine?"

He waited for Roger to lighten up, to break the ice with a joke, say something silly. But Roger took a canvas pouch from his shirt pocket, pulled out a pinch of tobacco, and began rolling a cigarette. Every movement was studied, pretentious. When Roger licked the paper to seal the cigarette, Artie cringed.

What a huge asshole this guy is, Artie thought, just before he went all hollow inside. This was how he must look. He was embarrassed for both of them.

"This bother you?" Roger asked, waving away the smoke.

"You can read my mind?"

"Telepathy is coincidence. ESP is a desire for belief." Roger took another puff. "I saw the look on your face."

"Maybe I shouldn't have come. You don't seem to be taking this too well."

"I *have* been looking forward to meeting you. Like in those stories of long-lost twins who're reunited." He turned to look out the window. Although it was only mid-afternoon, the sun was fading, the remaining light watery and disinterested. "It's probably me. I've been going through a rough patch."

"Maybe we could take a walk. You could show me this part of the island."

Roger rose from his chair and went to the closet. He brought out two parkas, handed one to Artie. "The afternoons get chilly this time of year."

The parka fit perfectly, as both of them knew it would. Nothing was said. Artie stuck his hands in the pockets, half-expecting to find some of his own things.

They left the cabin, heading down the dirt road, through a thicket of pines, out onto a forest meadow. The air was thick and damp. Artie could smell the rotting logs scattered about, and the lingering scent of Roger's cigarette.

They ascended a small hill. In the distance Puget Sound was a deep pewter. Beyond was a cluster of smaller islands.

"I needed to get away," Roger said. "No TV, newspapers, billboards. I think I'm feeling a little better, maybe even a little settled." He sighed, took a deep breath.

"Were you sick?"

"Not that way. Not so that the doctors could help. And you?"

"Sometimes," Artie said, looking away from Roger's penetrating stare. He owed him this one moment of honesty. But he would make it short. "When I was living back East. More so since my mom died."

"Anything help?"

"Keeping busy. Women." Artie could feel thoughts of Emily bubbling up. Quickly he added, "Reading comics."

"Nothing at all?"

"I keep telling myself it's the times."

Roger shook his head. "I don't think so. There've been other bad times, worse periods of history, but people still had hope. During the Great Depression men wore suits and ties. You don't get up in the morning and get dressed like that if you don't have hope. Now they're tattooing daggers on their necks. Permanent reminders that there's no future."

A clump of heavy gray clouds slid across the sun. "We should be getting back," Roger said. The two men turned and started down the hill.

"You ever try medication?" Roger asked as he stepped over a fallen log in their path.

"Once. In college. For a few days. Too many side effects. I started feeling better once I got laid." Artie stepped over the log, caught up with Roger. It was odd. They'd barely talked yet they already were beyond superficial chatter, as though getting to know each other was mere confirmation of what they had assumed before they met.

Roger shook his head. "I guess I can tell you now that I was dreading meeting you, knowing that there were two of us."

"Me, too."

Roger gave a forced laugh that scared Artie. How was he going to tell him about the others? He should have spelled it out in the letter. In person anything could happen. Though it was a ridiculous thought, he couldn't shake the worry that Roger might become violent.

Artie waited until they were back in the cabin, the two parkas hanging in the closet, and the two men seated in front of the fire. "There's more," Artie said, trying to anticipate Roger's response.

"Parents and all that? I presume your mother told you all this just before she died."

Artie said nothing.

"I phoned home last night. My mom swears that there was only me. What did your mom say?"

"That's not exactly it. Hold on a moment and I'll show you." Artie went outside, returned with the photo album he'd left in the car. He began slowly, the album in his lap, easing into the story of his mom and Sarah Woolfson as friends.

Roger rolled another cigarette, occasionally sneaking a sidelong glance at Artie. "Ten?" he said finally.

"I thought it was better to tell you in person." Artie held out the album. "You want to see the pictures?"

Roger pushed the album aside and cleared his throat several times. "There's an inherent ugliness in larger numbers. I guess I vote for regression toward the indefinite."

"Pardon me?"

"Mathematics of indeterminacy. Revert to a time before we knew." His voice dropped. "Have you met any of the others? Face to face?"

"You're the first."

"So you haven't seen—can't be absolutely certain?" Roger paused precisely where Artie would have, had he been speaking.

Artie balanced the album on his lap.

"We couldn't just leave it at the two of us? If no one else knew, wouldn't that be almost the same thing?" Roger's voice was higher and uneven. His expression was one of desperation and fear, spoke of hospitalizations and the assumption that you'd already read his chart.

"I've sent them letters. They do have the right to know."

"All ten? It's just that—yeah. You're right. Maybe you could do me a favor. Not mention me. Leave it at nine. No, that's not right, either. Oh boy." Roger downed the rest of his drink. "You want another?" he asked, motioning to his own glass.

Artie pulled out the ferry schedule. "I'll have to be leaving in a few minutes."

"There's no hurry. You could spend the night. The sofa's comfortable. It'd be no trouble. I'd love to have you." Roger was speaking rapidly. Artie felt frightened.

"My ticket's a cheapo no-refund one-day round trip."

"Right." Roger was standing with his arms at his sides.

"If you ever want the names of the others . . ." Artie said.

Roger shook his head. "We'll keep in touch. That's enough." Artie nodded. The two men moved toward each other as though to embrace. But they shook hands, looked away from each other, walked outside.

"There's more we could say. We've got entire lives to compare," Roger said, his hands on the open car door. Before Artie could answer, Roger added, "Have a safe trip. And a good Thanksgiving."

He closed the door and stood behind the car as Artie drove away.

SEVEN

U p in the high Sierras, an hour's drive northwest of Lake Tahoe, Sardine Lake was officially off-limits to visitors after October fifteenth. Last year Les Robbins had been able to stay an extra month before snow closed the roads and Bradley's, the general store down at the junction of 89 and Gold Lake Road. He'd hoped to do the same this year. The dirt path leading from the road to the lake was chained, the NO TRESPASS-ING signs posted, but the park rangers didn't mind. In fact they were glad. He'd leave the lake spotless, spending part of each day cleaning up the remaining scattered bits of tourist debris.

Though the daytime air was still warm with Indian summer, the evening temperature dropped down into the middle thirties. Les could smell the pines cooling. Some needles fell, others clung to their branches. Les applauded their effort, not turning, not giving in like the solitary maple ablaze in front of his small log cabin at the north end of the lake.

It was a time of isolation and meditative self-sufficiency. No sounds of radio, TV, boom boxes, dirt bikes, campers, or four-by-fours drifting over the lake. No roar of himself hollering at those who tried to whittle down his clearly posted cabin and boat rental rates. Without tourists the lake seemed darker, deeper; the surface was less apparent. Though it wasn't possible, he sometimes thought he could hear the faint breathing of the browns and the rainbow trout. He was glad he was a vegetarian. And that he could spend several hours each day floating on the lake clothed only in the dull gray skin of his aluminum rowboat.

He spent the mornings hiking in the nearby hills of the Sierra Buttes, the evening hours by his fireplace, reading and letting his mind wander.

Accusations were irrelevant. The world was collapsing under the weight of its own collected offenses, documented for eternity on a continuous loop of video coverage. Two years ago Les gave up TV, magazines and newspapers, yet the images persisted as though still broadcasting inside his head. Plane crashes, floods, famines, terrorism, assassinations, torture, earthquakes. The list was endless; there was no reward for completing it. Right now, if he wanted to, he could hear screams and cries of a world in pain.

No. He was here to forget. Cleanse his mind.

His one concession to modern life remained his Pentium Pro laptop that fit into a vinyl pouch on the back of his mountain bike. He preferred the printed page, the weight of a book in his hand, the smell of libraries and dusty book bins, but books would tie him to a place large enough to store them. CD-ROMs went anywhere. His latest CD of twentieth-century American literature weighed less than an ounce. His entire library was two pounds.

The individual word was without measurable substance. The most profound thoughts weighed nothing.

Perhaps that was as it should be.

The tourists had been gone a week when a park ranger dropped off Artie's letter at Bradley's. Les picked it up, but waited a few days until it was overcast and threatening before he opened it. He thought he was setting the proper mood for what he suspected was an irrelevant communication from the outside.

He read the letter twice.

Identical twin? He pictured a brother in investment banking, with monogrammed shirts, a copy of the *Wall Street Journal* in his back pocket, a stable of friends with pull and clout that could get him front-row seats at the Academy Awards and opening day at Dodger Stadium. Someone who sold easy listening to elevator companies. A professor of political science, or industrial psychology. Someone who used words like *downsizing, network, retrofit,* and *bonding.*

Or worse. Someone like himself.

Singleton said to get in touch. He would do just that. He would go to San Francisco, determine if Singleton really was identical. One meeting only, on Singleton's turf.

The cement overcast persisted. Les spent most of the next few days inside, pacing or sitting in his rough-hewn wood-and-canvas chair, staring at the fire, out the window. In leaving Los Angeles and moving to the mountains, he had hoped to peel himself back to whatever was the untainted Les, to the glistening pinkish-gray of his original mind.

The letter changed everything.

Les dropped to his knees in front of the fire, his hands together at his lips. It was his fire, his room, they were his ideas. He tried to calm his mind, but the fire's crackling was too loud, too obtrusive. The floorboards hurt his knees, each nail palpable. An annoying draft tickled the back of his neck. He got up, checked the door and windows, ran the back of his hand around each frame. Everything was secure. Nothing to fix. Winter was inside the room—brief flurries of chill rushed against his hands and cheeks. There were no detectable changes, yet his cabin had been violated.

He could think it through logically. Having a twin shouldn't concern him. If he could clear his mind of TV and newspapers, he could ignore one man a hundred and fifty miles away, someone he'd never met.

Three sleepless days and nights said that he couldn't. On the morning of the fourth day the sun rose bright and warm. The sky was clear. The lake was quiet, the Sierras shimmering on the glassy surface. It should have been a glorious awakening, but Les was a wreck. What had initially been a problem to solve had evolved into a condition, a reality he must bear.

As long as there was another, he could never be whole.

Les fitted what he could onto the back of his mountain bike—his sleeping bag, the computer and CDs in their vinyl pouch, his few personal belongings jammed into an old Nike workout bag. Though the day was pleasant and sun-drenched, he wore a parka over his wool shirt and faded corduroys, and Nike cross-trainers and a black baseball cap. It was the same outfit he wore each fall and winter day, the same as the outfit in his personal bag. Two of the same. He appreciated cleanliness; he had no use for style.

After locking up the cabin, Les pedaled down the road to Bradley's.

Duane Bradley had owned the dozen lakeside cabins for over forty years. Les considered himself fortunate to have seen the HELP WANTED sign in the store window while passing through several years ago. Since then he'd been the full-time guardian of the lake—from late April to mid-October—in exchange for room, board and enough money to coast through the rest of the year.

Duane was old. Each year his hands shook a bit more and his eyes grew more watery. Les was anxious to be on his way, but sorry to be saying goodbye. Something in Duane's expression intimated that he wouldn't be around next year.

It was a bad sign, a wrong mood for leaving. Departing thoughts tended to grow larger, to assume exaggerated significance.

Les spent the next hour keeping Bradley company, washing down two bowls of Duane's fiery black-bean chili with lemonade. Just the meal for the open road.

While he stirred small talk in with the chili, several locals came in, picked up their mail, pulled up a seat, gathered around the counter. Old men with weathered faces who were still thrilled by sunsets and mountain air. They all fussed over Les's leaving.

After a round of goodbyes he turned, walked out the front door and down the few steps leading to the dirt parking lot. He checked the bike tires and made sure his computer was secure in its traveling pouch. He turned back to the store. Several of the men were standing outside on the small deck. Some smiled, others nodded. Duane remained inside, looking out through one of the steamy windows. He tipped his hat as Les pedaled away.

The first half of the fifty-mile trip to Truckee was primarily uphill. Les was relegated to the bottom three gears of his eighteen-speed mountain bike. By Sierraville he was exhausted. He grabbed a quick bite at the cafe, then laid out his sleeping bag in the empty campground behind the park rangers' dorms. It was a spectacular night of shooting stars and a thumbnail moon. Les was all alone beneath his version of the universe.

Out of a clear black sky, snow began to fall. Not much, the flakes thin and dry, barely leaving a trace. But there was more on the way. Camping out was over.

The next evening Les checked into the Star Hotel in Truckee. It was an old Victorian with cheap rates, high ceilings, and a view of Main Street, including the town's original train depot with its jarring blue Amtrak sign.

After securing his things, he put out the do not disturb sign, locked his door behind him, took the back stairs, and crossed the tracks a block down the street. Soon he was on the slow overnight to Oakland.

Shortly after boarding the train Les claimed the empty dining car toilet. The door locked, the passing mountains in the tiny window his only witnesses, he stood at the sink and practiced sneaking up on his reflection in the mirror. "I'm Les," he said, extending his hand again and again, watching his movement toward himself. At Roseville he took his seat, confident that his voice was calm, his hand steady.

He repeated the exercise between Martinez and Richmond. *Ready or not, here I am,* he thought as he took the bus from the Oakland depot to San Francisco.

Somewhere between the bus station and North Beach he lost his nerve. Instead of walking into the store and introducing himself, he slouched in the shadows of a Kearny Street doorway across from Shazam. His cap low on his head, his parka collar up, he watched his double at work.

The noon sun angled across the front window, coating the glass with a thin yellow film. Superimposed was Les's dim reflection. Beyond, partially obscured by Les's reflection, was Arthur pushing his comic books.

Several times Les started to cross the street, only to slink back into the gray comfort of the darkened doorway. Arthur looked like him, gestured like him. Les suspected he smelled like him. They were definitely twins. Yet there he was playing the perfect fool, working his way through bins of outdated comics as though unveiling the great books of all time. Now and then he would look up and point to the front window sign for an upcoming sale. Each time Arthur pointed, Les ducked. He told himself that he was trying to avoid being recognized, but he knew it was more—the threat of dark secrets transmitted, bonds begun, feelings that could not be undone.

His skin felt prickly. He twisted in his parka, trying to find a position that fit, at the same time careful to avoid sudden movements that might attract Arthur's attention.

Arthur didn't notice; he was too busy with *Superman, Batman,* or *Plastic Man.* A merchant of pop culture, he would be the type that would wear a matching Giants cap and jacket, clothe his newborn in Elvis t-shirts and green leiderhosen, pepper his camper windows with stickers from every national park, theme park, major mall. Or wear railroad engineer's overalls and a conductor's cap while circling his life in a plastic replica of a Lionel model train.

They might be brothers in biology, but not in the soul, not where it counted.

He'd seen enough.

Artie's apartment building was a few blocks away. Les rang the manager's bell.

"You okay, Artie?" asked the manager, a middle-aged Asian man in a green velour warmup suit and black oxfords. "You look bummed out."

"Store's getting me down. Lost three sales because I refuse to carry the *Beavis and Butt-head* games. But you have to draw the line somewhere." He shrugged. "Then I go and lose all my keys. Maybe it's a sign."

"*Beavis* is what happens when you don't go to college," the manager said. He put his index finger to his temple. "Unless you're the one who dreams him up. Then it's big money and no more worries." He stepped inside his apartment, returning moments later and handing Les a spare key. "You lose this one, you're out ten dollars and a friend." He laughed, flashing a mouthful of dental decay and coffee and nicotine stains.

Arthur's apartment was three flights up. Before entering, Les stood with his hand on the doorknob, trying to anticipate what he'd find. He hesitated, fearful. Opening the door could mean anything. The layout could be just like his cabin at Sardine Lake or his room at the Star Hotel. Or it could be a clutter of memorabilia, middle Americana stacked to the rafters.

Which would he prefer? Similar or foreign? A chip off the old embryonic block, or transmogrification beyond recognition? It was a moment which begged for self-knowledge, but Les was uncertain. He'd seen Arthur at work; there was no doubt about their dissimilarities in interests. If the apartment was also alien, wouldn't that solve the problem? Two writers weren't identical because they used the same word-processing program. He could walk away and leave Arthur to his life.

He stepped inside, saw Bogart on the African Queen, W. C. Fields leaning over a dental chair, drill in hand, and the Creature from the Black Lagoon. Decorations he might have chosen if he believed in possessions.

Perhaps it was a matter of priorities, not tastes. Perhaps the comics were just business, not the real Arthur.

Les dropped down on the worn, cracked black leather couch. Not enough stuffing. He felt himself sinking, his legs losing leverage. Soon he would be immobilized, trapped. He pushed himself upright, then walked around the small living room. In different circumstances this could be his life.

On the mantel over a small brick fireplace, arranged chronologically, was a series of photographs of a woman that Les assumed was Arthur's mother. He looked closely, moving from picture to picture, examining the details. If he and Arthur were identical twins raised apart, this attractive and kind-appearing woman might be *their* mother, both of them carrying the genes responsible for the gradual broadening of her chin, the thickening of her jowls, the sloping of her shoulders. They were in a genetic free fall. Today's dissimilarities would drop away like the first soft hair of newborns, their paths merging in the way that you eventually became your parents.

He walked into the bedroom. On the nightstand were a half-dozen trade journals advertising comic book auctions and estate sales, a dozen thick catalogues for CD-ROMs, and the latest issue of *Sports Illustrated.* On the opposite nightstand was a single slim volume—Art Spiegelman's *Maus.*

Les stopped at Artie's bedroom closet. A single blue blazer, a couple leather jackets and an assortment of khaki pants and jeans. A purple satin Captain Marvel jacket, with Captain Marvel holding a brilliant yellow lightning bolt. *No. Don't.* Not listening, he tried it on. It was silky smooth, seductive, and in exquisitely bad taste. He would take it with him, toss it in a trash bin once he was on the street. No one should be seen dead in a jacket like this.

Later, back in Truckee, he would wonder why he hadn't thrown it away. Was he keeping it as a souvenir or as a reminder of what he might have become?

Off the bedroom was a tiny studio, barely larger than a closet. On a plain wooden desk was Arthur's Macintosh; Les flipped it on. Moments later he was scrolling through Arthur's credit card balances, reviewing recent purchases—these were numerical windows into his soul. He had to remind himself that this wasn't *his* apartment, that he was trespassing, that he didn't have forever.

He returned to the main file directory and kept browsing.

He stopped at Arthur's personal health records. Everything was in order, right down to a cholesterol level of 182 milligrams. Les was glad for Arthur's good health.

Below the most recent series of lab tests was a list of three MDS and three PHDS—two were in Boston, three in San Francisco, one in Berkeley. The interpretation was obvious, a comment on physical versus mental health—a single general practitioner might suffice for a patient's lifetime, but an army of therapists might not be enough.

Les counted his own. Six came to mind—the same number as Arthur's; could that be more than coincidence?—not to mention the assistants and residents when he'd been hospitalized. Initially he had refused to acknowledge them, intentionally not learning their names or remembering their faces. He fought all recognition as though his recovery demanded it. This behavior had extended to his parents.

He presumed this from their defeated demeanor, their per-petual undercurrent of guilt and sadness. His condition had infected them, had become their illness. They'd visit daily, bring-ing home cooking, false optimism, the promise of a swift recovery. They never mentioned the cost, which nearly had broken them.

He wanted to comfort his folks, explain that whatever was eating at him had nothing to do with them. He had said noth-ing, worrying that taking away their sense of responsibility might be more catastrophic. He was their only son. They doted on him, walked away from their own lives to concentrate on his. He knew that he must never mention that he was not their problem.

To everyone's surprise he did improve. Les was uncertain whether his therapy had played a role. He recalled with particu-lar fondness a single large sycamore tree immediately outside his hospital window. During the first few weeks, when he was unable to speak, he had spent countless hours listening to the branches of the sycamore scratching and pawing against the glass, reaching out to him. Les knew that the tree would do the same for the next patient. And the next. It was this precise combina-tion of blind acceptance and complete meaninglessness that seemed to help him turn the corner. He would later say he had been cured *beneath the tree of benevolent indifference.*

After returning to school, he had joked with his parents, his way of thanking them. He told his dad that a good therapist was like a playground supervisor, his primary responsibility being to keep the players on the court and the ball in play.

He couldn't remember if his father had laughed. He doubted it. Perhaps he'd nodded and patted him on the knee. That felt like what he might have done.

His mother would have baked something, kept her hands busy at the stove. "Here," she must have said, a gesture of constant giving.

It shamed him to realize the extent of their love, to know the degree of his own self-absorption that had led to his hospitalization. He'd moved to Sardine Lake to find what was good within him, what was worthwhile that he could sculpt into the shape of his existence.

Below the list of accessible files were others that were locked and required a password. Les opened the top right-hand drawer of Artie's desk. Sure enough, underneath boxes of paper clips, rubber bands, and a pile of loose papers, was an index card with columns of letters and numbers.

None worked.

Les tried the bottom line backwards, and the screen filled with a list of nine names. His was third from the bottom. Next to it was his post office box number. Most of the others had phone numbers and addresses.

On the next page was the letter he'd received. He hit PAGE DOWN and saw the same letter, only it was addressed to Harold Weinstein. On the following page the letter was addressed to Asher Newman.

He reread them to be sure, though he already knew. Maybe he'd always known—his episode of disintegration might have been premonition, not illness. He closed his eyes and took several deep breaths, telling himself to stay cool. At least this wasn't his mind, some bit of paranoia loose in his gears. For a fraction of a second he felt better. Until he considered the alternative.

He opened his eyes, wiped his hands on his jeans. He went through the loose papers in the top right-hand drawer, finding nothing. The bottom drawer was locked. But it was a flimsy factory lock that had come with the desk. Sliding his penknife across the edge of the drawer, Les was able to depress the bolt. The drawer popped open.

On top of a pile of papers was Sarah's letter to Arthur. *Nine genetically identical brothers.* Les looked at his shaking hands as though seeing them for the first time. He held his head and squeezed it, trying unsuccessfully to prevent the barrage of images from flooding his circuits. Inside his skull, in living color, played the old TV science programs. Clumps of cells being halved, quartered, floating out of view, cascading down the sides of his brain pan. In the distance was the babble of ethics, commentators choosing sides while the cells bubbled up, divided.

There was a parade of sheep with goats' heads. Striped cattle. Identical triplets doing synchronized swimming.

He returned to the opened personal computer file and began rapidly scrolling. There were a series of abstracts of articles on human cloning, all from esoteric medical journals obtained from Medline. The articles discussed theoretical possibilities. All ended by stating that human cloning had never been done. Underneath one of the journal abstracts was typed the word: *Bullshit!*

There was a noise outside the apartment door. Les jumped back from the computer and held his breath. Someone entered an adjacent apartment. Soon there was the muffled sound of a news broadcast. Les had the sinking feeling that he was already headlines. He searched the top desk drawer until he found some blank floppy disks.

Returning to the computer, he downloaded the personal files, including the names and addresses of the others, copied the list of letters and numbers on the index card, put it back in the drawer. He reread Sarah's letter a final time, which wasn't really necessary, each word etched into memory. He rearranged the bottom drawer to look untouched, then closed it. The lock snapped back into place. Arthur Singleton would never notice.

He took the next train back to Truckee. On his ride west the suburban sprawl between Sacramento and San Francisco had passed by, barely noticed, the expected industrial remains of the fading century. On the return trip the landscape oozed unfamiliarity. The train windows were tainted with a greasy sheen that soiled the edges of the Bay and coated the tired oil and sugar refineries in an otherworldly purplish-brown.

It wasn't until the train was above the Sierra foothills, the season's first snowfall thick on the low shrubs and pines bordering the tracks, that Les recognized the route with any certainty. Of course he had known that he was on the train. It wasn't a matter of factual disorientation, but a dislocation of his spirit.

The train was moving slowly. Other passengers were trying on new ski clothes, planning parties, comparing motel room rates. They laughed, nudged, kidded, and moved gracelessly forward into a future of tiny scale.

Time expanded, the air grew thinner, Les more impatient. He stared out the window and told himself that soon he would be back at the hotel. A good night's sleep and he'd feel better in the morning.

No. He must be on guard against false hope, against kidding himself into believing what isn't, that things are okay, will be okay, are tolerable, will be acceptable. Hope must have some basis, otherwise it is an insufferable deceit.

Les blamed his sleeplessness on the eighteen-wheeler traffic on West River Road, the trucks making a wide right turn at the corner, downshifting, then accelerating as they passed his third-floor window. Or the altered biological rhythms generated by a persistent cold front over the Sierras, Truckee's daytime high down into the mid twenties, dipping below zero early each morning. Or on the hotel's stale air and steam heating with its nocturnal banging of the pipes. Or on the positive ions generated by the neon STAR HOTEL directly outside his window.

Sleep was biological, serotonin flooding the brainstem. Insomnia was a chemical imbalance. He preferred the notion of his body as a temporarily out-of-tune machine to acknowledging the reason behind the look-alikes leering in his dreams, compounding his shadow, pushing him aside and stepping forward to answer to his name.

Salmon swam upstream. Humans spawned nightmares and imagined the worst.

It was only natural that his thoughts would turn to death.

In the blackness of approaching winter nights, like guests who had no intention of leaving, certain possibilities worked their way into inevitabilities. What-ifs evolved into skeletal plans which fleshed themselves out. Les stood aside, an impassive observer, watching his weary mind oscillate between destiny and choice.

His scalp was tight with tension, the muscles of his legs thick and heavy.

The sky darkened, the powdery gray lowering itself over the valley, stirring quiet afternoon breezes into a chilled wind that started up shortly after daybreak. The air smelled of snow. Les knew that the road from here was shaky. He'd been this way before, and it frightened him.

It was midweek, and the hotel was barely occupied. Ann Fritz, the day manager, agreed to save his room without charge, unless a new gold rush started up. Les had spent the last three winters at the hotel—he helped Ann shovel her car out from under several storms each winter, brought in firewood, mopped up after broken pipes. Never did he ask for anything in return.

Ann commented that he looked a little tired, "but then winter is never flattering."

He packed his few belongings on his bike and set out for Sardine Lake. He could pick up provisions at Bradley's, or, if they were closed, at the Safeway in Quincy. The lake would be deserted. He had the spare key to his cabin. He could settle in, build a fire, gather himself together. The lake would drive away thoughts of the others. Obsessions required a landscape. The lake was his, not theirs.

He pedaled twenty miles up 89 before the snow began—not cute little winter wonderland flakes, but a full-fledged storm that reduced visibility to inches. Les pulled off the road into a thicket of tamarind trees. He leaned his bike against a sawed tree stump, which he covered with a vinyl tarp he kept in one of the side pouches. His parka hood up, his hands warmly mittened, his feet toasty in high boots and two layers of wool socks, he loved the weather. Pure white nature.

It was noon. He would allow himself until three o'clock. If the snow stopped, he'd bike on to Sierraville. If not, he'd ride back to Truckee.

He sat on the stump, hands in his lap, watching the landscape fill up, then disappear. He imagined forgetting the sound of the human voice.

The sky grew as bright as if he were staring into the sun. All was whiteness, soft as cotton, clean as new sheets, a fresh beginning. There were no paths to order or disorder. Each direction was equivalent.

The snow showed no signs of letting up. His tire marks faded away. Eighty-nine would certainly be closed north of Sierraville; biking to Sardine Lake would be impossible. An hour ago the woods were full of possibility and sense of renewal. Now the storm was pushing in on him, shoving him back the way he had come. With a sense of resignation and retreat, Les repacked his tarp, secured his pouches, and started back toward Truckee.

That night, from the Shell station behind the Truckee Safeway, he booked an early morning flight from Reno to Seattle.

EIGHT

Artie was unprepared for Paul Lafora. With his shaved head, plain white sweatshirt and sweatpants, white socks and matching hightops, Lafora was straight out of the guru section of Banana Republic. Yet he was holding his own in a full-court game in the inner-city Portland playground, using plenty of elbow and hip under the boards, full of holler and hand-waving on defense. He had a nice, easy high-arcing jump shot.

Artie stood several feet behind the cyclone fence, trying to look inconspicuous. But he kept inching forward, transfixed by the shape of Lafora's head. Without hair it was long and bullet-domed, a department-store mannequin in the style of early Modigliani. Artie rubbed his own head, tracing the curves hidden beneath his thick dark hair as though following a path not taken.

Lafora stopped at midcourt, short of breath. He held his sides and looked directly at Artie. *Lead feet run in the family,* Artie wanted to explain to the teenagers who were laughing and pointing at him. Lafora waved to a gangly kid standing on the sidelines. The kid took Lafora's place. Lafora walked over to the cyclone fence and opened the gate.

"Art Singleton?" he said as he approached.

The two men shook hands, neither letting go right away, then both at once—perhaps Artie first. He wasn't certain, but he suspected that it might make a difference in their relationship.

"Good kids," Lafora said, rubbing his sweatshirt sleeve across the top of his head. "Almost all from busted homes." The two men walked away from the basketball court, toward the other side of the playground. "We try to be role models."

"We?"

"Let me take a good look." Lafora stopped, put both of his hands on Artie's shoulders, and gave him a slow once-over. He laughed, a loud nervous exhalation. "Peas in a pod. You have any other family?" he asked, wiping his eyes.

"Not any more. My mom died a few months ago."

"Sorry. I meant brothers, sisters."

Artie shook his head.

"Let me show you our church. It's only a few blocks from here." And they were walking out of the playground, Lafora's arm light around Artie's shoulder.

It was a rough section of central Portland. Many of the stores' windows were boarded up; most of the rest sold liquor and lottery tickets. Lafora's church was in the middle of an otherwise abandoned block, in what was once a tire store. From the outside there was the smell of old rubber.

Inside was incense and candle wax, and the faint odor of men in close confinement. Lafora led Artie to the doorway of the meditation room. A dozen monks in loose-fitting white pants and sweatshirts sat cross-legged on a large gymnasium mat. They faced a large door at the rear of the room. The door, floor-to-ceiling, was weathered, perhaps siding from an old farmhouse. It had no doorknob or handle.

"What's behind the door?" Artie asked.

"A wall."

As Artie watched, the men rocked slowly in a succession of flesh-capped waves. The combination of shaved heads, similar clothing, and synchronous posturing created an impression of frightening oneness. Artie could hear in their chanting the reduction of their souls, a low bubbling sound like soup simmering away unattended. Emptiness as a goal? In Artie's book flushing the mind wasn't transcendence—it was submersion, a scary descent down the evolutionary ladder.

And the height of arrogance.

The drone of the men grew louder. Artie felt trapped, wanted desperately to leave.

"If you'd like to join us, we have spare clothing in the men's dorm. After we have some tea." To Artie's relief Lafora led him down a hallway into a tiny sitting room. It was stark, with two cushions and a cheap pine table adorned with a single flowerless vase.

They drank from sand-colored ceramic bowls. Lafora knelt at the small ceremonial table, his sneakers squeaking as he shifted his weight. He sipped the green tea, his gestures as slow as Roger Ligott's.

"Your life—is it good?" he asked, holding his cup in midair.

"The usual ups and downs." Artie winced at the ordinariness of how he'd described himself. A store, a Peugeot, an ex-girlfriend, maybe a work of hypertext fiction one of these days. The more he said, the less he'd be. He glanced up at Lafora, who was contemplating his cup of tea. What right did he have to be so judgmental, with his rocking and mumbling and protracted silences? So Artie sat, not wanting to give Lafora any edge. Two could play this game.

Lafora was in better shape. Practice makes perfect. Out the single dusty window Artie thought he could see the seasons changing. His foot was going numb. Artie cleared his throat, trying to remember who'd dropped the handshake first. Some clue to hierarchy felt essential.

According to Welinda's printout, Artie had been born two days before Lafora. He was senior, dominant. If a few minutes made a lifelong difference to identical twins, two days must be exponentially more important. Artie threw back his shoulders, pleased with this bit of information. He'd tell Lafora the whole story, then see how smug he was. But he didn't, couldn't. Instead he asked, "You always this quiet?"

"They say that identical twins can have extraordinary bonds. That would be beautiful, like an infinity of invisible brightly colored streamers flowing between us."

"I think it varies from one set of twins to another."

Lafora laced his fingers together. "I never had an inkling. Some intuition." He dropped his hands onto his knees. "Am I adopted?"

"It's not that simple." *Okay, you asked for it.* From his briefcase Artie brought out the photo album. With a calculated deliberateness he turned the pages, naming names. He finished by showing Welinda's list from the DMV.

Lafora shifted on his cushion, picked at the edge of one of his sneakers. He pulled his hand away and dropped it into his lap.

"I've met one of the others," Artie concluded. "I think you'd like him."

"Yes, I'm sure."

Artie waited for the expected questions, but Lafora was silent. And blinking rapidly.

"You okay?" Artie asked, half wanting to take back the words. Lafora nodded. "Was he pleased? I mean, glad to see you?"

"Hard to say. It *is* a weird circumstance to find yourself in."

"Here we try to think of all of us as brothers. It's the only way, if there's to be any future." Lafora straightened up, tilted back his head. He was repositioning himself as best he could.

"I think he was hospitalized, probably several times. Is there anything I should know?"

"Falling is natural. Embarrassment is pride's handmaiden. Did the two of you find a common ground?"

"We hit it off all right. Would you like to meet him?"

"He's physically well?"

"I think so."

"And doesn't appear to be in need?"

Artie shook his head.

"Then that wouldn't be necessary. You could explain our church to the others. They'd be quite welcome. We give seminars, weekend retreats."

"There are ten of us. You have any feelings?"

Lafora sat for some time, then rose. "It will take time. Would you like to stay for dinner?"

"That's okay." Artie stood and handed Lafora one of his store cards. "In case you ever need me," he mumbled. He hated appearing so ridiculous. Superfluous. "We should talk again. Check in on each other."

"Yes." Lafora put Artie's card alongside the teacup. The two men walked out of the room, said their goodbyes at the front door. One of the monks passed by, stopped, turned, and bowed ceremoniously, first to Lafora, then to Artie. The man looked from Artie to Lafora, lowered his head and scurried away.

Lafora smiled at Artie. "My heart is your heart." He bowed, his hands in front of him. He leaned forward and gave Artie a firm hug.

It was what he and Roger would have done, if they'd allowed themselves. He felt Lafora's cheek tight against his. Roger's last words echoed in his ear: "Have a nice Thanksgiving." Artie realized that he had his arms around Paul, not Roger. He was gathering up the beginnings of a family.

"You stay well," Lafora said, drawing back, his arms falling to his sides, his eyes glistening.

"We come from tough stock," Artie said, the sensation of Lafora's sweatshirt still on his fingertips. "Have a good Thanksgiving."

Artie was out on the street, in the gathering darkness at the center of a foreign town. A green neon cross on the roof of the converted tire shop crackled and came on. Lafora was a seeker. Ligott was also, in his own way. Artie wondered how that related to him. He'd done his reading. They were supposed to be similar in tastes, traits, desires. Did this mean that he'd somehow turned away from what should have been, might have been the real Artie?

There was so much he didn't know about himself. He'd have to sit down and take stock. If he made it out of the neighborhood alive. To his surprise, he was glad to have some specific terror to overcome. The gangs in the neighborhood were nothing compared to the constriction in his chest.

He put himself on big city vigil, looked carefully up and down the street, at the alleyways and driveways. He took a last glance at the neon cross before running full tilt to his rented car.

NINE

Dulled by the flight, the delay at the car rental, and the ferry ride, Les Robbins struggled to focus on the task at hand. His actual plan remained elusive, without sharp edges. Which was just as well, since nothing was necessary, not even checking for a pulse. Roger's jeep was parked in the dirt driveway; the front door was unlocked. Roger was on the couch, his mottled feet draped over the armrest, his head tightly wrapped in a clear plastic bag, propped up on a loosely rolled sleeping bag. His face was the color of fresh halibut meat.

Arthur Singleton's business card was on Roger's burled coffee table. At the bottom was a handwritten home phone number and an email address. Judging by the schedule that Les had downloaded from his computer, Arthur probably had been here sometime yesterday afternoon.

The position of Roger's body left no doubt that he had committed suicide.

Les moved closer, kneeling alongside the couch, his face inches from Roger's. The sight of Roger's lifeless body was alarming, yet he could not turn away. They were identical. Roger's hand was cool, his fingers clenched as though at the last moment Roger had tried to pluck something from the air.

Death was incomprehensible. He was touching it, was right on top of it, staring it in the eye, yet his mind was like Roger's empty hand. Death had no specific dimensions, its meaning arbitrary, determined by those left behind—anything from the unnoticed disappearance of a heartbeat to a national catastrophe.

Once he'd spent an afternoon in the University of Nevada library playing and replaying a CD-ROM of the Abraham Zapruder film, John F. Kennedy slumped forward, his brains flying out the back of his head. Metaphysically, this moment was the yardstick against which all arguments were measured.

On a battlefield such a wound might result in a man sinking soundlessly to the ground, to slowly decompose without fanfare. He'd seen photographs from the Civil War, death no more than a greasy bulge in the mud, unless elegized by rank. Generals were mortally wounded. Privates became numerical, relegated to the deepest interstices of government statistics.

On his recent trip to San Francisco he'd passed a lifeless woman in a Sixth Street doorway, covered by a frayed overcoat, and an even thicker layer of street grime and a lifetime of rejection. On the sidewalk, only feet away, milled the usual curious, and those peddling drugs and bodies.

Les had watched from the Airporter bus. Through the double glass panes he thought that he heard someone mutter that she was better off. Someone else asked if she still had her watch. The bus accelerated; tourists pretended the woman was asleep. From the bus the dead woman seemed small.

Not at all like Kennedy's death, millions grieving, raising death's ante, every millisecond of recoil of the head ratcheted upward into history.

Where was Roger? Was his death a tragedy or a necessity? Les recalled why he had come. If Roger'd been alive . . . Was a death by suicide less than by murder? Was the scale smaller, more manageable because a suicide occurred as a final icy act of separation while murder always reflected the residual heat of a relationship that had caught fire?

Had he planned to kill Roger? Did he have it within him to murder? He needed to know, but the questions, though urgent, had a curious dreamlike insubstantiality, as though they had not yet been specifically assigned to him. He could walk away, the unanswered questions falling lazily, harmlessly, onto a terrain he had already abandoned.

He moved his hand back and forth an inch above the bagged face, tracing Roger's features in the air. He was careful to keep from touching the plastic. He ran the fingers of his other hand slowly over his own cheekbone.

He'd read where identical twins often have a similar distribution of dental fillings. Les wondered how he could pry open Roger's mouth and take a look. Impossible without running the risk of tearing the bag.

He continued to stare at Roger's cloudy features. Even through the mist of early decay there was no doubt, right down to the thin lips and prominent chin—and the red-and-black checkered Pendleton shirt. Clothes don't make the man, he told himself. But the same shirt?

Through the open door Les could see an occasional light come on; the nearest house was a good quarter-mile away. He closed the front door and walked to the kitchen, returning with a straight-backed wooden chair. He pulled it alongside the couch and sat down.

Moved out here to get away from it all. Away from TV and bad thoughts. I understand completely. A wise decision.

Darkness settled over the living room. Roger was barely visible in a quarter's worth of moonlight.

They won't understand. Can't understand. You shouldn't blame them. I'd have killed you. Not that I wanted to. I've never killed anything. Not a fly, a spider, nothing. The thought sickens me. I want you to know that it isn't your fault. If you'd come for me, I'd have understood. You or me, that's the proposition. I think you knew that.

Perhaps you can send word to the brothers. It'd be better that way, their knowing that it's not personal. That I'd understand if the tables were turned.

Les reached out and put his hand on Roger's shoulder. His body was continuing to cool. Les accepted this. He was more bothered that he hadn't been entirely truthful. Once he'd come across a deer crushed in a bear trap. The deer was beyond saving, and was looking at him. Les had slit his throat with a single sweeping motion, apologizing and crying, then getting sick in a nearby bush. But he'd done it.

He'd carved the deer free, covered it with some loose topsoil and leaves.

For weeks he'd kept an eye on the area, hoping to catch the man who had set the trap, which had caught not only the deer, but himself. One day the trap was gone. A few scattered bones were all that remained.

Les sat for a while, eyes closed, concentrating on Roger's presence and paying his final respects, but he found himself edgy, curious. Guided by the tiny white beam from his halogen penlight, he wandered through the four spartan rooms of Roger's life. The smallness of the cabin and the dearth of possessions made it easy for Les to see himself living there. He could get up in the morning, slip on the checkered Pendleton, step into Roger's job (whatever that was). He could easily spend several months working through the adequate selection of books. The kitchen was stocked with many of his personal favorites, including a trail mix hard to find in all but the most particular health food stores.

He had to remind himself that this wasn't a healthy way of thinking, that it was blasphemous to Roger's spirit. One man to a soul. Wasn't that what this was all about?

On Roger's bedroom bureau was a snapshot of a lovely young woman standing at the rail of an interisland ferry. She was barefoot and wearing a long flowery skirt which billowed around her. She was smiling and waving.

A sister? Hardly likely.

He opened the top drawer of the bureau. At the back of a thin black leather address book was a neatly clipped strip of four arcade snaps of the same woman. Over the bottom photo was the inscription: To the shyest of loves. Suzanne.

In the larger snapshot the woman was smiling, but also had an air of apprehension. *Will you be well without me? Can you manage? Will I be seeing you again?* her eyes asked.

She must have loved him very much. Knowing it was a suicide will make it all the harder. Perhaps he could write, say that Roger had some incurable disease and considered this the best way out.

The leather book had few entries and only one Suzanne. He jotted down her home and email addresses on a scrap of paper from his wallet.

At the back of the top drawer, underneath a stack of underpants, was a packet of perfumed letters sealed in a plastic bag. Les slipped them into his jacket pocket. They would help him draft his letter.

He completed his survey, combed the closets, the bookshelves, the tool shed at the back of the house. Satisfied he'd gathered what he could, he returned to the living room to resume his vigil.

TEN

FROM: Newsadvisory <remailer@cypherpunks.ca>
TO: Arthur Singleton

>I am dead.
Roger

Artie stared at his single piece of email. He was weary and nauseated by his visit with Paul Lafora and the bumpy return flight. He wasn't interested in what he suspected was some web surfer's idea of a practical joke. He walked to the kitchen and poured himself a grapefruit-flavored soda. *If you were the main character in a crime novel, you'd be belting down a shot of Jack Daniel's,* he told himself, cursing his defective biology that transformed alcohol directly into pain.

Roger had headaches. In all probability so did one of his biological parents. Artie shifted away from this line of thinking. He had only fragile recollections of his own father—a big face, warm hands, deep, gentle voice, the smell of some lemony cologne, riding on his shoulders at the beach, holding hands. Love.

The memories were delicate and had to be protected from the confusion of acknowledging and exploring a separate parentage.

Already he was having trouble assimilating his mom's final years. He could visualize the torn-up tracks of her mind—neurons exploded, fibers frayed—but the images couldn't convey her loss of self. Identity seemed to be more than brain cells. It was what you *were*.

His mother had proved that idea wrong. She had gone hollow on him, disappearing while her body continued to function, her appearance altered only by her empty, fallen expression. Her death had been a dismantling of the already abandoned.

Now the question of identity had shifted to himself.

He returned to the computer and took another glance.

```
>I am dead.
Roger
```

Artie picked up the phone, dialed Ligott. An answering machine clicked on: "Please contact the coroner's office for further information."

The coroner's assistant was matter-of-fact; he could have been reading a weather forecast. "The final report will be ready in about a week. Ten dollars and a self-addressed stamped envelope. It happened last week. A suicide by suffocation; typical right-to-die death manual stuff—a plastic bag over his head." The assistant paused, his voice suddenly lower and more personal. "Was he family?"

"An acquaintance."

Artie hung up and sat down on his couch. He'd known that Roger was unstable, but to kill himself right after his visit. There was no doubt; he'd been the messenger. Artie cringed as he saw Roger sending his email, fumbling with the plastic bag while exercising his final responsibility—to contact his newfound brother.

Artie was surprised at the heaviness in his chest. Roger had made him uneasy; after the visit Artie had concluded that he probably wouldn't see Roger again. Now he wiped at his eyes and wondered if there'd be a memorial service. As much as he hated funerals, he wanted to pay his respects. Of course it wouldn't be possible—family and friends would ask questions.

He considered typing a note to the others, but only Paul—who was not the epitome of well-balanced—knew that Roger existed. There was no one he could tell. Even Welinda was off-limits. It'd taken some doing to convince her that Sarah's list was a clever prank from one of his comic book distributors.

No one should know.

The following day Artie found himself in the push and shove of McCarran International Airport, behind a group of white-shoed Elks, a women's softball team in matching jackets and caps, and a pack of golfers with hooded clubs and expressions of impending joy.

Perhaps identity wasn't such a good thing after all, he mused while the Elks stampeded to the available cabs. Artie stood at the back of the line. He was in no hurry.

Fifteen minutes later he was in the shredded back seat of an ancient Checker cab, hurtling toward downtown Las Vegas.

It was his first time in Las Vegas. He'd seen movies of the early days—gangsters, gun molls, hookers on the half-shell. Tumbleweed rolling up to the front door of some ranch house casino. But that was long ago, before the era of theme parks and air-conditioned family vacations. Artie passed by facsimiles of the Sphinx, the Tower of London, the sunken city of Atlantis, an exploding volcano, a miniature mountain that featured roller-skiing. What kind of alternative Artie could possibly live in such a place? If taste was in the genes, did it mean that Las Vegas represented a repressed urge?

A chilling idea, he thought as he entered the over-air-conditioned lobby of Day's End. "Hal Weinstein?" he asked the room clerk, a short, squat, bald man in a Hawaiian shirt and red Bermuda shorts.

"Not here. You his brother?"

"He was supposed to meet me. Did he say where he went?"

"Didn't have to. He plays every afternoon and evening over at the Glass Slipper."

"Could you be more specific?"

"Sure. You go out the door, turn left, keep going until it gets even sleazier. It's three blocks further down."

"From here, or where it gets even sleazier?"

"Both."

"Where in the casino should I look?"

"Stand plumb in the middle, near the poker room. Wait for a loud moan. That'll be him, taking a beating." The man squinted. "OK. That's enough. I've got work to do."

"He didn't leave a note?"

"God damn, Tuna. I told you, I've got work. Try the long-lost identical twin bit on Rosalie. She's fresh up from Nogales. She'll believe anything."

"Tuna?"

The man looked out through the top of his bifocals. "You told me this morning that your brother was coming, and that he would look like you. Then you come back in some new threads. Good. You'll give this dump a little class. You look beautiful. What else do you want me to say?"

"Thanks for the directions," Artie said, opening the lobby door and walking into a wall of heat.

The Glass Slipper was a 1950s version of a theme park gone belly-up. A fifty-foot cowgirl, one leg raised in a mockery of dancing, blinked savagely in the hot afternoon air. The lights around one garter were out, those around the other were flickering. The woman had some incurable neon disease.

Inside was the sound of coins against metal, laughter and the scream of numbers, bells, an overhead hum of electricity. A series of flashing arrows pointed to the poker room tucked behind a bank of slot machines and another row of video poker machines. Eight tables covered with green felt cloth. At the far table, next to the coffee machine, was Hal Weinstein. He wore aviator-style dark glasses, a blue cowboy shirt with silver collar tips, and jeans. Artie stood behind one of the video poker machines and watched.

Weinstein was up to the coffee machine, down in his seat, lighting a cigarette, motioning to a cocktail waitress, standing up behind his chair, looking at his cards, then throwing them away as though he had been personally affronted, shot, stabbed with bad fate. Artie suspected cocaine, or a dozen cups of coffee. The man was wired.

Obnoxious.

He talked over others, he blurted, ignored, knocked over the water glass of an elderly Asian man to his left. He swallowed his apology, his sentence tapering off into a snarly accusation at the dealer. Artie considered backing away, taking the next plane home.

But Weinstein was leaving the room, coming toward him. "Over here," he said, putting his arm around Artie and ushering him from the center of the casino. The gesture reminded Artie of Lafora.

"It's quieter next door," he added, rushing Artie into Marge's Coffee Shop at the rear of a run-down mini-shopping center behind the casino. He took a booth at the rear, quickly ordered each of them a cup of coffee and a Danish. "Heavy on the filling," he said to the waitress. As an afterthought, he asked if Artie wanted anything else.

"You seem to be in a hurry," Artie said.

"Not really. Been a slow day. Cards've been running like paraplegics." Weinstein stirred his coffee, leaned back in his seat, took a good look at Artie. "I'll be fucked." He shook his head.

"Like some ten-cent TV show. I thought it was going to be hoaxville."

"Not exactly."

Weinstein was checking his watch.

"You have another appointment?"

"They collect time every half hour. Four bucks. No big deal when you're winning. Right now I see eight dollars an hour as mucho dinero." He paused. "This week, mind you. Temporary setback while the cards get reoriented."

Artie decided not to waste time. He gave a compressed version of the biology, and a summary of his meeting with Sarah.

"There are others?" Weinstein asked.

"You're the third I've met." He watched Weinstein for signs of surprise, instead saw only a knitted brow and dancing, scheming eyes.

"Reasonable facsimiles?"

"Any more and we'd have to be in the same place at the same time." Artie decided not to mention Roger's death. He couldn't imagine Weinstein caring.

"Slow down and run this by me again."

"You sure you have the time?"

"A few minutes one way or the other. No big deal. Not compared to these possibilities."

"The room clerk called you Tuna."

"Nine of us. You're shitting me."

Artie shook his head.

"Little nickname I got when I first came to town. Tuna. You know, as in big fish. By the time I got even, the name had stuck. You might as well join in."

"Tuna Weinstein?"

Weinstein shrugged and wolfed down his Danish, at the same time eyeing Artie's.

"Go ahead," Artie said, shoving his plate over to Weinstein.

"You sure?"

"I filled up on plane peanuts."

"Thanks." As Tuna bit down, a small chunk of raspberry jam fell onto his finger. Tuna licked it off, the side of his finger now glistening and streaked with pink.

"How'd you settle on Las Vegas?" Artie asked, fascinated and repulsed. He tried not to stare, but couldn't help himself.

"The wheel of fortune rolled off my car. Broke down out in Henderson, walked the rest of the way. I've always been good with numbers. Las Vegas seemed like a good percentage proposition."

"And?"

"Five years, long enough to get black lung and pissy breath from feeding on tourists. Though now it's more like dieting. Too bad, these theme parks. Tourists used to think the purpose of the place was losing. Blow two weeks' salary and feel like a man." He took another bite of his Danish. "Now they bring their wives and kids, fuck off their cash on camel rides and virtual reality arcades. Used to be I'd clear a grand a week with my eyes closed. Now it's all I can do to beat the time."

Artie started to ask if he was thinking of leaving, but Tuna interrupted. "You got any health problems? Discs out, bone spurs, carpal tunnel? Something that'd show up on tests?"

"Excuse me?"

"You know. Something I could use in a slip-and-fall. Nothing better than before-and-after films. I go down over at Lucky's. The company doc gets an MRI of my back. It's normal. I thank them, tell 'em I had a dramatic recovery. I don't file, which establishes character. A couple of weeks later I take a dive at Ralph's. Now we've got pre-fall normal, and you slip into the machine for a popped disc. Megabucks. No middle-man shyster—we split it fifty-fifty."

"My back's fine."

"Any head stuff? Something that might show up as atrophy, brain wave irregularities?"

Despite himself Artie answered, "I've got cluster headaches."

"Red wine and champagne?"

Artie nodded.

"Me too. But it's the wrong kind of migraine, doesn't sour the EEG. I've already checked." Tuna motioned to the waitress for more coffee. "T cells? Not that I'm prying. A quirk in the immune system'd work for toxic exposure. Fumes in the motel room, carpeting in the casino."

"I feel fine. At least I did before we started talking."

"Just an idea. If you come down with something, you'd let me know, wouldn't you?"

"You are definitely the last word in brotherly love."

"Fifty-fifty and I do all the paperwork. It's a no-lose proposition. You get something major, enough to cover travel expenses, we do a road show."

"Does nervous breakdown count?"

"Only if we can set it up before you see the docs."

"Because I think I'm having one."

"This is no joke. We've got a chance of a lifetime. You check with the others. Certainly we can't all be a hundred percent." Tuna glanced at his watch. "Think about it. I've got to get back before they ante my life away." Tuna dropped a five-dollar bill on the table. "If it comes to more," he said to the waitress behind the counter, "I'll catch you tomorrow."

"I'll be here," the waitress said, not bothering to look up.

Artie put down another five. Tuna eyed the bill before walking up the aisle, his hand in the small of Artie's back.

"Glad you came. Maybe we could catch dinner later." They were outside the cafe, on the hot parking lot asphalt.

"I've got to be going back. I've got a special one-day round-trip ticket." The explanation sounded worn and recycled, but

Artie was certain that impatient Tuna wouldn't notice, or worse, wouldn't care.

"Then another time?" Tuna said. He paused, started to say something else, then quickly patted Artie on the shoulder. Before Artie could say anything, Tuna had turned away and was hurrying back toward the Glass Slipper.

ELEVEN

Les had a week to study the self-help suicide manuals and pamphlets he'd picked up at the Seattle airport book store. The older books mentioned short-acting barbiturates and the newer analogs of Valium. None were optimal; given orally all took ten to fifteen minutes to take full effect. The most recent manuals recommended car-fentanyl, a synthetic ultrafast narcotic. Initially developed in back-street laboratories as a "designer drug" alternative to heroin, car-fentanyl was two thousand times as potent. It wasn't long before the drug was legitimized by the major pharmaceutical houses. In pill form it was a cheap, rapidly acting, potent analgesic, and quickly became the treatment of choice for a variety of pains ranging from postoperative to terminal cancer. It also turned out to be a sensationally efficient anesthetic agent.

He logged onto Medline, using Arthur's password. Administered by nasal spray, a single inhalation of car-fentanyl produced deep anesthesia nearly instantaneously. It was the method of choice at most zoos; the largest of animals could be quickly subdued without restraints.

He was about to look up the pharmacology—how the drug was metabolized, whether or not it could be traced—but stopped himself. It wasn't necessary. Traces of the drug in blood or urine were irrelevant. Car-fentanyl was widely discussed in the press; already it was a frequent mode of suicide. The most recent self-help manual, released last month, was already in its third printing.

In the back of the book was a list of laboratories that could provide direct sale or mail order veterinary solutions. Not classified as pharmaceutical houses, the labs had effectively sidestepped FDA regulations requiring a doctor's prescription. One of the laboratories was in Carson City.

Les hopped on a bus to the capital and purchased a lipstick-sized canister. Then he took the bus from Carson City to Reno.

The Biggest Little City in the World had a side street filled with pawn and gun shops, including several that specialized in the latest self-protection equipment. At a place called Fear-No-More, Les bought a high-power stun gun, a scary matte-black wand that telescoped, at the push of a button, out of a metal cylinder that looked like a cigar container. This was not your magic wand of the old-fashioned fairy tales, Les thought as he slid the gun in his plastic bag, alongside the vial of car-fentanyl. Perhaps stun guns would be included in the modernized versions.

He had plenty of time to think it over; the bus ride from Reno to Portland took twelve hours. There were only half a dozen passengers, all bunched together in the first few rows. Les sat at the rear of the bus, reclining across several empty seats, watching the afternoon sun fall across the high desert, then the snow-capped Sierras. Soon it was dusk, the dense forests leading to the Oregon coast a succession of shadowy figures. He felt isolated from his surroundings by the heavy double-paned window that held his dim reflection. Soon the other passengers would gather their belongings and step off the bus and back into their own lives. Until Portland they were a group, loosely bound together, but it was a temporary co-existence of no particular significance. If the bus were to crash and they were to die, he would be one of eight victims headed toward Portland. He would be a fraction identified by his destination.

If he were to get off the bus and disappear into the night, he would not be noticed; or if he were, he quickly would be forgotten. His image would be filed away in some dimly lit memory storage site, a bit of useless unlabeled minutiae. Unless he went ahead with his plan. It was the unstated reason for collecting chance memories—the hope that one day they might be worth something.

"Why, he sat right behind me on the bus," he imagined hearing the girl in the front seat say to the police. "He seemed . . ."

Les did not listen further. Not necessary, knowing how those who'd never talked to him felt about him, would feel about him. How they'd describe and analyze him. They weren't entitled. Taking away memories of him was a form of stealing.

He slid down lower in his seat, out of the line of sight of the driver's rearview mirror, out of sight of the others. Who were they to judge him?

He was the judge. It was his opinion that mattered, and it was a difficult call. For a time he sat with his hands open in his lap, as though they were cradling Paul Lafora's lifeless head. He'd seen Roger Ligott. Paul would look the same.

How would it feel, Paul's head in his hands? It felt like a combination of murder and suicide. And neither.

Better Paul than me, he muttered to himself, trying to convince himself that his idea wasn't unique, that the others would think of it once they'd had time to consider the consequences.

According to Arthur's planner that Les had downloaded at the apartment, Arthur's visit was scheduled for yesterday. Also on the planner was Paul's address and a notation mentioning his private quarters at the rear of the church.

He had a moral obligation. Better one life saved than ten squandered. Ethics came from the heart, not from laws. A prosecutor might argue otherwise, but the prosecutor would be quoting case law while Les's circumstances were without precedent.

He put his hand flat on his chest. He knew what he felt. If he didn't proceed, he would be the dead one. Without self-defense there could be no self-discovery.

He was the last passenger to deboard. He kept his head down, his back to the driver who was busy filling out his time sheet. The terminal was in the low-rent industrial section of Portland, a fifteen-minute walk from Paul's church.

Paul was at the rear of the church, in a freestanding corrugated metal shed once used for storing worn tires waiting to be recapped. The strong smell of old rubber was further accentuated by the circumstances of the meeting. First smells were important. They spoke of priorities and preferences, of body chemistry and self-acceptance. Les was glad Paul didn't smell of aftershave, his room of furniture polish—not that there was much to polish.

His quarters were spartan, lit by a single kerosene lamp. On the floor was a mattress, a short squat wooden stool, and a small shrine consisting of a vase of dried red and yellow flowers. In one corner was a small folding card table. There were no books, posters, or other decorations.

"Arthur told me about you," Les said as introduction.

"Sorry about the lighting." Paul pointed out at the darkened alleyway beyond the shed. "I've debated bringing in electricity, but somehow I can always hear the hum." He invited Les inside.

Paul sat cross-legged on the mattress; Les sat on the stool, his elbows on his knees. Hanging above them by a thin woven cord was the kerosene lamp, the smoke rising up, collecting under the low metal ceiling before it drifted out through a series of crudely punched holes high on the metal walls.

The two men cast similar shadows on the dirt floor.

"From a scientific perspective it's remarkable," Paul began.

"I wish I could believe that."

Paul smiled. "A quirk of biology. It's not like we have the same souls."

"You're not bothered at all?"

"It's too soon to say. Self-honesty hasn't kicked in yet." Paul laughed. "I'm still comforted by the notion that this won't be our only existence."

"You don't plan on telling anyone, do you? This *is* just between us?"

"There's nothing to hide. It's not like we're mutants or Martian androids."

"Your room smells like mine. We could exchange lives. That's not how we were meant to be."

"I had those thoughts, when I first heard. But that's pride. We can do better."

The two men discussed how they had outgrown former lives, how they were presently searching. The more they spoke, the more Les saw himself in Paul's wanderings and yearnings.

"Perhaps you could spend some time here. Get out in the community and help some of the less privileged. If we were less self-absorbed, this wouldn't seem such a problem."

"We?"

"Yes, we."

The two men nodded at each other. Nothing more needed to be said. In the flickering light, Les thought how easy it would be to get up, embrace Paul, and say goodbye. A simple gesture of affection. In the distance he could hear the prosecutor recreating the moment, his pointer loud against the chart he was using to convince the jury. But the jury was in his mind and it wasn't listening. Les reached into his pocket, fingered the stun gun. The sensation of the metal drove away the prosecutor's eloquence, the pointer fading into silence. His mind emptied itself and waited for further instructions.

TWELVE

From NEWSADVISORY <remailer@cypherpunks.ca>
To: Arthur Singleton

>I am dead.
Paul

Not possible, Artie thought as he dialed Lafora's church in Portland. An older man answered.

"You're the one who visited last week?"

"Uh huh."

"It's strange. After your visit he seemed subdued and spent much of the following day praying. That's not unusual for him, and he seemed in good spirits. One of the brothers found him in his room the next morning."

"What happened?" Artie asked, already suspecting.

"It was horrible, right out of one of those dreadful suicide manuals."

"He used a plastic bag?"

"And some pain pills. The coroner's still running tests." The man paused, then said, "We think he was glad to have seen you. We really do."

"I'm sorry. Please give me your address. I'd like to send a contribution."

Artie said goodbye, hung up the phone, picked it up again.

"No, Tuna's not here," the room clerk said. "Haven't seen him in three days."

Artie's heart pounded as he phoned the Glass Slipper to have him paged. The operator put him on hold.

"He's not answering," she said.

"Try again," Artie insisted.

There was a hum, then a click. "Yeah," a voice almost identical to Artie's answered.

"Tuna?"

"Who is this?"

"Artie Singleton."

"Hey, bro. You copacetic?"

"Sure. And you?"

"That's it? Long distance for just checking in? You asking about me? I'm okay, considering this has been a three-day marathon. Was up almost four grand. What a rush of cards. Right after you left, like you were some good luck charm."

"Was up?"

"Little backslide the last twelve hours. Still got twelve hundred. Probably should call it a night, but the game is *so* live."

"I just wanted to say it was good meeting you." Artie considered mentioning Roger and Paul, but Tuna's cheerful indifference put him off. "You might try to get some sleep."

"When I get tired. Deal me in," he said, his voice directed away from the phone. "Listen, I've got to run. Anytime, give me a call. And don't forget about the x-rays."

Artie hung up and put the phone back on its base set. He tried sitting down but was too agitated. He paced the living room, his arms wrapped around him. Three visits, followed by two deaths, both by the same method, the same message on his computer.

Could the form of the suicide notes have been dictated by genetic similarities? Surely biology didn't extended to semantics.

Welinda was minding the store. Artie had the rest of the day to himself. From his briefcase he pulled out a selection of computer printouts he'd culled before his trip to Las Vegas. He had started to thumb through them several times, but had always made some excuse to himself. He no longer had the choice.

The first article was on similarities between twins. There were long lists gathered from questionnaires of identical twins raised apart: They fold their clothes the same way. When they are putting things away, they button up every other button on their shirts and blouses. They leave their bedroom doors slightly ajar. Similar obsessive habits, such as counting the wheels on a passing truck. They read the same magazines and novels. Similar nightmares.

Artie was relieved at the banality of the so-called similarities. You'd find the same responses in any large sample group.

The second article was on personality differentiation of twins raised together—the problem of a collective awareness versus individual consciousness.

```
I used to wake up in the morning, see my twin in
her bed and think, How do I know I am me?

I treasure my middle initial because it is dif-
ferent than my brother's.

I recognize that I am a copy. My brother is the
original with an exact duplicate.

We are absolutely identical. In fact, it is pos-
sible that my sister is really me and vice versa.
```

The Macintosh beeped. Artie looked up; there was a new message waiting.

```
From NEWSADVISORY <remailer@cypherpunks.ca>
To: Arthur Singleton
```

Obsessed, bewildered
By the shipwreck
of the singular
We have chosen the meaning
of being numerous.

Email normally was sent instantaneously. Could the sender have set up a time delay? Was this an additional electronic suicide note from Roger or Paul?

He phoned Netcom. The representative checked. The note was anonymously sent from a remailer service. It was stripped of headers; there was no return address or any detectable site of origin. "It's impossible to trace."

"No way of determining when it was sent?"

"Our email can be preprogrammed for later delivery."

"Thanks," Artie said and hung up. His mind raced with possibilities, none of them good. He turned back to the computer, half expecting another message. He stood for some time, then bolted from his apartment, half running down the street. It wasn't until he reached the corner that he realized where he was headed.

He entered the confessional at Saints Peter and Paul Church on Washington Square. He wasn't Catholic. He wasn't religious. The smell of incense was less sweet than he'd experienced in Portland. He chose not to sit or kneel, closing the door behind him and standing with his cheek against the metal grate. The dark air reeked of abandoned sins, desperation, all sorts of penitence.

"Is anyone there?" he asked.

"Yes."

"This is my first confession. How much time do I have?"

"As long as you need."

"This is going to sound strange. But first, I need to be assured of complete confidentiality."

"Are you in trouble?"

"This is strictly between us?"

"You are in the house of the Lord. Our conversation is privileged."

Artie had no idea where to begin, or what to say. He could no longer remember how he had decided on confession. He was considering leaving when he blurted out, "I am a clone." Then he waited.

"We're each alone, but not in the eyes of God."

"A clone. As in a biological freak." Artie told of the letter and the others, including the two suicides.

"How long have you had these feelings?"

"They aren't feelings." Artie's voice rose. He had to remind himself that his purpose was not to convince some invisible cleric of the truth of his circumstances. "I've seen three of the others. We're all the same in appearance. There's no doubt."

"And you're concerned that you contributed to the two . . ." The priest paused, weighing the next word. "Deaths?"

"Partly. And, I think I'm trying to hear how it sounds, admitting this to someone." Artie looked down at his hands, the same hands as Roger, Paul, and Tuna had. He found himself on his knees, facing the grill, in a posture of prayer. Kneeling felt right, appropriate, but he knew in his heart that he was beyond deliverance. What kind of god would not have foreseen, taken precautions against the eventuality of scientific trickery? "Fresh eggs for sale," he imagined some merchant biologist barking.

The priest was suggesting that he see a counselor. "Someone better equipped to handle this type of problem."

"Yeah, I'll just look up a clone counselor in the Yellow Pages." Artie stood abruptly. "Thanks," he said into the grill.

"The Lord has put away all your sins," said the priest. "Go in peace. Pray for me, for I am a sinner. Consider one of the clinics. They have someone on call twenty-four hours."

He walked up the side aisle, past a group of mourners in black dresses and suits. Some of the women were sobbing; many of the men were dabbing at their eyes. Everywhere was the sense of loss. Though he had no idea who had died, Artie was reluctant to leave, lingering at the periphery before dropping five dollars into the collection box and stepping out into the lengthening shadows.

After closing the store, Welinda would be coming by his apartment to pick him up. She was playing at the Kearny Street Saloon—an evening of Professor Longhair, Pinetop Perkins, Dr. John, and Memphis Slim. Welinda's solo performances were invariably a combination of great blues piano and witty asides; there would be plenty of women and laughter.

Welinda from Louisiana, with the bayou in her blood, blues in her heart, computers and games on her mind, was a curious combination of nostalgia, romance and nerd. Artie was sometimes sorry that they were more comfortable as friends than lovers, but appreciated the special relationship their former intimacy allowed, and the shared knowledge that they would be friends long after their affairs with others had turned to dust and recriminations.

Certainly longer than Emily, Artie thought, as he hurried home to search through Medline.

```
A large and consistent body of evidence supports
the influence of genetic factors upon personal-
ity. The evidence taken as a whole is overwhelming.
We are led to what must for some seem a rather
remarkable conclusion. The degree of monozygotic
(identical) twin resemblance does not appear to
depend on whether the twins are reared together
or apart.
```

Our findings do not imply that parenting is without lasting effects. The remarkable similarity in social attitudes of identical twins raised apart does not show that parents cannot influence those traits, but simply that this does not tend to happen in most families. This is true for a wide variety of social attitudes, including religious interests.
(Thomas Bouchard, Jr. and Matthew McGue. Journal of Personality 58:1, March 1990)

Religion in the genes? He read further.

Of 69 identical twin pairs in which one twin was diagnosed with a manic-depressive disorder, 46 co-twins had manic-depressive disorders, and a further 14 had presented other psychoses or marked affective personality disorders or had committed suicide, revealing a concordance rate between siblings of 87%. (A Danish Twin Study of Manic-depressive Disorders. British Journal of Psychiatry April 1977)

Of 62 identical twin pairs in which one twin committed suicide, there were 9 in which both committed suicide. Suicide in Twins. Archives of General Psychiatry Jan 1991)

The odds of Tuna Weinstein winning the World Series of Poker were better than betting on their own mental stability. Judging by the behavior of Roger and Paul, each of them had a nearly ninety percent chance of serious mental problems, and over a ten percent chance of suicide.

He had the same chance of killing himself that a woman had of getting breast cancer. At least there were mammograms, and a woman could examine her breasts as often as she wanted, hopefully getting a jump on the disease.

How did you examine yourself against the possibility of suicide?

His occasional lapses—the high school counseling, the clinic time at Harvard, his present uneasiness—made sense without invoking a genetic imbalance. What if the explanations were irrelevant, after-the-fact?

How do you check for, or fight against, bad programming?

Who was he? To continue to believe that he was Arthur Singleton and that he was in charge of himself was to go against everything he was learning about himself. Unless he could prove himself, could meet the enemy head on.

With a sense of inevitability and grim determination he went to his bedroom closet. The freshly pressed shirts were wrapped in glistening plastic.

You prop the bag open and just imagine. He pulled the bag from one of the shirts.

As he turned away from the closet, Artie had the sensation of something wrong. He went quickly through his clothes. His Captain Marvel jacket, a gift from a wholesaler, was missing. He couldn't remember if he'd left it somewhere. He was annoyed and momentarily distracted. Until he saw the plastic bag in his hand.

He propped up the pillows at the head of his bed. Had they been dressed or undressed? It was a significant distinction, how they offered themselves. Naked was how he'd go, Artie thought, slipping out of his clothes, including socks and underpants, dropping them in a heap alongside his bed.

Naked in transparent plastic.

He slipped the bag over his head, leaned back, being careful to adjust the lower edge of the upper flap to mid-chin level. To be doubly sure, he held both hands against his cheeks, lifting the plastic from the sides of his neck. He checked, taking in some deep breaths. There was no impediment. The ventilation was fine.

He closed his eyes and saw Roger's tiny cabin, Paul's shed at the back of the monastery. Soon his cheeks were damp and hot, his mind tight against Roger and Paul's collapsed worlds, trapped within the thin moist stale air.

You'd really have to want to die to kill yourself this way, he thought, trying to shake his rising anxiety and sadness. So deliberate, an insistence of rationality, a final definitive statement. To whom? To Artie? To the world? It was the opposite of the self-destructions of a gun in the mouth, razor to the wrist. It was an effort to die intact, unmarked by the world that had beaten you. An arrogant refusal to bow to unacceptable circumstances.

Roger and Paul: men of principles wrapped in plastic.

The moisture increased, the air wet and palpable. An occasional drop of condensation fell onto his cheek, flowed down the side of his neck. Some he caught with his hand. Others hit the floor.

A bead of moisture fell directly into his nose, causing him to half-sneeze, half-cough. In trying to catch his breath he sucked a fold of the dry-cleaning bag into his mouth. He bolted upright. He saw only blurry outlines. He instinctively yanked out his hands. The bag stretched when he pulled at it.

The doorbell rang. It was Welinda. Artie stumbled to the door, threw it open, his free hand clutching his throat.

"Aren't we being dramatic?" Welinda said. "I'm five minutes late and you throw a tantrum." She shrugged, walked past Artie, not intending to humor him. She flipped on Artie's stereo, turned to the local jazz station. It was early Ornette Coleman and the sound of a migraine.

Artie grabbed at the bag. This time it came away easily, as though no struggle had been necessary. He threw the bag in a wastepaper basket alongside his couch.

Welinda looked up into Artie's red eyes. "A little kinky, are we?"

Artie wiped his eyes with his underpants, slipped them on. "Did I loan you my Captain Marvel jacket?" he asked, dressing quickly.

"You want to talk?"

Artie considered telling Welinda about the two suicides. But he didn't, wouldn't, couldn't. "Your gig starts in ten minutes. All the decent women will be taken."

"I'm your friend," Welinda said. "We're not going anywhere until you level with me."

"Tonight you play. Tomorrow we talk."

"Dr. John can wait."

"It's not what you think. I had no intention of killing myself."

"I'm not letting this drop," Welinda said as they stepped out of the apartment. "You talk to me or I turn you in to higher authorities. They lock you up, give you the ice bath and elec- troshock treatments. Or we have dinner, a nice bottle of Beaujolais, and you tell me what's eating you. Is that a promise?"

"I already gave you my word. Now let's drop it."

THIRTEEN

The autopsy reports arrived, the descriptions so cold that Artie's hands trembled. Other than the differences in clothing, the two reports could have been carbon copies. Artie put them down, wandered around his apartment, picked them up again. He was sliced open, staring inside at his own long-term weather report complete with advisory warnings.

> The heart weighs 412 grams. The outer surface is without scarring. There are early fatty streaks in the coronary arteries, but no stenosis or calcification. The valves are smooth, without vegetations.
> The brain weighs 1307 grams. The arachnoid is clear and glistening, the cortex a uniform gray. There are no areas of discoloration or bruising or other signs of trauma.

Artie turned to the other report.

> The brain weighs 1306 grams. The heart weighs 415 grams.

One gram difference in the two brains. What did that extra gram do? See? Feel? Or was it merely an artifact of measurement, no more than a standard deviation of error? What if the report had read 1306 grams for both Roger and Paul? Would that be remarkable or statistically irrelevant?

And the heart? Despite himself, he checked to see whose was bigger. Estimates would range between 410 and 420 grams. Utterly useless information, yet absolutely transforming. His insides had become numerical, coded for disease and wear and tear. In the future, any thought of his heart would be followed by the modifier—415 grams, plus or minus five. But what did the heart's weight mean?

Bighearted. Lighthearted. Heartfelt. Heartthrob. Hearty. Faced with a minute description of each vessel, tag of fat, the color of the fiber, he had slipped beneath Valentines and Cupid's arrows, into the land of raw meat and dry bones.

The external genitalia are of normal size and shape.

The lifeless penis's final stop was the pathologist's metal table, flesh reduced to a psychiatric artifact, its last function being to point the finger, level the accusation, or, in the present cases, reveal possible clues to minds unraveled. Congenital disfigurements, herpetic scars, piercings and tattoos—everything from the pain of diseases regretted to oddly cherished moments—held up to a tightly gloved scrutiny like a packet of forgotten love letters read aloud on judgment day.

What did the pathologist see that he didn't record? Himself? Of course not. He had no relationship to the flesh between his fingers. It was gristle to be discarded, incinerated, buried to decompose.

The image of the autopsy protocol made Artie sick. He could see himself lying on a cold metal table, hear the buzz of saws, gurgling of drains. He told himself that he wouldn't feel the chill of the metal; he rubbed the back of his neck, picturing a huge block of melting ice.

The aorta has a significant amount of fatty streaking and some early atherosclerotic changes.

The biliary system is somewhat underdeveloped, with a narrowed common bile duct.

There are multiple areas of hypertrophic spurring along the lumbar vertebral bodies.

Both reports read the same. Their model had the tendency toward early atherosclerosis, gallstones, arthritis. They did. He did. All of them.

He flipped back to the initial section, knowing the images would be indelible. He started with Roger.

The plastic bag is carefully freed from the duct tape ligature surrounding the neck. It is a standard dry cleaning bag, inscribed with the words: "We appreciate your patronage." Underneath, in purple script, is: "Please keep away from small children." The bag is generic, without further identifying features.

There is some residual moisture on the inner surface.

There are no signs of struggle.

The face is modestly suffused, consistent with asphyxia without strangulation.

Paul's report read the same, except for the bag's warning, which was in English and Spanish. Momentarily reassured by this minor distinction, Artie mentally traced their last steps to the different laundries, then their walks or drives home, freshly pressed clothes on the hanger, under the arm, hung in the closet. His mood slipped as he focused in. Did they read the fine print before or during their last thought: *please keep away from small children*? Or would the bag be too close to the eyes, the print blurry hieroglyphics, Roger and Paul beyond warnings and consequences?

The toxicology reports listed a minimal blood alcohol level (Roger), a moderate level of car-fentanyl (Paul), negative VDRL and HIV (both). Artie had seen enough. He put the two reports into a large envelope and slipped it in his bottom desk drawer. As he did, he was aware of some alteration in the drawer's landscape, but he dismissed this as being a shift in his orientation. He locked the drawer, walked to the kitchen, then returned to double-check the lock.

Welinda said he should talk to someone. Sure. He could have another session with Doubting Thomas over at the church. He could go to some uptown shrink and be next month's journal article. "*A.S., a twenty-eight-year-old single male . . .*" He would be presented as the end of the millennium's update of paranoia. Fifty years ago the FBI eavesdropped through the family Motorola. Then the CIA tapped your wires. Now it was *The Case of the Multiplying Egg.*

Bring on the butterfly nets.

Or worse, he could be believed—the shrink a bearded mass of joy bombarding the Internet.

If only he could find a blind, speechless bartender without a memory.

When Artie could no longer take care of his mother at home, she had been sent for brain scanning at the UC-Berkeley neurodiagnostic laboratory. In order to qualify for long-term nursing home placement, her health insurance carrier demanded laboratory proof of mental incompetency, which was defined as a greater than sixty percent reduction in brain metabolism on a PET scan. One of the doctors in the lab, Janine Richards, had taken Artie aside and shown him the results. Artie knew little about medical science; the scan looked like a Christmas tree with most of the bulbs burned out.

That had been over two years ago. Since then there had been a few feature articles in the *Chronicle* discussing Janine's latest scanning techniques as a possible way of unraveling a metabolic basis for a predisposition to violence and suicide.

As Artie phoned, he wondered if Janine would remember him. She said that she did, though Artie wasn't sure if she remembered him or his mother's scan. An hour later they were sitting in her cramped Berkeley lab. Janine wore a starched white coat, silk blouse and linen skirt, her legs crossed as she perched on her high stool. Artie had not remembered her as being so striking, with thick dark hair, intense blue eyes, and, despite the seriousness of their discussion, the hint of a sly smile. Artie had to look away, down at his paper cup of instant coffee, and remind himself why he was there. In a near mumble he explained that two cousins, one in Seattle and one in Portland, had recently committed suicide. He was concerned that there was something amiss in his genes.

"First of all, this kind of information is strictly preliminary. We think it's correct, but we need to do a lot more testing." Janine pulled out a notebook and asked for names.

"Roger and Paul," Artie said.

"Don't worry. This is confidential." Janine's voice was soft, with a trace of a southern accent; under other circumstances she would have been reassuring.

"If you discover something, you won't name the gene after us?"

"Everything's numbers these days."

"Roger Ligott. Paul Lafora."

"They're first cousins of each other, and you?"

Artie nodded.

"Mother or father's side?"

"Mother."

Janine drew a series of connected lines. "How many others are there?"

"I'm not sure. The family's not close. Skeletons in the closet, bats in the belfry, mystery afoot . . . My mother always changed the subject."

"You'll find out and fax me?"

Artie agreed. Janine closed her notebook, motioned to the examining table in a partitioned section of the lab. Artie lay down. She adjusted the scanner; it fit like an electronic crown.

"We need to determine your norms," Janine said, injecting Artie with a radioisotope. She explained that the machine worked by measuring the metabolic rates of different areas of the brain, and that these rates were known to change during mental and physical maneuvers. She had Artie read, clench his fists, tap his fingers. Each action produced a different pattern of activity seen on a large overhead video monitor. The data was stored in a computer beneath the monitor.

Janine checked her watch. "You in a hurry?" she asked, her voice lighter, a hint of mischief in her eyes.

Artie started to shake his head but couldn't. "Uh uh."

"Just a scientist's curiosity," she said. She left the room, returning with a Victoria's Secret catalog. She held it in front of Artie, flipped through a few pages, then turned to watch the results.

The pattern on the overhead monitor changed. There were now symmetrical hot spots in both temporal lobes. There was also a region of increased activity in the left frontal region. Janine laughed. "See that single area up there? That's the motor cortex. It controls the movement to your right hand."

Artie blushed and the activity disappeared.

"So much for baseline." Now she showed him a sheet of paper containing several short passages. "I want you to read a paragraph, then close your eyes and think about it. You have to remain perfectly still for five minutes after you've finished the reading."

The first paragraph was from a Camus essay on suicide.

In a sense, killing yourself amounts to confessing. It is confessing that life is too much for you or that you do not understand it. Dying voluntarily implies that you have recognized, even instinctively, the ridiculous character of that habit, the absence of any profound reason for living, the insane character of that daily agitation, and the uselessness of suffering.

The second was a journal entry by Antonin Artaud.

If I commit suicide, it will not be to destroy myself, but to put myself back together again. Suicide will be for me only one means of violently reconquering myself, of brutally invading my being, of anticipating the unpredictable approaches of God. By suicide, I reintroduce my design in nature, I shall for the first time give things the shape of my will.

Following this quote were a series of suicide notes.

After Artie had finished the testing, Janine busied herself at the computer keyboard. There was a distinct change in her expression. After a few minutes she looked up. "If you don't mind, I'd like to try something else."

Janine opened a book that contained a series of photographs of violent crimes—rapes, murders, morgue photos. Included were several handwritten confessions of serial murderers describing sexual pleasure, even ecstasy, associated with killing.

At first Artie was shocked, not only with the material, but also by knowing that Janine had collected such information. But soon he was busy looking and reading. It was repulsive but strangely fascinating.

The overhead monitor continued to register the ongoing brain changes.

Janine removed the scanner. "It'll take a while to collect all the data. How about you take a walk around the campus and come back around six?"

"Maybe I'll hit the gun shops," Artie said, bothered by the Janine's suddenly all-business manner.

He spent the next three hours in Sproul Plaza, watching the newest crop of students, and preparing himself. He tried to tell himself that tendencies weren't the same as predictions. Anyone who ever bet sports knew that being an odds-on favorite wasn't the same as a guarantee. Still . . .

Artie knew immediately by the expression on Janine's face. "Not here, not in the lab. It won't seem so serious over pizza," Artie said.

Janine smiled; Artie tried to interpret. He settled on sincere and humoring. Janine turned off the machinery, grabbed her battered leather briefcase, locked up the lab. During the short walk to north campus Artie noticed that Janine limped.

"Skydiving," she explained, anticipating Artie's question. "The instructor landed on my foot, proving the old adage, those who can't do, teach. The orthos say it's probably permanent, but then they always were at the bottom of the class. If you're interested, we jump every weekend."

"Still?"

"Free-fall gets in the blood. You should try it, at least once." She shrugged and turned into LaVal's, a north campus pizzeria.

"It must be an unwritten cosmic requisite, one red-and-white checkered tablecloth restaurant per university," Artie said, sliding into his chair. He felt the push of words at the back of his throat—he was geared up to chat, divert, small-talk himself out of his situation. Janine sat quietly, her hands in her lap—perhaps the way she sat before jumping out of a plane.

"When giving a fatal prognosis, always present a cool demeanor. Patient Management 101." Artie spoke as though reading from a textbook.

"It's my nature. Like your scan. It doesn't mean anything."

"How about us doing the evening news first? This way I'll know how much to order." Artie cleared his throat. "And you can skip the disclaimers."

"These are cousins, right?"

Artie nodded.

"You won't shoot the messenger?"

Artie waved his hand.

Janine shoved aside the plastic-webbed candle in the center of the table. From her briefcase she pulled a series of scan photos. "Your patterns are a little unusual. In families with a strong history of suicide, there's relative hypoactivity in the medial frontal structures. And this doesn't change much with the provocative readings." Janine pointed to one of the scans. "Right here. You can see the darkened area?"

Artie nodded.

"We think that smudge is the PET scan equivalent of a genetic marker for a tendency toward suicide." Janine pulled out a second scan and placed it alongside the first. She pointed to areas of increased uptake in both anterior temporal regions. "These correspond to the amygdaloid complexes. They control fear and rage. There's a much higher incidence of increased activity in these areas in those convicted of violent crimes, especially multiple violent crimes."

"That's what the gruesome photos and the serial killer confessions were testing?"

Janine pulled out a third scan. She handed all three to Artie. "See what you think?"

Artie mulled over each of the scans. This was no time for hasty judgment. After some deliberation, he answered. "The third scan seems like a combination of the first two."

"We haven't seen this pattern before, not exactly like this. But then, we're using new radioisotopes and we've only tested families with strong suicidal tendencies, and mass murderers. We've never had the opportunity to test a family that had both." Her tone of voice was one of quiet sharing of confidences, as if she were idly speculating about someone else.

"This is me?" Artie said, holding up the scan.

"We'd have to repeat it on other members of your family, to be certain. There's always the possibility of a lab error, or some technical artifact."

"You ever tested a group of poets or novelists?" Artie tried to smile, but he felt brittle, ready to snap.

"It could be nothing."

"But you don't think so. You think these scans are going to be a major breakthrough, don't you?" Artie could hear his shrillness.

"It's not like saying that you have a fifty percent chance of killing someone, or yourself. Nor is it like detecting the gene for, let's say, Huntington's Chorea, where a positive test is . . ."

"I know what a positive test for Huntington's means," Artie interrupted. "And I understand tendency. My question is, what are the odds?"

"Your mom was OK until . . . ?"

"Absolutely."

"I only met her that one time, in the lab, but she seemed like a lovely woman. She cared a lot about you."

"When you saw her, she couldn't talk."

"You could see it in her eyes, when you were sitting with her. I'm sorry. It must have been awful. If that happened to my mom, I don't know what I'd do. You'd probably have to commit me."

"You did medical school, internship, a residency in neurology, no less. That takes a stomach the size of Yankee Stadium."

Janine shook her head. "I do research. Disease is easy to study but impossible to accept. Sick people scare me."

"So you skydive?"

"Not the same. Not at all." Janine paused, as though there were more she wanted to say. Instead she asked about Artie's father.

"Died of a heart attack in his early fifties. As far as I know, there wasn't any history of depression or suicide or violence. He was a gentle man, full of love."

"Grandparents?"

"More of same." Artie was exhausted. It made no difference what he said; the scan was impervious to deceit. It was biology, not love, that Janine was questioning.

"Perhaps we shouldn't have done this."

"I already suspected. Two cousins that never met each other, both killing themselves in the same way, within two weeks. I figured that some gene kicked in."

"Relax. It's not like either is your twin. Your immediate family history sounds fine. The test may only be a marker, like a white forelock or multi-colored iris."

"That's reassuring."

"Don't worry. I'm not in the habit of having dinner with potential mass murderers." Janine put the scans back in her briefcase. She looked away, at the steady stream of students passing beyond the front window.

"My second year in medical school—it was physical diagnosis —my instructor wanted us to get rid of any feelings of embarrassment, so he made us examine each other. I pulled the short straw and had to go first. There I was, my face and neck in flames, slipping on the gloves while some Phi Beta Kappa from Princeton gripped his ankles and pleaded for tenderness. A week later he asked me out."

Janine turned to Artie. "By the way, I wouldn't jump to conclusions. I just wanted you to know that I've seen worse than your scan." She laughed, redness spreading over her neck and cheeks. She looked down at the menu.

Artie watched carefully, struck by her loveliness, at the same time trying to decide whether or not she was humoring him, or liked to live dangerously. Or both.

FOURTEEN

After flying from Portland to San Francisco, Les took the bus from SFO to the Amtrak terminal in Richmond, then the early afternoon train to Truckee. When he arrived, weary with travel, the town was asleep, the main street dark and abandoned. Worse than the bitter cold was the lack of music, as though he might wake up in the morning and find all the birds gone.

Overhead was the sound of grating and flapping, the first tinsel Christmas decorations hanging from light poles, dark metallic shreds against the night sky. The muted tinkle of desperation, a couple dozen merchants trying to salvage a bad retail year. In two months the sales would begin, the windows covered with pleading and begging, the whole town marked down.

He was glad to step inside his hotel. Ann Fritz was at the front desk, finishing up the day's books.

"Your trip go okay?" she asked.

"Relatives, not okay."

Ann smiled and reached for a pot of mint tea steeping on the side counter. Without asking, she handed him a cup. Les buried his nose in the mist, the steam warm against his cheeks. Abruptly he pulled back.

"You think the word *relative* originated to stand in contrast with *absolute*?"

"I gather you're not big on family."

"The more the murkier," Les said. "You whip up a soufflé for too long, it collapses like a punctured tire."

"Excuse me?" Ann enjoyed chatting with Les, partly because of his frequent non sequiturs, but also because of his strong sense of self and his unflaunted rugged good looks. If only he weren't so unsettled, she might be seriously interested. Not that he'd ever indicated that he noticed her. Maybe this winter it would be different.

"Family meetings. Everyone trying to blend together. A little goes a long way."

"Didn't you tell me your folks lived in Santa Barbara?"

Les nodded.

"You see them often?"

"I used to phone fairly regularly. Now I email them a couple times a month. Saves on the uncomfortable pauses."

"Strange. You go out of your way to sidestep modern life, yet you spend so much time with your computer. If they ever invent one with"—Ann looked down at her well-developed chest—"us girls will be completely obsolete."

Les gave a small smile that Ann could not interpret. He finished his tea, then handed her the cup, lightly touching her hand as he did.

A minute later he was in his room, on his bed, reading the letters from Suzanne.

On the light blue stationery the script was elegant, bordering on calligraphy, suggesting that the letters were to be saved. Not downloaded like email, but tucked beneath a stack of underpants, to be reread again and again, savored and cherished.

Les pulled out the larger snapshot and the strip of arcade photos and balanced them on his thigh, rereading the letters. What did Roger have that was so special? Was it something that all of them shared? What if *he* were to show up on her doorstep?

Would Suzanne notice a difference? Would he feel the same as Roger would have? If he did, what would that say about love?

He walked to the pine dresser opposite the foot of the bed. He leaned the two photos against the single ceramic-base lamp, lay down to check the angle, rose again and readjusted them. He dropped back onto the bed, Suzanne now in clear view.

Would she love them all?

Paul Lafora? It seemed unlikely. Lafora was a man of superficial solutions, right down to that ridiculous door hanging in the prayer room. It's symbolic, Lafora had explained, barely containing himself and his neat proprietary smugness.

He looked over at Suzanne. *Believe me, you wouldn't have liked him.*

Les stopped himself. There was no reason to be personally vindictive and spiteful. This wasn't a competition to be won. Much better it should be a series of isolated events, without narrative or judgment. Proving a point wasn't the point.

He turned on his computer and logged onto Travelnet. Arthur would be arriving in San Diego early Friday. His return flight was late afternoon. Les would arrive later that evening. He lay back on his bed, closed his eyes, and prayed the flight over the Sierras would be smooth.

On the way to the airport and having time to spare, Les stopped by the small Church of the Lake to listen to the women's choir practice. He took a seat at the rear. In the front, forming two rows to the left of the altar, a dozen women sang a single dark pool of medieval melody.

The music had started in monasteries, brothers alone in their cubicles, singing in unison, yet barely knowing each other. All alone, together alone, polite strangers despite a lifetime of proximity. When death came, heads would bow, rice bowls would be passed, a mass would be sung. New monks would replace the old.

Les hated knowing that there would have to be an autopsy, a humiliating exposure of organs that weren't meant for public viewing. And the administrative detail, the rustle of papers and the roar of saws that would drown out the fleeting whisper of the soul escaping. This he wished he could have spared Paul.

They would find nothing.

Following Paul's death, Les had not watched the news, read the newspapers, or listened to the radio. Paul's death remained a distant knowledge, without public confirmation.

From Paul's dresser he'd taken only a single thick bronze silver-dollar-sized medallion—*Portland Inner-City Man of the Year*. It had a nice feel, a weight beyond its size. He hoped that Paul would be missed, though it was doubtful that his memory could survive for long in that bleak downtown landscape. Les would carry the medallion in the coin pocket of his jeans.

The women were finishing up, putting on their coats, filing out. One older woman glanced at Les as she passed. A flicker of fear passed over her face and she hurried from the church. The look saddened Les. Last summer he had pulled a child from Sardine Lake. It was impossible to forget the blank stares of the bystanders—the horrible unspoken acknowledgment of human fragility. He'd given the child mouth-to-mouth until it was clearly hopeless. Before stopping, he'd looked to the parents, advising with his eyes, yet allowing for their decision. They were speechless, and turned away, holding each other, leaving him with their lifeless child.

Les sometimes thought that he could still taste the child's last moments on his lips.

Mental illness was that way—onlookers overwhelmed by any display of irrationality that hinted that they, too, could fall from the tenuous grace of a day successfully negotiated. He'd seen the look on the ward clerk, the housekeeping crew, the orderlies, that time in 1991 when he'd been *uncertain*. That's what he'd said to the intake psychiatric resident at Santa Barbara General. "I feel uncertain." The resident had smiled, as though they were sharing a private joke. But Les had seen the expression on her face. Human beings were time bombs with blurry timers and hidden fuses.

For some time he sat in the deepening shadows, the late afternoon light seeping through the stained glass windows above the side aisles of the church. Then he biked the mile to the bus station, where he locked up his bicycle and caught the five-thirty express to Reno International.

FIFTEEN

Thomas Bunker III wore tasseled loafers—no socks—a sweater tied around his neck, tortoise-shell-framed sun glasses, and a white painter's cap. He and Artie sat on the deck of the Valencia Hotel in downtown La Jolla, the Pacific at their feet pushing up the lunch price.

"Harvard? Must have been a culture shock for a human being. I got the nod, but weighed the course catalogue against the local maps and surf charts, which made for thumbs down. Bunker rule numero uno: it's easier to fake culture than weather. So it was the MBA from UCLA. Then the tap from Goldman Sachs. Regional office opening right here in beach city. But La Jolla's mostly retired military and Easterners who aren't afraid of the sun. They still think in terms of breeding and credentials. I've got nothing but LA on the resume. Not good, personnel says, shaking its Grecian Formula head. I plea bargain and do two big ones in New York. Dropping Wall Street's big out here, like saying your father landed at Normandy."

Bunker propped his feet up on an adjacent chair, sipping his white wine spritzer. "Not bad. The bell rings at one Pacific Daylight. Fifteen minutes later you're riding the waves. So you're in comics?"

"And CD-ROMS."

"Games?"

"Some, but I specialize in interactive fiction."

"Not much on sales, I'd guess. No one reads anymore."

"San Francisco's different. Maybe it's the fog. We do a fair mail-order business. Slow but steady, good word of mouth. I'm only three blocks from the old City Lights bookstore. Ever heard of it?"

Bunker shook his head. "Trading's trends. Tradition is measured in milliseconds. Make a buck and get out. Retire to the mountains, read Thomas Merton, eat brown rice and tithe some world peace organization."

"Is that your plan?"

"Sure. It's as good as any. Why? Don't tell me you don't like Merton."

"How does he relate to the stock market?"

"Excuse me?"

"Isn't there some inherent contradiction between a life of meditation and playing the market?"

"The Dalai Lama repairs Austin Healeys and old clocks. What's the big deal? It's not like consistency is a virtue."

Artie was reminded of Tuna. "Do you happen to play poker?"

"Not any more. I get enough rush from the ticker and the surf. Why? Do you gamble?"

"Never had the urge."

"I'll give you two weeks on the floor. Then we'll see. It gets into the blood."

"I hate losing."

"That's because you see each event in isolation. There isn't any final tally, not until you're dead, and then you can't read the numbers. Trading's like riding the waves. You catch some, miss others. No big deal as long as you're in the water."

Artie thought of Tuna's marathon in Las Vegas. He could have quit four thousand ahead, but he was more concerned about staying in action.

"So," Bunker continued, "how similar are we?"

"So far we've all had different hair styles. Not a trace of similarity there. And there've been differences in posture, gesture."

"Overall," Bunker said impatiently. "The net-net."

"Conservatively speaking, I'd say ninety-nine percent plus."

Bunker looked out at the ocean. "Of course it was only a matter of time. If you'd bought GenePlus in '91, you'd be rolling in dough. Bigger, better, smarter cattle. Higher lean body mass, lower fat content, smaller turds. It's already split three times." Bunker stopped, ran his finger around the rim of his glass, making a whistling sound. He looked over at Artie, his expression suddenly serious.

"Are we supposed to feel like brothers? I mean, once we get beyond the curiosity?"

After visiting Janine, Artie'd tried to put the scan out of his mind. He leaned on Janine's comment that it could be nothing but a family marker, without any definite implication.

He knew better; he'd seen the terror in Roger. Paul's was less obvious, but certain in retrospect. They were both haunted men.

Artie needed to meet the others. An afternoon with each would be enough to detect any major mental aberrations, especially depressive tendencies. He could inquire about suicidal gestures. Once he'd met them all, he could calculate the odds. Though his plan made perfect sense, it came wrapped with a subtle dread. He tried to tell himself that it was because figuring out the odds was exactly what Tuna Weinstein would do. And Bunker.

He was not an outsider looking in. Whatever stains were carried in their genes affected them all.

What would Bunker's scan look like? An investment banker might have a hot spot for violence, but the hypoactive areas of depression? Not likely, though in October 1929 hundreds had jumped from office windows. It was impossible to think this

through further. Hidden depression could drive a man to suc-
cess, yet be revealed only in a martini count. Psychiatry was
retrospective.

Were the scans more predictive? Would those who jumped
from their boardrooms test differently than those who walked
downstairs and sold apples?

Bunker asked him a second time how they were supposed to
feel. His bravado had slipped; he saw that Artie recognized this
and began inspecting a torn cuticle.

The question was perfect, and Bunker was the least likely to
have asked it. His barely concealed vulnerability was alarming.
Artie saw Bunker standing at the window of his high-rise office.
It could be in a position of power, or . . . it was hard to know.
Perhaps one bled into the other, according to circumstance. Artie
was unsure how to proceed. "It's too soon to say what I feel. It's
going to take time to sink in."

"I considered taking you to meet my parents. But . . ."

Artie waved his hand dismissively.

"I don't think they received the letter from Sarah Woolfson.
They have no idea that I know."

"You're not going to tell them."

"No point. It'd cheapen everything they've done for me. My
dad was in aerospace. When that folded, he took two jobs so that
I could hang out on Melrose. Never complained. Always said
how lucky he and my mom felt having a son. They're from the
old school, where having children means everything. Me, I say
kids are expensive toys that you can't get rid of when you're tired
of them." Bunker straightened up in his chair, motioned to the
waiter to bring the bill. The sun highlighted a glimmer of moisture in his eyes.

"It's hard, thinking about this," Artie said. He started to reach
over and touch Bunker's hand, instead grabbed his glass of water. "That's why I thought I should meet each of us separately."

He decided against telling Bunker about Roger and Paul. There was something unsettled, even unravelled, in Bunker's demeanor.

"House of cards, all fall down," Bunker said. "One moment you're this, then the next you're—well, what are we? Do we adopt each other, go our separate ways, have a few more drinks and forget this ever happened? Goldman Sachs would send it to committee for a recommendation from the experts. What do you say?"

"Do what feels natural," Artie said without much conviction.

"Nothing feels natural. I keep looking at you and seeing myself. I've had enough trouble growing into this body and mind, without having to put myself in your shoes. Don't get me wrong. I'm really grateful for my folks. Love them. That kind of thing. But more family? What would that accomplish?"

"Accomplish? Family's not a matter of purpose." How utterly cold and cynical Bunker sounded. Or was he being truthful? Not knowing his own views or what he even wanted of Bunker was so disturbing that Artie felt himself being cornered into defending a position he wasn't sure he held. All Bunker probably meant was that each of them would be better off alone.

"Take my advice. Sell the nuclear family short. Prices'll be going through the floor. Or you can spend needless energy and ride sibling rivalry all the way to the bottom."

"Aren't you being a little excessive?"

"I don't know," Bunker said. "You seem like a nice guy. We could talk once in a while. Check up on each other. See what happens."

"I didn't mean to upset you."

"Don't worry. I'm not going to jump in the ocean over this. No way. There are people walking around with someone else's heart, liver, kidneys, lungs. They manage not to go to pieces over amalgamated identities. We're just another step along the road." Bunker finished his spritzer, then the last of his glass of water. He added up the bill and dropped a twenty on it.

"Let's try to keep in touch," Artie said. He handed a twenty to Bunker, who stacked Artie's bill on top of his own.

"Absolutely. Through thick and thin." He handed the money to the waiter. "I've already put you in my personal planner. No chance you'll get misplaced."

Artie and Bunker walked to the front of the hotel, then out into the parking lot. The valet drove a '97 Mustang convertible up and handed the keys to Bunker. He glanced back and forth at the two men.

"No big deal." Bunker handed the valet a five. "He's my clone from Mars. Here for the weekend. I told him that if he isn't a good boy, we're sending him back by Greyhound."

"Have a beautiful day, Mr. Bunker," the valet said. He turned to Artie. "Enjoy your stay."

"You earth people are curious," Artie said to the valet as he slid into the passenger seat. Bunker was racing the motor. "Always insisting on enjoyment, happiness, pleasure. It's as if you know nothing about biology. Very gnarly." He winked at the valet as Bunker gunned the Mustang out into the street.

"It could be a kick, hanging out together," Bunker said as he dropped Artie at the San Diego Airport.

"It's something to think about," Artie said, getting out of the car.

The two men shook hands. Artie was reminded of Roger Ligott, standing in front of his house. "You're okay?" he asked.

"Please," Bunker said. "We're going to be just fine."

"Right." Artie nodded, then headed into the terminal.

SIXTEEN

Artie and Janine met at the Stinking Rose 2, the Berkeley branch of the hip Columbus Avenue restaurant that specialized in garlic, right down to garlic-flavored after-dinner mints.

"You sure this is what you want?" Artie asked Janine as they waited for a table. At the table next to the front door two women in jogging suits were *ooohi*ng and *aaahi*ng over milky bowls of high-octane garlic yogurt. Three tables over, two couples were spooning chunks of roasted garlic onto french bread. The fragrance was overwhelming. Artie felt like ducking whenever someone laughed.

He took Janine's arm and guided her to a table by the window.

Janine ordered linguine with garlic and clams, and a side of spinach with garlic.

"Give me a grilled chicken breast, hold the garlic. Salt and pepper only," Artie said to the waiter.

"One chicken breast without garlic," the waiter said loudly to the grill cook. Several of the customers turned and booed. "Will there be anything else? We have raspberry Jell-O and fresh tomato aspic."

"One of each," Artie said.

"I was just kidding," the waiter said.

"I wasn't."

Earlier in the week, Artie and Janine had met for coffee, working through biography and incidentals. Janine was from West Virginia, one of seven sisters, a roller-skating waitress at a drive-in outside Wheeling, full scholarship to the abbreviated six-year undergraduate-MD program at Duke. Residency in neurology in Boston, post-graduate work in Manhattan.

Small-town and big-time, quiet southern ways and a steely determination—how she seamlessly juggled power and grace, practicality and lusciousness was unclear, but Artie didn't care.

A squat woman appeared in the front window. She was waving wildly. "Sorry," Janine said under her breath to Artie as she motioned the woman inside.

"Lynn, this is Artie Singleton." Janine turned to Artie. "Lynn's a therapist, so please excuse her."

The woman kissed Janine's cheek, ran her hand through her dark crew cut, pulled up a chair, scanned the menu. She nodded to the waiter, pointed to the bowl of yogurt at the next table. "I've only got five minutes," she said as the waiter approached. "So don't bother to introduce yourself."

"I was going to say that my name is Dennis, but I guess it won't be necessary." The waiter pouted his way back to the kitchen.

"I've got this great case," Lynn said to Janine, ignoring her comment. "This guy thinks he's an Internet discussion group. He's got a dozen voices, speaks a line or two in one, then switches to another. I thought of you and your machines. I wonder if you could see different brain patterns with each of the personalities."

"I'll bet he's real pleased to know you're broadcasting his dirty underwear," Artie said.

"I'm fond of him," Lynn said, talking and eating, still looking at Janine. "He's a good man. Decent." Lynn glanced at Artie. "My supervisor wants me to start Clozapine. I think he's getting better the old-fashioned way."

Artie clinked his fork on his water glass, glad to hear of someone else's troubles. Being on the Internet without a computer—now that was a problem.

Lynn lowered her voice. "It's strange, but he seems to be getting some pretty good advice from some of the voices on the discussion group. It's like group therapy for one."

"You're joking," Janine said.

"Not really. He states the problem of the day in his own words. Then he breaks into voices, which contradict, advise, analyze, then he makes his own summation. I mainly sit and try to keep my jaw from dropping."

"Does he have any idea why he's hearing voices from the Internet?" Janine asked. "I mean, is he being clever or are they real?"

"Hard to say. He works in computers. Perhaps the Internet has a special significance. I'm not sure that he knows." Lynn shrugged. "Well, got to be going." She blew her breath out on the back of her hand. "Pretty ripe. Hope tonight's group is all stuffed up. Thanks for dinner." She got up, straightened her windbreaker, leaned over, gave Janine a hug. She looked at Artie, said, "I forgive you," and pinched his cheek before hurrying out the door. She did not turn back to see Artie and Janine staring at her.

"Maybe next time we can meet in the city," Artie said. "Just in case whatever's she's got is contagious."

"Before my accident we took tap dancing together. Can you imagine the racket?"

"You? Tap dancing?"

"Complete with spangled shoes. Lynn wanted to combine the dancing with skydiving—she thinks it'd be neat to tap on a cloud." Janine gave Artie a wry, whimsical look. "I hear that she's a great therapist and that it's standing-room-only for her groups. By the way, I think she liked you."

"And?"

"And."

Artie entered his dark apartment, dropped his coat on the couch, turned on the lights, and went through his mail. Junk mail, a condolence card, and a reproduction of his scan, which Janine had sent. Artie extracted the rolled five-by-seven photocopy from the mailing tube; he considered tearing it up and tossing it in the garbage, but he didn't. Instead, he walked into his study and dropped it in his bottom desk drawer, where it came to rest alongside the letter from Sarah. Rolled. The scan reminded Artie of his college diploma. Only this was a different kind of graduation.

He opened the card; he didn't recognize the sender. He slipped it on top of a pile of unanswered letters on the corner of his desk. One day soon he would have to respond. But how do you write to people you don't know? Maybe he'd have Janine over. She could sit on the couch, reading; he could finish off the entire pile. The evening would have melodrama, romance, sympathies everywhere.

But not yet, he thought, looking up to see the new message on the computer monitor.

```
From: NEWSADVISORY <remailer@cypherpunks.ca>
To: Arthur Singleton

>Me, too.
Thomas Bunker
```

Artie groaned and slumped into the chair in front of the computer. Not possible, he kept thinking as he picked up the phone and dialed; Bunker's line was busy. Maybe that was a good sign. Or maybe it was the police, using his phone to call the morgue ambulance. He switched to the speaker phone mode and punched redial, the busy signal filling the apartment, Bunker's life on hold, in the balance, Bunker neither dead or alive until someone answered.

Bunker's line remained busy.

The taped message from the coroner's office said to try back in the morning. The *San Diego Tribune* confirmed that the death had been reported two days ago. The cause of death was not listed, though the woman at the *Tribune* suggested that the obituary phrasing indicated suicide.

It had been four days since he'd seen Bunker. The email was sent only minutes ago, but the message could have been delayed at the remailer, held for sending until a specified time.

He went back over the three messages. They were similarly worded. Newsadvisory had a particularly threatening quality, not the tone of anyone's last words.

He pulled up the password-protected file with the other names.

```
Jefferson Lippe
Asher Newman
Mark Caputo
Les Robbins
Harold Weinstein
Bernard Sadler
Thomas Bunker
Paul Lafora
Roger Ligott
```

He moved Ligott, Lafora, and Bunker into a separate column and stared at the remaining names.

"She tires easily. If you need anything, I'll be in the kitchen." Carolyn, Sarah Woolfson's day nurse, led Artie down the narrow hallway to the bedroom. Artie held his breath, the smells of his mom's nursing home still fresh in his memory. But the room was bright and cheery, the window open, the air vaguely sweet.

Sarah was in a wheelchair at the window, looking out over her garden. She was smaller than he'd remembered her. She turned slowly and took his hand in hers. He felt bone on bone, a thin grinding. How different from his mother, who had died with her hands strong and muscular. But she hadn't known what to do with them. He remembered those hands, picking idly at her robe, flitting over her face and through her hair without direction.

"I guess I'm losing my grip," Sarah said, her voice indistinct. The morning sun shone on her scalp. She continued to hold his hand while she looked him up and down. She nodded in approval and motioned for him to have a seat in the easy chair alongside her.

"You've seen them?" she asked after Artie was seated.

"Some."

"And?"

"They're doing fine. I've visited four so far. All okay."

Sarah looked at him with a puzzled expression. She shook her head. "Something's wrong." She wiped at her mouth with a crumpled tissue.

"You couldn't have known. No one could have anticipated." He stopped as Sarah's face darkened with worry and guilt. She was a dying woman. Let her go in peace.

"Known?"

"I shouldn't be burdening you. Besides, I mainly came by to see how you're feeling."

Sarah waved her hand. "We did something wrong?"

"Not at all. Everyone came out perfectly."

She continued staring at him. "What is it?"

"I'm not sure." Artie turned to look out the window. He started by discussing Roger.

"I've always wanted a family so big that you'd have to rent Candlestick Park for reunions. It couldn't have been him just finding out he had brothers. No. It has to be something else," Sarah said.

"Do you know who our real parents are? Maybe there's something in the genes."

"Henry didn't want me to know. He made me promise not to ask."

"But he worked at a clinic. Which one?"

Sarah reached out and touched his hand. "You think he'd think badly of me? I mean, circumstances have changed."

Artie saw Sarah as a little girl, asking her parents for forgiveness. "I'm sure your husband would understand."

Sarah deliberated. "You won't let it change your feelings about your mom?"

"Of course not."

"The Samson Clinic. I think it was bought a few years ago by some conglomerate."

"Last time you mentioned a brilliant scientist and a famous novelist. Can you remember anything more?"

Sarah's shoulders slumped. "It seemed like such a good idea. Henry got the very best." She looked at Artie, her eyes glistening with a combination of shame and pride. "Henry said the man had won a Nobel. But I didn't ask. Honestly."

"In—?"

Sarah shook her head. "That's all I know." She sighed, becoming even smaller as though some part of her had fallen away.

"You must be tired. I'll let you get some rest." Artie stood up to leave.

Sarah shrugged. "You won't tell anyone that I told you?"

"Mum's the word."

Sarah took his hand and held it in hers. "You'll visit again?"

"It'd be my pleasure," Artie said, being careful not to be the first to let go.

A quick Internet search revealed that the Samson Clinic had been purchased by American Hospital Systems in 1991. Later that year AHS had been acquired by General Foods. The clinic—renamed Clinic for Reproductive Assistance and Genetic Counseling— was located on Van Ness Avenue, in an art deco building that once had housed British Motor Cars, an upscale auto dealership. As a kid Artie had loved to look at the red MGs and racing green Austin Healeys in the window.

He hated to imagine what window displays the clinic would have.

There was no need to worry. The elegant marble and granite ground floor had been subdivided into a labyrinth of administrative cubicles. Artie had to explain three times, to three separate interviewers, that he wasn't interested in having a child, or any specific gene testing, that he was a reporter for *Mother Jones*, and that he merely wanted to discuss the history of the clinic with the head physician. *Yes, it is going to be a favorable piece on the advances of science. No, it will not get into the ethics of embryo freezing and preservation, pre-implantation embryo cultures for prenatal genetic information. No, it will not compare costs and results. No, it isn't sponsored by any pro-life, anti-vivisection, or midwifery group.*

"I thought it would be of historical interest to recount the early days, before many of the techniques were perfected," Artie repeated for the fourth time, now addressing Dr. Crea, a short, dark, intense man in his early forties. He was wearing a stiffly starched lab coat, his name embroidered on the label in mauve.

"I joined up with Samson after my residency, worked with him until he retired. A brilliant man, a brilliant career, over a dozen textbooks and hundreds of journal articles. *And*," Dr. Crea paused for emphasis, "completely honest. A scientist from the old school."

As he described Samson's accomplishments, Dr. Crea escorted Artie up two flights of stairs and down a maze of hallways. They reached a locked corridor. A large metal yellow sign read NO ADMITTANCE WITHOUT AUTHORIZATION. Dr. Crea started to unlock the wire gate.

Artie shook his head. Beyond the gate, inside the labs, would be, Artie imagined, row upon row of white-smocked techs nudging and manipulating tiny bits of matter into being. "I'm a little pressed for time. Maybe if you had any snapshots of the original clinic, the founding staff? Or of some of the earliest equipment? That could make an interesting cover."

Crea took Artie back to his office. In a glass case on the bottom shelf of his bookcase were the first micropipettes and fine wire loops that the clinic had used. "These were developed by Henry Woolfson. A quiet man who never got his due credit. Dr. Samson used to say that Woolfson's instruments were the real breakthroughs behind the first embryo implants. That and his perfection of the nutrient solutions. You realize that this was one of the first three *in vitro* fertilization clinics in the country and the first on the West Coast? We did our first implants in late '79, the year after Louise Simpson was born in England. Samson told me privately that they could have begun years earlier if the religious right hadn't stalled the FDA for so long. Too bad. Think of all the women who were turned away."

Dr. Crea shoved aside a pile of papers. Underneath, in a filigreed silver frame, was a small faded photograph of two men. Behind them was a jungle gym's worth of glass tubing. "That's Woolfson," Crea said, pointing to a burly man with a black beard and a kind, timid smile.

The man who had stolen him into existence. Artie wondered what Woolfson must have thought, all those nights scheming and planning. He'd seen the admiration in Sarah's eyes. He, Artie, was their life's work. So were Roger, Paul, Bunker. All dead now. The only one he'd visited who was still alive was Tuna Weinstein. Hardly what Henry would have envisioned.

"Is there any chance I could borrow this picture? We could have it duplicated and I'd have it back to you in a couple days."

"You're going to emphasize that we operate under the strictest of controls? And stress that we are not working on cloning. No sidebars with photos of cute sheep. Every time an article appears we get all kinds of crank calls. You promise me that, the picture is yours."

"Do you think human cloning is possible? I mean, it seems so simple to accomplish in animals." Artie tried to appear as casual as possible. But Crea stiffened up. "Just kidding," Artie added.

"It's not a laughing matter. There're lots of kooks out there who think we're transplanting Hitler's brain into innocent little children."

"I saw that movie. It made no sense."

"Some screenwriter's idea of genetics gone wild. It's totally irresponsible."

"I can promise you that's not the purpose of this article."

"Anything to rev up the public," Crea said.

"I'll leave out any mention of cloning. That's probably better than saying it isn't possible. Denial sometimes sounds like you're hiding something."

Crea nodded. "Scientific discovery has its own pace. Public acceptance operates at a slower tempo. Any larger overview, if there is to be one, comes still later. Waves of controversy are nothing more than the natural tides of understanding. Look at the history of the atom bomb: a surge of feverish research followed belatedly by lukewarm apologies from a handful of senior scientists well past their creative years. *Forgive me for I knew not what I did.* Or: *If only I'd known.* As if the direction of science was mysteriously hidden from their view until their grants ran out. That's utter baloney. It's in the DNA of science to continue inexorably forward. That's the way it is, and the way it will be." Crea slipped the photo out of the frame and handed it to Artie. "Don't worry. I've got the original negative. I'll redo it, make it bright and fresh again. There's nothing like the chance to update history."

Artie took the photo and put it in his jacket pocket. He walked over to the glass case and stared at the pipettes. Crea opened the case and carefully handed him one, balancing it in Artie's palm. "The new ones have a smaller bore and a more finely beveled tip. But essentially they're the same."

Artie moved his hand up and down, trying to assess the difference in weight between an object and its implications. *It's just a piece of glass,* he told himself.

"Easy," Crea said. "You squeeze it, it'll break."

"Sorry."

"Come on. Take a quick look." Before Artie could decline, Crea took the pipette and put it back in the case, and motioned Artie to join him. Crea led him down the hall to one of the OFF LIMITS labs. He pushed the door open.

Artie was stunned by the lab's ordinariness. It was narrow and cramped, two lab counters separated by an aisle barely wide enough to accommodate the two young women sitting back to back on tall metal stools. Both wore pink high-top Keds, faded jeans, and white lab coats. The woman at the far table was wearing a Giants cap on top of a white surgical cap. The woman nearest him wore a Mickey Mouse cap. Both had their handbags tucked beneath their stools. Both were leaning into microscopes.

B. B. King was blasting from a portable CD player on the counter. The woman nearest Artie wore a huge half-moon earring which hung motionless even as her feet danced along the lower rung of the stool. Artie was reminded of a juggler.

Above the din the two women were comparing recipes for *linguine con vongole.* "This is where we do the embryo separations." Crea nodded at the woman tapping her foot. He looked into the second set of eyepieces on the microscope, then back at Artie. "She's separating one cell from an eight-cell pre-implant embryo. When it's done, she'll transfer it to a separate petri dish. We let it grow for a time, then use PCR to get adequate genetic material for testing."

"PCR?"

"Polymerase chain reaction. A way of reduplicating genetic material. It allows the single cell to act like a gene factory. We can detect Huntington's Chorea, cystic fibrosis, certain kinds of muscular dystrophy—the list is growing daily."

"Here. Take a look," the woman said like a ventriloquist, holding the blunt end of the pipette firmly between her teeth. She pointed to the second set of binocular eyepieces.

Artie wanted to say no. Instead he found himself squinting, the field slowly coming into focus.

"Careful not to jiggle the scope," the woman said. Manipulating the pipette in her left hand, she held the embryo motionless. With her right she slid a fine wire loop into the center of the embryo. After some delicate maneuvering, one of the cells floated free. The woman sighed.

"Pretty slick. We just pop this guy into its own bed, add some oregano, rosemary, and PCR and this mother turns into a genetic workhorse. Modern science making the world a better place." Behind her, B. B. sang the blues.

"You left out the garlic," Crea said, looking at the label on the medical chart adjacent to the microscope. "Mr. and Mrs. Pelligrini would like some garlic."

"I didn't know you were a cook," the other woman said to Crea.

Artie had seen enough. He stepped back from the microscope and leaned against the far end of the counter. He took a couple deep breaths. "Looks like you guys have a lot of fun here," he said, trying to smile.

The woman with the earring said, "It beats cancer research. This way, if I suck up something, I don't worry that it'll kill me."

"I think she's saying that this isn't exactly a job for a respectable woman," the other woman said with a smile. "All day with your lips to the tubes." She turned to Crea. "And don't say a word. Remember, I scream harassment and you get a year of night call."

"This lab is more informal than I might have hoped," Crea said with a shake of his head. But he was smiling, and so were the women. As Artie imagined Henry Woolfson might have, sucking up the little speck of life, bringing it home, where he could raise his own idea of family.

The room filled with a ferocious guitar lick. The woman with the Mickey Mouse cap, her head to the eyepiece, said softly, "Play it, B. B."

Artie wondered if there'd been music the day he'd been separated out. Jimi Hendrix? Lawrence Welk? Bob Dylan? Or all three? That might be the explanation, some fundamental dissonance deep within his original cell.

"I thought what we did would make more sense if you saw it in context," Crea said.

They walked down the hall to the elevator. While they were waiting, Artie asked, "In the beginning, what were the charges for *in vitro* fertilization?"

"It depended. Before it was covered by insurance, the clinic took what the patients could pay. Some of those better off made donations, which helped pay for the others. And there were donors. I mean financial donors. They're listed downstairs."

The elevator arrived, the two men descended, exiting on the ground floor. At the back, behind the rows of interview cubicles, was a large granite plaque filled with names. "The first group of contributors. We keep it to remind ourselves of our beginnings."

"You wouldn't have a list of names? It might make an interesting footnote to the article."

"Sure. It's in one of our brochures." Crea walked over to a rack containing a dozen brightly colored pamphlets. Artie had the feeling of being in a travel agency specializing in exotic countries. Crea handed him a couple of copies of the pamphlet that outlined the history of ivf. On the back cover was a photo of the donor list.

"Thanks for everything," Artie said.

"Remember. I have to approve the article before you print it."

"Absolutely." They shook hands. Artie turned and walked out into the main floor, through the succession of interview cubicles.

A couple in their late thirties sat across from each other at a small desk, reading from a series of brochures. Another couple sat at an adjacent cubicle, listening to a nurse-specialist spout statistics. At the front of the building, in a small, tastefully furnished lobby, a young couple waited. They were holding hands and talking softly, as though in church.

Waiting to be called.

Artie held his breath until he was out in the street.

SEVENTEEN

When they were juniors at Cal Tech, Les Robbins and his dorm roommate had spent much of their free time developing a computer-generated poker strategy. Les was intrigued by the mathematics, his roommate by the potential profits. During a series of dry runs in the dormitory, the system seemed infallible. Despite his habitual skepticism, Les found himself anxious to give it the acid test.

To avoid being obvious, they chose the Bicycle Club in Bell Garden, a big LA cardroom. In the main gambling area were over a hundred and fifty poker tables, nearly all jammed. In an adjacent room were an additional hundred tables offering a variety of Asian games.

Les lasted thirty minutes, overcome by an increasing lightheadedness and a fear that he might faint. Later that semester, when his roommate and another classmate had won enough money to move into a swanky condo in Marina Del Rey, Les tried to understand why he had bolted from the casino. He had no moral position against gambling nor did he have any specific objection to making a quick buck. He was superb with numbers. The system was completely legitimate and worked as well with three as with two.

The offer still stood for him to join in.

He complained of working indoors, the lack of fresh air, the cramped tables, cigarette smoke, artificial lighting. He had a litany of excuses.

He never mentioned that he couldn't bear to see the look on the players' faces. The intensity of their desires scared him, the undisguised need to win at all costs. Insignificance, not money, was the issue that haunted the players pounding the tables, ripping the cards, screaming, laughing, taunting, threatening.

The casino was a temple to victory, cause and effect, effort and cunning rewarded. It was what men did—whether it was the stock market, a pickup basketball game in the gym—or at the tables. It was as much a part of life as hating yourself. And equally distasteful.

He worried that his disinterest in winning was a coverup for stronger, more violent urges in that direction, undercurrents of feeling that, if acknowledged, might be uncontrollable.

He stopped visiting his two friends in their poolside condo and dropped out of school the last month of his senior year. He'd only had a senior paper to finish. "No," he said to his advisor. "Count me out."

If he'd sat down at the poker table, joined in, he'd have been one of *them*. Not himself. If he'd finished the paper, he'd have been one of the graduating class, a statistic for the alumni association—though he had to admit that by dropping out he represented another statistic. At least it was a smaller number that hinted at individual reasons for not graduating.

Including mental imbalance. Quitting school at the last minute was a classic pattern of the passive-aggressive, the refusal to graduate a reflection of a thinly disguised hostility. But that wasn't it, not in his case. He wasn't angry at anyone, not at his parents, the university, his graduating classmates.

Dropping out had its own contradictory messages. So be it. It was not possible to strip language of contradiction. If one got beneath words and symbols, there would remain the act, if some-one cared enough to take the time to look closely.

He moved to the mountains.

His visits to Seattle, Portland, and San Diego—booked using a fake ID, paid for in cash—had closely followed Arthur's itiner-ary as listed on his Travelnet account. Anyone who investigated beyond suicide would see that the deaths occurred in the wake of Arthur's visits.

This was the first departure from his plan. He'd initially come to Las Vegas the day after Arthur had visited Harold Weinstein. But Harold had stayed at the table for three days, getting up only to pour coffee, hit the john, and grab a succession of hot dogs at the nearby snack bar.

For three days Les had tried to stay out of sight. Several times he heard passing players say that Weinstein was on a hot streak. Les smiled at the irony. But the smells of the casino and his in-creasing fatigue eventually drove him away. Too exhausted to think straight, he needed time in the mountains to regroup.

He waited until the following Sunday. Shazam would be closed, Arthur would have no obvious alibi. Les booked the flight to San Francisco with his fake ID, and the round-trip flight from San Francisco to Las Vegas with a touched-up ID—Arthur Singleton.

Over the phone, the manager of Day's End was short and un-cooperative. "He's here when he's here. If not, then not."

"He owes me a bunch of money," Les said.

"Then definitely not."

"I owe him a bunch of money?"

"Leave it at the front desk. I'll watch it for him."

"I'm from out of town and will be leaving soon?"

"Not now. Sometime later, but not specifically."

"You should wear a hat when you're out in the sun," Les said before slamming down the airport telephone.

It was important to be inconspicuous, Les thought as he approached a side entrance to the Glass Slipper. Like a magician, the first line of defense was misdirection. He wore Arthur's Captain Marvel satin jacket. In Las Vegas no one would notice, yet if there were an inquiry, everyone would remember.

The automatic doors opened and Les stepped inside. The noise was overwhelming, a thousand lives caught between giant metal gears. The grinding went directly to his head, spreading out into a buzzing, a beating, a rhythmic droning that he could not dislodge. It was worse than he'd remembered from the first visit, the commotion of slot and video poker machines competing with keno numbers being broadcast over an infinity of overhead speakers, as well as two country-and-western lounge bands wailing away in different keys.

Being off-center was dangerous. He took several deep breaths, sucking in stale smoke and the smell of sour drinks, then eased his way through two aisles of brooding slot machines.

The poker room was shielded from the rest of the casino by high clear plexiglass walls. At a distance the players appeared to be underwater, trapped in a brightly lit aquarium. Les scanned the faces. Sure enough, adjacent to the coffee pot was Harold, opening three packets of sugar and pouring them into a cup of coffee.

"That's my machine," an elderly woman said without expression. Les was startled, puzzled, until he looked over at his hand clutching the woman's slot machine lever. He let go, floating free in the aisle. His legs were rubbery, his chest was constricted as though he were trying to inhale coins. He hit himself in his chest several times with his fist until he realized that he was breathing just fine, that it wasn't the air that was stuck in his windpipe.

The similarities in their appearance should have been old hat. But with each meeting the horror was more intense. Roger could have been a twin. Meeting Paul could have meant triplets. Arthur and Thomas would mean quintuplets. Sarah's letter said there were ten. Why stop at ten? Fifteen or twenty would be another order of magnitude more terrible. It was a dreadful equation that defied mathematics—the greater the sum, the less the total. Ten times one was less than one.

He tried to distract himself by focusing upon differences. He reminded himself that he didn't use sugar in his coffee. But he once did, before he became concerned about processed and refined foods. Now he used three teaspoons of honey.

That had been a bad choice. There were other differences, the most obvious being choosing to spend time in this godforsaken casino in this godforsaken town. At least they didn't have that desire in common.

The other meetings had taken place privately, without prior letters, phone calls, or faxes of introduction. Les had scouted Roger's cabin, Thomas's condo, and Paul's small shed behind the monastery, dropping in unannounced when he was sure that each of them would be alone. By occurring in unfamiliar surroundings, at night, without the verification of letter or photograph or the presence of others, the meetings already had assumed a dreamlike insubstantiality. They felt flat and two-dimensional, easily tucked away beneath memory like important letters slipped unexamined into a bottom drawer, letters that should be kept but not read.

Les knew that he would have to look one day, but not now while he was accumulating the raw data. Later, when he was whole again, there would be plenty of time.

Harold was back in his seat, looking at his cards, his visor down, his eyes deep in shadow. Les wondered what stakes he was playing for, as if that might make a difference in his plan.

Leave him alone, Les told himself. *He's not you, not by a long shot. Leave the casino, get on the plane. Once you're back in Truckee it'll be like this never happened.*

A pleasant thought, but impossible. Roger's bagged face taunted like a dark cloud nailed to the corner of his mind. Often Les would find himself replaying how it might have felt, pulling the bag over his face, fastening the duct tape, then waiting to run out of breath. So deliberate, the equation having only one answer, Roger knowing that it wasn't possible to continue in a diluted diminished way.

Paul and Thomas—Les had seen their eyes at the last. They knew—all of them.

In freshman biology Les had read of the crested penguin. The mother lays two eggs a season, one small and one large. Given the harshness of her Arctic surroundings, she only can rear one bird to maturity. If both are hatched, the smaller penguin acquiesces to being killed by its larger sibling or the mother. The textbook suggested that this was a Darwinian urge built into the genes, the smaller bird willingly sacrificing itself for the smoother perpetuation of the species. *An example of genetic altruism,* the instructor had called it.

As evolutionary biology it made sense.

But as human behavior?

All of them understood that existing as a group was not an option. Roger's death underscored that assumption.

It was a sign of inner strength that Roger had taken his own life rather than passively waiting to be struck down. His suicide had been an act of pride. So would have been going on the offensive. If one of the others were out looking for him, that would be understandable, acceptable.

The country music had risen above din and was quickly approaching the level of pure pain. A Loretta Lynn look-alike was singing off-key. Les knew that he would only last a short time.

Harold was glued to his seat.

Les had hoped to get him away from the tables—a walk to the back of the parking lot, a chat in his motel room, a stroll in a park, if Las Vegas had one. Somewhere out of sight. It would only take a minute.

The woman to his left hit a jackpot and the machine ejaculated quarters to accompanying bells and whistles. Personnel would be arriving to clear the machine and pass out free drinks so that onlookers would not be disappointed with their fate.

He slipped out of the slot machine area and made his way to a courtesy phone in front of one of the exits. Moments later Harold Weinstein was paged.

It was a side exit, one seldom used. If they were seen, it would be a matter of two brothers, one in a Captain Marvel jacket. Les had the operator page him three times, the last time mentioning to ring him in the poker room.

Harold didn't show.

Les sucked in his breath and walked back to the slots, where he could again see the poker room. Harold was gone. Les rushed back to the side exit.

Nobody.

He phoned the operator. "There's no Mr. Weinstein here," she said. "Or he's not answering."

Les hung up. He checked the men's rooms and the bars, then the poker room again. Harold had disappeared. Les phoned the Day's End. Weinstein hadn't been in all day.

Vanished. Gone.

Perhaps he'd seen him and had been waiting to make a getaway. But to where? Where would he go if he were Harold?

Les spent the next several hours scouring the casino and phoning Day's End. Harold's seat was now occupied by a fat middle-aged man with a shiny forehead that collected the overhead light into a purplish pool. It was as though Harold had never been.

The evening passed in slow motion. Les took a room in a nearby motel, paging, phoning, checking the cardroom every hour. By the following afternoon he was exhausted. Somehow Harold had eluded him, he conceded. Les took the early evening flight back to Reno.

On the flight home he tried to convince himself that his trip had been successful, that he had accomplished what he'd originally intended. Out of sight, out of mind. He tried to feel better, but it didn't work. Harold being gone wasn't the same as being *gone.* Glumly Les accepted that he'd have to return to Las Vegas yet again.

EIGHTEEN

Janine phoned Shazam; she was on her way to give a lecture at the California Academy of Science in Golden Gate Park. If Artie could meet her in half an hour at the Chinese-Italian restaurant at the foot of the Ninth Street offramp, they'd have enough time for a quick bite. Artie rushed home for a shower and a clean shirt. Lovely Janine, he was thinking as he unlocked his apartment door and stepped inside.

"How's tricks?" Tuna Weinstein asked, rising from his seat on Artie's couch. "I hope you don't mind the manager letting me in."

"What're you doing here?" Artie's voice rose in a combination of anger and panic. "You didn't tell him, did you?"

"Tell your manager? Hey, don't go all paranoid on me. This is going to be all calculated, choreographed, right down to the press releases."

Artie started to interrupt, but Tuna wasn't finished. He kept talking, at the same time pacing the room, picking up the ceramic statues, putting them down again, checking out the bookcases, fingering the leather of the couch. He was wearing the same style jeans and denim shirt with silver collar tips that he'd worn when Artie'd first met him. He gave off an unpleasant smell of stale cigarette smoke and perhaps a bit of mildew. "Nice place you've got here. Pretty comfy. I could adjust to this. Not the day job, mind you, but the accoutrements. Good stuff," he said, patting the sofa.

"Which brings me to the point. Individually each of our bodies is worth five, maybe ten bucks. A little calcium, a few pounds of sweetbreads—if you include the brain—and a few yards of tripe. In India you might get two grand for a kidney. That's it, tops. But collectively, the sky's the limit. We start with National Institutes of Health. They sign us up, start their data files—questionnaires, a few blood tests, sperm and stool samples. Nothing you can't spare. Once we're on the payroll, the tests under way, they couldn't even think of dropping us. We've got 'em by the short hairs, a government-backed lifetime free ride. It's better than T-bills or Ginnie Maes.

"The future is genetics, and we've got the keys to their puzzles. We're going to need lawyers, patent and copyright specialists. No one's going to be stealing any ideas from our bodies."

"Not now. I've got a dinner date in fifteen minutes." Artie motioned to the door.

"I can wait until you get back."

"Five minutes. Then you're out of here. So, feel free to sit down and take a deep breath. One only."

"Not necessary. The last week I've been checking. A whole bunch of science organizations have spent all kinds of money studying identical twins. Think what they'd pay for ten of us."

"Eight," Artie interrupted. He decided not to mention Bunker.

"That's what I'm coming to. Maybe we've got a bad gene. We've got to negotiate from strength, before they start doing the lemming two-step."

"Tuna. I hope you're not serious."

"You bet. I don't have a Harvard sheepskin to fall back on. One busted semester at Cal State is the total resume. It's been strictly hustle for a buck, no security, no benefits, no cushy family money in the reserve tank."

"Doesn't being your own self mean anything to you?"

"Not a bit. You think I want to be like this, that I chose to be hardwired for gambling? I tell myself I could have been anything—a songwriter, a mathematician, an astronaut, an investment banker. But I'm so addicted I'd rather piss in a glass than leave the table and miss a hand. You say, 'Try Gamblers' Anonymous, therapy, will power.' Sure. The power of positive thinking. If you believe that, you might as well try fucking the tooth fairy."

Artie again motioned for Tuna to sit down. Tuna shrugged, dropped onto the couch. Artie took a chair from his kitchen, straddled it backwards, his arms on the wooden back, his chin on his hands. He spoke slowly, looking down at the carpet.

"I think everyone wants to believe that they're somehow special, unique. It's what makes us tick."

Tuna shook his head. "Down deep we're nothing. Anyone who's taken Zen 101 knows that."

"Whatever," Artie said with a note of irritation. "But I have no intention of being part of some humiliating study."

"You don't own the rights to our bodies. You give me the list and I'll contact the others. Let them decide. One man, one vote. Majority rule. It's the American way."

"No." Artie made a point of checking his watch.

Tuna got up, stood with his arms folded across his chest. "When you get back we're going to discuss the NIH proposal, right?"

"Wrong. I'll talk to you tomorrow."

"Wrong," Tuna said, matching Artie's inflection. "Wrong, wrong, wrong."

"Suit yourself," Artie said, stepping around Tuna, walking into the bathroom. He closed the door behind him, aware of the peculiar sensation of leaving yet not leaving the living room. It was like trying to walk away from his shadow.

"Relax. You, me, we're worth waiting for," Tuna said when Artie stepped out of the bathroom. "You show up on time, women think you're anxious to please. It sets the wrong precedent." Tuna was standing in the middle of the living room; he was wearing the blazer that Artie had bought for his mother's memorial service. "Fits perfectly," he said, moving his shoulders, burrowing into the coat. "I'd feel better wearing this while we discuss government grants. It'll be like a dress rehearsal for when we show up with the others. I think conservative gray flannel slacks and this sportcoat would make a great team uniform."

"Take that off." Though he was furious, Artie also saw a younger version of himself pulling some similar college prank in a pathetic attempt at being noticed. But this was no laughing matter. Tuna's hands were deep in the jacket's pockets, as though claiming this new territory. Artie prayed Janine was stalled in traffic.

"I know. Being a civil servant isn't exactly first choice. I've considered private organizations. Genentech and Biogen would have nicer examining rooms and lots of freebies. But biotech is so iffy. They get swallowed up by United Fruit, we end up as tomato research."

"Your life would never be yours again," Artie said as he put on a fresh shirt. The sight of the plastic wrapper made him queasy; he balled it up and threw it in a wastebasket. He slipped on the blue sweater hanging from the knob of his bedroom door. "You couldn't go anywhere without people stopping, staring, asking questions, snapping pictures."

"So what?" Posing at the window, Telegraph Hill behind him, Tuna looked like a Las Vegas imitation of soiled gentry. "Consider public attention the cost of doing business. You told me about Roger Ligott, that he apparently valued individuality more than his life. That's as stupid as a poker player thinking a run of bad cards is personal, a malignant message from the gods. It may *feel* that way when the losing's right on top of you, but feeling shouldn't be the same as believing." Tuna waved his hand. "Someone should have sat Roger down and straightened him out."

"What about Paul Lafora?"

"Yeah. That kind of bothers me, too. *You* I can see getting all nutty. But from the way you described Lafora, he should have been cool about it. Of course we don't know he killed himself. Maybe he was knocked off by one of his less enlightened brethren. Seeing someone else approximate nirvana while you're still trying to get the morning news out of your head must be a real downer."

"I talked with the coroner. They're pretty sure it was a suicide."

"You think it might be in the genes?" Tuna said, his voice uncharacteristically soft.

Artie wondered what Tuna would think if he showed him the scan. Would it worry Tuna or appeal to his mercenary streak? Artie couldn't shake the additional concern that he was indirectly responsible for Tuna. If he were a doctor, not mentioning Bunker or the scan would qualify for malpractice. But he wasn't Tuna's doctor. Sarah had designated him as messenger, not healer. Who was she to tell him what to say? He had no contract with the others. He slipped on his shoes and socks, pointed to the door.

"Would you feel better if you thought that Lafora had been murdered?" Tuna asked, ignoring Artie's gesture. Before Artie could answer, Tuna said, "I know that I would. Murder's meaningless, without implication. We should go up to Oregon and investigate. We pin it on one of the other monks and we can consider Roger's suicide as a bad beat, something off the oddsmaker's chart."

"Listen. I'm in a real hurry. Can you get that through your head?"

"I'm busted." Tuna sprawled out on the couch, his hands behind his head. "Flat stone tapped out. Lost the last of my bankroll on some fool tourist's inside straight. Knocked me right out of my seat. No point in going back to the motel. The manager at Day's End has given me three days, then it's out in the street. I had to cash a bad check for the round-trip flight to talk turkey with my only known family." Tuna sighed. Despite his arrogant posture there were signs of defeat reflected in the deep lines of his face and the weariness in his voice.

"You're not suggesting—?" Artie asked. But he already knew the answer.

"Consider it a loan, or better yet, an investment. I'm overdue for a major score. We take part of the proceeds and ante up into the World Series of Poker. Last year's winner made over a million for three days of playing. You could handle that, couldn't you?"

"Let me get this straight. I'm supposed to get real excited about advancing you poker money because you're so good that you're going to be next year's world's champion? And, correct me if I'm wrong, your recent losses are nothing but some fluky aberration that happens as often as Halley's Comet. Right?"

"This way you'd have some time to think about the NIH grants. I realize that you're a conservative business man and have to mull it over, run it by your accountant, crunch the numbers in some retirement software package. Believe me, I'm a patient man, a man of principles. You help me out, I'll keep my mouth shut *and* play with responsibility and purpose."

"How much are we talking?"

Tuna began counting on his fingers. "Room and board and a bit of operating expenses. Let's say two grand a month, until the NIH money starts rolling in."

"Get out. And take off my jacket before you go."

"I could squeak by on eighteen hundred. And please don't threaten me."

Tuna was a loose cannon. For a quick buck he'd phone the *National Enquirer* or some TV exposé. Artie quickly calculated.

He couldn't afford more than a few hundred without borrowing on the store. He countered. "I'll cover this month's rent, then half the rent until we get this squared away."

"Rent's only six hundred. It's the food I'm worried about. Eating healthy costs bucks. Plus I'll need a nubbin of a bankroll. Fifteen hundred."

"A thousand. That's my last offer."

"Before the first of the month? So there won't be late charges."

"I can't believe I'm doing this," Artie said. "It's pure extortion."

"You're the one who's dragging his feet on the opportunity of a lifetime. Fifteen hundred a month is peanuts compared to what NIH could be dishing up."

"I thought we settled on a thousand."

"I was just making sure." Tuna eased himself off the couch, walked over to Artie, who was now standing at the door, and slapped him on the shoulder. "You did real good," he said, breaking into a laugh. "I thought you'd go for thirteen, maybe fourteen hundred. You sure you never played cards?"

Tuna kept his hand on Artie's shoulder. The man had just extracted a thousand a month from him and now he was caressing him like a long-lost brother. To his surprise Artie looked directly at Tuna and started to laugh.

"You're really pretty good," Artie said. "Walk into my apartment with a one-move checkmate."

Tuna smiled. "Yeah. From now on you're going to be *my* checkmate."

"That's not what I meant."

Tuna put both hands on Artie's shoulders. "You're not going to regret this, not one bit. Playing with family money'll give me a whole new perspective. I should be flush again in no time."

"And then?"

"I get ahead enough, we put aside your money for the World Series entrance fee." He gave Artie a final pat, jammed his hands in his jeans front pockets. "Relax, I'm going to make you rich. In the meantime, if you find yourself short, I'd suggest that you strongly consider the NIH route. Swallow your pride and it'll be a lifetime of drinks on the house."

"Alcohol gives us headaches," Artie mumbled as he pulled a folded check from his wallet, wrote out the first month's payment. Tuna bowed, slipped the check in the blazer breast pocket, opened the door, stepped out into the hallway.

"The coat," Artie said.

"Yeah, I almost forgot. Thanks. It's a real beauty." Tuna turned and started down the stairs.

Artie wanted to say something, but there was no point. He waited until Tuna was out in the street before locking up and running down the stairs two at a time.

By the time Artie arrived at the restaurant, Janine had left. "Not too pleased, if you ask me," the hostess said. "And her language. You keep her waiting again, I suggest you have first-rate catastrophic medical insurance."

"Stick to reading off the specials," Artie said, angered with himself and Tuna. He ignored a volley of stares as he abruptly turned and left the restaurant.

Not in the mood for a solitary dinner, he grabbed two burritos at a corner taqueria. Eating standing up made him feel less lonely, gave him a sense of purpose, of being on the go. But the destination was home. By eight o'clock he was back at his computer. It was a simple matter to cross-reference the donors named in the Samson Clinic brochure with a list of Nobel prize winners. Richard Fleischer was the only name appearing on both lists. Within minutes the Internet coughed up the references and the abstracts of two hundred scientific articles and seven technical books. There was also a book of essays that was not abstracted.

Fleischer had won the Nobel for his research in the physics of superconductors. After winning the prize he'd left academia to work on his own theories of consciousness. There were a series of articles in which he had debated his ideas with Francis Crick, another Nobel laureate who had turned from hard science to metaphysics. Apparently the two men had violently disagreed. Crick had accused Fleischer of suffering from an excess of artificial intelligence. That was their last recorded debate.

Artie keyed into *Who's Who*. Fleischer's wife, Harriet, had written three critically acclaimed novels. The most recent, *Failing Light*, was published fifteen years ago. "A heart-wrenching narrative written from the point of view of a young boy dying from a malignant brain tumor. It is a work of great courage and unexpected beauty," said the *Washington Post Book World* blurb.

Under *family* was listed Benjamin, died age nine. There were no other children.

Artie checked the dates. Shortly after Benjamin's death, Dr. Fleischer had resigned from UC-Berkeley. There were no further books from Mrs. Fleischer.

"Benjamin Fleischer," Artie said aloud, gazing absently at the screen. Artie was acutely aware of the notion of hierarchy. Although scientifically the case could be made that they were all identical and equal, Artie acknowledged that Benjamin was the original, the only intended. Artie recognized that the distinction was more philosophical than biological, but it made no difference. Benjamin's ranking was based upon natural law. He was the Fleischers' son. The rest of them . . . ?

Dead of a brain tumor—a fate worse than Alzheimer's. Artie's mother had been spared the pain, the blindness and paralysis—the outward stigmata of the failure of one's own mind.

He thought back to age nine. How would he have reacted? With great courage and unexpected beauty? He doubted it.

His mood sank. Artie imagined Benjamin stumbling around his house, bumping into his father's Nobel prize, knocking it over, then apologizing, misunderstanding his father's tears.

For a moment he had the crazy idea of phoning the Fleischers, explaining that there were others. He would leave out what had happened, what was happening.

Artie got up from his computer, walked to the living room, started to sit down, but didn't. Earlier Tuna had been sprawled on this couch as though he owned it, as though he were better at occupying his couch than Artie was.

If only he could be as disinterested as Tuna seemed to be.

Artie opened the living room window, stuck his head out into the cool evening air. Below, a group of Asian children were playing jump rope in the pink of the mercury street lights. He was momentarily calmed by the rhythmic swish of the rope and bursts of children's laughter. One of their parents came out. The children begged to play another few minutes, before obediently trudging inside.

It was five flights down, enough distance to do serious damage.

He desperately needed to talk to someone. He left a message on Janine's machine apologizing. "Sudden emergency at the store. Life hanging in the balance. Family catastrophe. Stopped traffic in the fast lane. Take your pick." Followed by, "I'm really sorry. Call me when you get in."

He went back to his study and his computer, idly made his way through some public discussion groups. He paused at a couple sex bulletin boards, but was quickly bored and irritated by a succession of feminist attacks on pornography interspersed with readers exchanging second-hand masturbation fantasies. He wanted to talk with those with an interest in *his* problem.

Janine's therapist friend, Lynn, had a patient who communicated with himself via an imaginary Internet. Lynn had mentioned that her patient actually got advice and comfort from the other voices.

Maybe he could do the real thing. It would be easy enough to arrange—he would announce on one of the literature chat rooms that he was researching a science fiction novel and wanted reader input. He could set up a discussion group in which he would describe the cloning, but emphasize that it was strictly hypothetical. Then he would tell them how far he had gotten in his story, ask how they would feel, what they'd do, thoughts they'd have.

He would poll them on whether or not they found the story plausible, whether or not they would believe in three suicides. If they did, would they continue to track down the others, and what would they say?

It would be anonymous group therapy in cyberspace, a real confession presented as a fiction.

He phoned Netcom, who recently had begun offering discussion groups. The service manager thought it was a swell topic—provocative and certainly original. He gave Artie immediate approval and an untraceable alias. Artie typed in the basic plot to date and asked for suggestions.

Within minutes his screen was filling up, people responding to his story line and to each other's comments.

```
>Nuke 'em.

>Three suicides in a row is hokey. Two is plenty.

>Three suicides makes perfect sense. If you can
think of a reason for living, please respond.

>I had three cousins who killed themselves. Sui-
cide is no laughing matter. Your book is sick.

>What's the big deal? Everyone knows that the
FBI, the CIA, the Secret Service, and the DEA
already use clones for front line work. It's
common knowledge that George Bush was the first
working model. There've been significant improve-
ments since.
```

>It's not possible. Cloning of humans is against natural law.

>There's no difference between humans and animals.

>Not true. Animals don't carry grudges.

>That's not what I meant. Animals are a lower order. Humans have the potential for personal dignity. Clones don't.

>Sure they do. Clones are conceptually no different than athletic teams. Have you ever seen an entire baseball team standing, hats over their hearts, listening to the Star Spangled Banner? What you see is a group dignity and respect for the flag, a submersion of the self in a higher collective order.

>That's not dignity, that's a corporate stance. Those guys pull down five mil a year. Give me a big one a year and I'll stand in line with a hundred clones. That's my price, not a penny less.

>Well said. Personal identity is what "they" say you've got when they don't pay you. I see it as an either/or. Starving artist versus corporate sell-out. Personal identity is the consolation prize.

>Write it in hypertext. Then you can alter the order and distribution of the deaths. The randomness would be a wonderful metaphor for marginal causality among identical biologies. Forget identical biologies. It's all of us, isn't it?

>If god didn't believe in science, he wouldn't have invented scientists.

>Men invent. God creates.

>Clones are part of the evolutionary process. The first phase was to give man two arms, two

legs, two kidneys, two eyes, etc. Now there's the possibility of greater protection against dis- ease, accidents, etc. It's survival of the fittest to the third power.

>I doubt that was what god intended.

>Will your book have a religious subtext?

>Of course his book will. This is modern man's dilemma, technology outstripping moral values.

>Boooooring. It's been done to death. Why don't you send them off to a new galaxy/planet? See how they'd evolve in an entirely new environ- ment. If personal identity is, from the Darwinian perspective, a mental survival tactic, show how they'd behave under extraordinary circumstances. If they truly needed each other for survival, their deaths would have greater significance and create a greater tension.

>Why not call the book Scrambled Eggs?

>Cellmates.

>Wrong Division.

>Split Personality.

>Shipwreck of the Singular.

Artie paused at the title *Shipwreck of the Singular*. The phrase was familiar, but he could not immediately place it. It's been a long day, he told himself, turning from the computer screen, walking to his bedroom. The electronic conversation continued to silently fill up the screen, but he was no longer interested. It was folly to think that the Internet could provide answers.

 "We need to talk," Welinda said, rushing into Shazam. Artie was behind the counter, halfway through the first chapter of a stale-smelling library copy of *Failing Light*. Looking around to be sure the store was empty, Welinda approached Artie, leaned over the counter, and closed the book. "Now."

"I was reading," Artie said.

"It can wait. We need to talk about you."

"Me? I thought we were square."

"It's not about money. It's about you. You look like shit."

"I haven't been sleeping well."

"No. You've been up all night playing bulletin board."

"Excuse me?"

"Let's cut to the chase. Last night I got home after my gig over at Moose's. I'm all fired up with nowhere to go, so I start wandering around on my computer. Guess what I run into? Come on, take a guess."

Artie shrugged.

"Here's this guy pushing this science fiction plot about cloning. And three suicides." Welinda swatted the side of her head with the flat of her hand. "I go all déjà vu, except I haven't heard the suicide riff before. I get to thinking about how my good friend Artie seems to be wearing the full twelve-bar blues. I tell myself it's time to cut the crap. That's what friends are for."

"Welinda."

"Don't condescend me."

"I'm not asking for any help," Artie said, trying to cut the conversation short. "Besides, it's *patronize*."

"OK, wise guy. Let's play a moment of 'what if?' What if you did want my help? I'd imagine the first thing you'd be concerned about would be absolute secrecy." Welinda took two fingers and made a cross over her heart. "Mum's the word. I won't even tell my dreams."

Two customers walked in. Welinda held a finger to her lips. She waited until both customers were elbow-deep in the comic bins. "See? Not a peep. But tonight we talk. Drinks are on me, the onus is on you."

Artie had the day to consider. Sure, Welinda was sometimes annoyingly eccentric, but that was Welinda. Artie knew that theirs wasn't a friendship of convenience, one that would fade once one of them got married or moved out of town. In her own way she was family.

In the store Welinda sometimes seemed unbalanced, even possessed by the computer games, as though moving into self-absorbed nerddom. But there was the other Welinda, the first-rate blues pianist who spent hour after hour practicing and composing on her electronic keyboard in her minuscule studio apartment down the street. There were the four-times-a-week sessions at the martial arts studio on Stockton Street. Once Artie commented on the sharp contrast between Welinda's delicate touch on the piano and her black belt in karate. Welinda replied by hammering her way through a particularly strident Mose Allison piece. "If that's not violent music, sign me up for a hearing aid. I'll bet Mose could break a brick with a single chord."

Welinda was the genuine article—her run-down life style was not a pose of the *artiste*, her performances were not filled with phony riffs and easy changes. She played like a woman possessed, the circumstances of her life playing a distant second fiddle to what mattered.

She was offering her friendship.

They met at Le Petit Menu. Welinda knew the boss and sometimes played the six-to-eight PM shift in return for dinner and drinks. She was soaring through "Pine Top Boogie" when Artie showed up. Welinda finished by inserting a bit of Mozart, then playing the final chorus at double time. She banged the piano seat three times with her hand in an imitation of perfunctory applause before sitting down with Artie.

Welinda drank house red. Artie stuck with a non-alcoholic beer. For the first few minutes neither said anything, both pushing bread crumbs around the tablecloth as though guiding their thoughts into position.

"So, what if I agree to talk about it?" Artie said at last.

"You don't have to say anything. I was able to slip into the DMV's limited access files. A neat hack a friend once showed me." Welinda reached into the inside vest pocket of her oversized cheap black suit jacket. She made a show of fumbling around before bringing out the pictures. "All the ID photos scanned into memory. How convenient."

Artie glanced around the restaurant to make sure that no one was listening or watching. He shifted his body so that he would block the view of anyone trying to see the pictures, though there were only three couples in the restaurant, none of whom had given Artie and Welinda a second glance since they sat down.

"Pretty much the same, if you ask me." Welinda spread out the nine drivers' licenses in front of her. She was gesturing broadly, her body in constant motion, a whirling dervish in a restaurant booth. "Maybe a little difference here," she said, pointing to Bunker's smirk. "And here," indicating Lafora's shaved head. "Let's see. This one is Roger Ligott, this one is Paul Lafora. This one is Les Robbins. Or have I got them mixed up?"

"Don't ask me. I can't tell them apart, either."

"So?" Welinda asked. "You going to fill me in, with me swearing to secrecy, or am I going to draw my own conclusions and spread them all over town?"

"I was under the impression that one picture was worth ten thousand words. I think these photos say it all."

"Details, man. I've got the big picture, but let's hone in on the details. Then we can work on the three deaths. Not suicides, not murders. Deaths. There's no point in jumping to conclusions before we've established the ground rules."

"Ground rules? This isn't some game." Artie tore off a piece of French bread and dipped it in Welinda's glass of wine. The bread turned pink as though it were bleeding. Artie took a bite, the bread soggy in his mouth. "Not bad. Has a nice bouquet," Artie said, sniffing. If he didn't have such terrible cluster headaches, he'd have been halfway through a bottle of it.

"Not for you. You're too involved." Welinda held her hand as though shielding her eyes. "Up to here. That's why you need a cool outside assessment. A simple suggestion. Let's divide this into two parts. Your personal feelings go in Box A marked 'spill your guts out, no holds barred, and I'll listen and try to understand.' How you proceed goes in the B box, labeled 'game theory.'"

"I just told you. This isn't a game."

"That's not the point. Grant me that your life has turned into a puzzle. No matter what you call it, you're down to game theory as decision-making. For starters, we need to know the author's intentions."

"Author?"

"Sure. Every game has an author."

"This is my life we're talking about."

"Let's not go all philosophical. This is pure pragmatism. Get in, solve the problem, get out. You watch some gorilla show on PBS in order to see our raw 'nature' in action. But always there's the nagging question—'how did this come to be?' Whether you're an atheist or a true believer is beside the point. Somehow the programming came into existence. To me, real introspection requires acknowledging the presence of some kind of programmer or author and figuring out what she had in mind."

"I didn't know that you were religious," Artie said. Despite himself, he was smiling.

"Not religious. Practical. Better to know that you're programmed for high-strung than to spend a lifetime telling yourself to relax, meditating yourself into craziness."

"I'm supposed to look for an author that I won't be able to find, and by imagining what this imaginary invisible author had in mind, I will know what happened to Roger, Paul, and Bunker, *and* I will know what to do about it?" Artie paused and looked at Welinda. He took a large gulp from Welinda's glass. "Are we talking metaphor? Is this what this conversation is all about?"

"Yes and no. What I'm really saying is, I'd love to try to help you. I've got a few ideas and a different frame of reference. Two heads are better than one. Need I go on?"

"And these photos, you'll keep them to yourself?"

"Under my bra, where no one can get at them."

"The inquiries aren't traceable?"

"The DMV was a piece of cake, all done anonymously from one of the online computers at the main library."

"Just the two of us, right?"

"Like Nancy Drew and Butthead."

"What more could I ask?" Artie said, dipping his bread into Welinda's wine.

NINETEEN

The following night they met at Welinda's tiny apartment. Sheet music and CDs were piled everywhere—in stacks on top of the studio upright, at the foot of her unmade sofa bed, on a low pine dresser that doubled as nightstand. A panama hat was atop the piano. On the doorknob to the bathroom was her porkpie. A bowler was sitting on the piano stool.

"The cleaning lady's on sabbatical?" Artie said, squeezing his way between the sofa bed and the piano.

"There *is* a difference between style and dirt." Welinda went to her closet, pulled out a wooden folding chair, shoved it under a card table jammed in a corner of the room. Artie sat.

In contrast to the surrounding clutter, the tabletop was empty, except for an ornate chess set of carved ivory. Artie picked up one of the pieces and cradled it in his hand.

"Did I ever tell you that those were my grandfather's?"

Artie nodded and put the piece back on the board, which was also ivory.

Welinda squared away the men and said, "White or black?"

"It's late. You dragged me over here to play chess?" Artie started to stand. Welinda put her hand on Artie's shoulder.

"Humor me for just a minute. All I want you to do is make an opening move. Any move. Then I've got some news for you."

Artie looked down at the men, started to shove one of the pawns forward. Welinda stopped him, grabbing his wrist.

"Why that one?" Welinda asked.

"Because I don't know anything about chess and care even less. One man is as good as another."

Welinda flashed a lewd smile. "OK, move him."

Artie moved one pawn forward one square. Welinda took all of her white pieces off the board, then removed all of Artie's except for seven pawns.

"Your move," Welinda said.

"Let me guess. I'm supposed to say 'I can't make a move if there's no opponent.' Then you say something like 'Are the men still chessmen if they don't have a game to play?' Then I'm stuck with some metaphysical quandary as to the essence of identity and meaning in the absence of defining circumstances. Big deal."

"Don't be so preppie. I was just trying to get you inside the killer's mind. Right now you've got seven pawns without orders. One of them's your killer, but he's a counter-puncher waiting for you to make your next move. If you don't know what to do, then neither does he. When you visit one of the others, he hangs behind, in your shadow. If you just ignore the others, let the whole thing slide, he might also."

"If there is a killer." Artie was already convinced, had probably known for weeks, but didn't want to believe his own conclusions. And he couldn't exactly discount the moment he'd stuck the plastic bag over *his* head.

"There's a killer," Welinda said. She reached over and grabbed a stack of sheet music. Stuck in the middle of the pile were several computer printouts. "Here, you read them."

Artie looked at the autopsy protocols of Ligott, Lafora, and Bunker. "I've already seen them. Those are the copies I gave you."

"Look again." Welinda jabbed her finger onto the final page of Lafora's record. "The toxicology report lists a moderate level of car-fentanyl. Bunker's report reads the same. Now, read this." Welinda handed Artie three pages of photocopied pharmacology text. "I downloaded it last night. See? 'In pill form death occurs in ten to fifteen minutes.'"

"So?"

"I went over this pharmacology printout four times before I figured it out." Welinda flipped back through the pages of Lafora's record. "Right here. 'The stomach and small intestine were free of food or other foreign material.'" Welinda then read from Bunker's. The words were the same.

"Car-fentanyl's primarily used for sedation and pain relief, in low doses. In order to manufacture it in pill form the drug company adds inert, non-absorbable bulking agents. Lafora and Bunker's blood levels were higher than you'd get by taking a single pill. If they took several, there should be some amount of undissolved pills still lying in their stomach and small intestine.

"No pills, not even a trace. Which means that they didn't take it in pill form. There were no signs of any injection, no syringes or paraphernalia. This morning I phoned the vet who used to treat my parrot. He's also part-time at the zoo. He told me that car-fentanyl spray is the preferred anesthetic for the big animals. One whiff is enough to have King Kong sawing z's. So inhaler's the method, except that there wouldn't have been time to dump the inhaler. Which boils down to, nix to suicide."

"But Ligott's autopsy didn't show any car-fentanyl."

"It could be lab error. The assay is difficult; maybe some lab tech fudged it the way I used to in high school chemistry. Anyway, that doesn't make any difference. The main thing is that Lafora and Bunker didn't give themselves the drug."

Welinda swept the seven pawns up into her hand, shook them up, as though preparing to throw dice, then threw them out onto the chessboard. "Take your pick."

Artie looked up at Welinda, who was staring at him. "You don't think that I . . . ?"

"Of course not. If you'd done them, you'd have no point in telling me. No, after due deliberation, I've counted you out." Welinda reached over, took one of the pawns off the table and held it in her hand. She arranged the remaining six pawns in a circle in the center of the board.

"How would this supposed killer have known who I was visiting? The letter I sent out only brought up the possibility that each might have an identical twin. The others still don't know, except for Tuna, and he didn't know until after Roger and Paul were already dead."

"You told me that Tuna was in your apartment. He could have booted up your computer. You booked the flights on the Internet; it would be simple to look them up."

"I have a secret password."

"Where?"

"In my bottom drawer."

"Ooh, how original. You don't think that he could have figured that out?"

"I suppose. But Tuna? He wants us to go on the road like the Dionne quintuplets."

"If he waits long enough, it'll be more like the Andrews Sisters."

"No. Tuna sees us as a cash crop, nothing more."

"But he was able to get into your apartment, right?"

Artie nodded. In the back of his mind was the vague sensation that something had been different about the last time he had looked into the bottom drawer. Nothing precise, but a subtle shifting of contents. He'd check when he got back home.

"You talk to your manager. Ten to one he's had to pass out a spare key when you lost yours."

"I didn't lose mine."

"Earth to *Artie*."

"I know. It's just so impossible. Someone gets my flight numbers, follows me, does each of them in and makes it look like a suicide?"

Welinda grabbed another computer printout from atop a stack of sheet music. "Maybe we should start with Mark Caputo." Welinda handed the sheet to Artie.

Once into the DMV computer, Welinda had been able to tap into the state welfare files. Caputo had been on disability and Medi-Cal for twelve years. "For eight of those years the state laid out more than a hundred grand in medical payments. Which means he was hospitalized. So I ran the hospitals against his name. He was in Napa State for five years, and another three at Agnews State. After that it's been a series of residential facilities in the Central Valley. Big bucks means mental illness. I'd bet on schizophrenia."

"The DMV has his address?" Artie asked.

"Not the DMV. Welfare." Welinda took the paper back. "Some board and care home in Escalon."

"Where's that?"

"Outside of Manteca."

"And Manteca?"

"That's near Lodi."

"And Lodi?"

"Close to Turlock."

"And . . . ?"

"You pack the sandwiches," Welinda said. "I'll bring the map."

From Manteca east to Escalon, a succession of small vineyards and some plowed-over fields rolled by. Off-season, the vines barren, the almond trees short of leaves, the farmland had a bewildered helpless look as though a low-lying seasonal plague were upon it. Frequent potholes in the road didn't help Artie's mood either. He gripped the wheel of the Peugeot with both hands and prayed for his shock absorbers. The metaphor wasn't entirely lost on him. He worried about how he'd react if Welinda were right, if Mark Caputo was schizophrenic.

Welinda leaned forward in the passenger seat, her feet tapping, her hands in constant rhythmic motion on her thighs.

"Do you think you could cool it for a minute?" Artie asked. "I'm trying to collect my thoughts."

"Sure thing, boss. I was just trying to imagine Artie number two."

"You're going to stay in the car. I'll go in, talk to the head nurse or warden or whatever, and then we'll see."

"I thought we were in this together. Hello, my name is Arthur Singleton and this is my friend, Welinda Dupré. We shake hands, you do the small talk while I analyze, intuit, scope out the scene, make conclusions, solve the problem. If I'm relegated to staying in the car, you might as well go in there blindfolded."

Artie chose not to answer Welinda. He continued in silence, his jaws clenched as he rehearsed his introduction. He was unnerved about how he might react, what he might say. He certainly wasn't interested in having Welinda's off-the-wall comments as an additional concern.

Before leaving the city he had phoned the residential house supervisor for directions and the visiting hours. She seemed surprised, perhaps excited, that Mark was going to have a visitor. Artie sensed from their conversation that Mark had been abandoned. He had wanted to ask if Mark had been out of town at all during the last month, but knew that he'd stand a better chance of finding out during the visit.

After passing through the center of town, they pulled up to a shabby, faded blue Victorian on a treeless side street. The surrounding houses were in various states of disrepair, with collapsed porches and abandoned cars in the front and back yards. Several of the front lawns were overgrown and full of weeds, the houses lifeless.

Artie wiped his hands on his pants and got out of the car. Welinda was opening her door. Artie shook his head and started toward the house. Welinda hurried up alongside him, half-jogging to keep up with his long stride.

"It's nothing but one pathway in an interactive game. You don't like what you see, you change directions. One keystroke and Caputo's *kaput.*"

Several of Artie's former psychiatrists had said that he took life too seriously. Artie wished he could have seen how they'd handle this one. "Easy for you to say," he wanted to tell them. But instead he found himself walking up the wooden front steps, Welinda tagging along, jabbering away like some high school computer geek. Mutt and Jeff simulating *Mission: Impossible.*

The supervisor was a wiry, tanned woman in her late fifties. Her voice sounded like three packs a day, half a fifth in the evenings. She'd seen it all, too many times to count; her weariness hung from her like her ill-fitting gray cardigan. She gave Artie a once-over, then shot a glance at Welinda. "He's expecting you," she said without any further introduction.

They passed by the living room where several elderly men sat staring at each other, at their magazines and newspapers, at the TV which was set too high on the reds and yellows, the faces bleeding sideways as though pressed against the inside of the screen. Artie had expected the smells, the ones that he remembered from his mother's last days—and the muted light that seemed to come from another time, filtered through ancient plexiglass sconces lining the walls of the living room and the corridor that led to the back of the house.

They stepped out of the corridor into a back porch that had been enclosed and converted into a solarium. A man in a wheel-chair looked out onto the rear garden—a bruised bit of overgrown lawn and a few dusty rose bushes—his back to them. His head was slumped forward; he did not turn when the super-visor addressed him.

"Mark. Your brother is here to see you." Without waiting, she turned and left the solarium.

Artie swallowed hard. For a moment he stood still, as though Mark would turn his wheelchair around and make the first move. But Mark continued to slump in his chair, his head tilted at an awkward angle, his hair as mussed as the weeds he was watching.

Welinda crossed the room and stood directly in front of Mark. "Hello. My name is Welinda Dupré." She said her name twice, then looked up at Artie and shook her head.

Artie came forward and stood alongside Welinda. Caputo's features were coarsened; Artie guessed from medications. He had an institutional pallor as though his skin had been buttered into whiteness.

Caputo wore a thick terrycloth bib secured behind his neck by two strips of black Velcro. Somehow the Velcro said more about his helplessness than his puffy slippered feet and blank look.

Artie gave a long sigh.

"Sorry," Welinda said. "It never occurred to me."

"It's not your fault. I should have talked to the supervisor first." Artie went over and took Caputo's hand. Their fingers were simi-larly long and tapered, but Mark's were without calluses, his skin soft and shiny, the fingernails cut straight across, as if tended by machine or a pair of shearing scissors. Artie stroked Mark's hand as though it were his own hand that had gone to sleep and he were trying to awaken it.

After a moment he gently put it back in Mark's lap, his own hand damp from touching Mark's bib. Artie made a point of not wiping his hand on his pants leg. He doubted that Mark would notice, but he could not be sure.

Welinda started to say something, but instead nudged Artie at the elbow. "It's been great to see you," she said to Mark.

No response.

Artie took a last look at his brother, Mark's image oscillating between profound similarity and utter strangeness.

After a short talk with the supervisor, Artie and Welinda were back on the two-lane highway winding through Escalon. For a time they rode in silence, each afraid to start the conversation. Finally Welinda spoke.

"You want to leave me by the side of the road? I'd understand."

"No. I'd still have me inside the car." Artie concentrated on the road, relieved to have the distraction of a series of sharp turns. But the distraction was short-lived. Soon they were on the freeway, heading back to the city.

"The supervisor was right," Welinda said. "It probably was some intrauterine infection, something toxic during pregnancy. Some form of cerebral palsy."

"Never talked. Never did anything. He's been like that all his life." Artie shook his head. "Did you see his eyes? So empty."

"On a brighter note, at least we know he's not the murderer."

"That could have been me in the wheelchair. A different throw of the dice and I could have been assigned to the Caputos. And vice versa. It's like we're characters in one of your damned games." Artie rolled down the window and stuck his hand out, deflecting the cool afternoon autumn air over his face. "I used to love this time of year."

TWENTY

For the last three weeks there had been no new entries in Arthur's Travelnet account. Les considered the possibilities.

Arthur wasn't flying. He was driving to each destination.

Arthur had figured out that one of them was a killer and was developing his own counterplan.

Knowing that three of them died following his visits had scared Arthur off.

Les considered the last option first. What if the others didn't know? If they lived their lives in ignorance of their biological connection, would that be enough? Certainly that would be a decent alternative. Let them live in peace and ignorance.

But Arthur had sent the letters or made the calls to each of them. Each knew of the possibility of having an identical twin. If Arthur didn't follow up his initial contact, sooner or later they would contact Arthur. Perhaps Arthur wouldn't say more, especially if he felt responsible for the suicides. On the surface, Les thought that could be a possible solution, except for all the complicating details. A curious brother would check his hospital records for information about the other twin and his biological family, etc. Five minutes at the computer would be enough time to find out that he wasn't the product of a multiple birth.

And there remained the problem of Harold Weinstein. Les's two visits to Las Vegas had been like having asthma attacks. His chest ached at the thought of the casino bells and whistles, yet he had to go back, once he knew Arthur's plans.

He considered Arthur's discussion group entries. Arthur specialized in interactive fiction, so was probably great at games and puzzles. By now he'd have figured out that the deaths weren't all suicides.

Once Arthur suspected murder, he'd realize that someone had tapped into his computer, and that that *someone* had to be one of the others. Any future information on Arthur's computer might now be a lure. So might lack of information. He might even be flying to visit the others but not booking through Travelnet.

Arthur could no longer be trusted.

The following morning Les borrowed a lightweight suitcase from Ann Fritz and packed it with his few belongings, including his computer. In his room he left behind his mountain bike and some of his heavier winter gear. He rode down to San Francisco in the back of a casino tour bus, slumped in his seat like a welfare check loser.

The bus let him off at Sixth between Mission and Market Streets. At a nearby thrift shop he bought a used Oakland A's baseball cap and a pair of sunglasses with mirrored lenses. Over the next two days he wouldn't shave—a couple days of stubble would be perfect. Most people never took a second look at the homeless; he could walk the streets as anonymously as if he were invisible.

He checked into a cheap rooming house on Eddy Street. The clerk wasn't interested in IDs or credit cards. It was cash in advance, fifty bucks a week, no peeing in the sink, no paraphernalia flushed down the toilet, no condoms out the window, and no excuses. Pay on the first of the week, or be out by six PM. Les signed in as Arthur Singleton.

On the bureau he put Suzanne's photographs, her packet of letters to Roger Ligott, Paul Lafora's Inner City Man of the Year award, and a Montblanc pen engraved *Goldman-Sachs* that he'd lifted from Thomas Bunker's desk. Each of these items represented evidence, but only if and when the police suspected a crime. Which they didn't. Wouldn't. It wasn't likely that Arthur would contact the police. Judging by his discussion group entries, Arthur feared public exposure as much as he did.

He could keep his heirlooms on display.

They kept him on course. When he'd kept them hidden underneath his mattress he felt confused, uncertain as to what had actually happened.

He was glad for the precise dense weight of Paul Lafora's medal. Each morning, just after awakening, he would hold it in his cupped hand and feel Paul Lafora's presence. The medal was emblematic of substance, of history and a world outside his own personal dimensions. As were the other items.

How terrible Suzanne must have felt when she heard of Roger's death; he wished he could console her. He would put his arm around her, touch her forearm, offer her a glass of juice or a cup of tea. Judging by the letters, she'd loved Roger deeply, which made his suicide more difficult to understand. Sometimes it's hard to accept that kind of love. Perhaps he didn't feel worthy. Or . . .

There were plenty of possible causes, but the real answer was Arthur. If Arthur hadn't visited, hadn't pulled the plug on Roger's sense of identity, Roger would be enjoying the quiet of Whidbey Island and the love of Suzanne.

Arthur's visit was inexcusable. He might as well have put the bag over Roger's head.

Paul and Thomas were different. He'd talked with both of them, and they seemed understanding, willing to accept. Both had been gracious and open, glad to see him. The stun gun's effect was instantaneous; their last thoughts would have been of a heartfelt reunion between lost brothers.

Not like Arthur giving Roger the news and just leaving, inviting despondency in his wake.

Les stood at the cheap pine dresser and stared at Suzanne smiling in the arcade photo booth. Despite the harsh light she was lovely, with a gentleness that you didn't often see in women these days. He traced his finger along her face, paused, replaced the photo on the dresser before pulling out his laptop. He snapped the modem interface into the bedside phone and hacked onto a rental terminal at Café Network on Eddy Street. Using the Café's email address, he sent Suzanne an anonymous letter introducing himself as a friend of Roger and proclaiming the depth of Roger's love for her. After posting the letter, he reread it several times, his chest heavy, his eyes watering, as though he had expressed his own feelings rather than Roger's.

If only one day they could meet. . . . He could explain that he and Roger were twins separated at birth. But it was a hollow, cheap fantasy. If she did shift her affection from Roger to himself, it wouldn't be the real thing. He did not want her affection by proxy. Love must be earned.

He waited, sitting cross-legged on his bed, the line open, the cursor poised. The room was alive, charged with potential. No return email appeared; there would be no connection. He turned off the machine, stared at the letters and photographs that now lay in his hand like a collection of paper jewels.

After a time he slid the photos back in one of the letter envelopes and put the entire packet in the top dresser drawer. The drawer was otherwise empty and gave off the smell of pine and camphor. Les was reminded of a child's coffin. He quickly closed the drawer, telling himself that the drawer's contents were Roger's life, not his.

The purpose of his exercise was to avoid such confusion.

His operative term was *consolidation*.

He returned to his computer and pulled up Arthur's list of others. To date he'd managed to clearly establish Arthur at the scene of each death. But he no longer knew if Arthur was visiting the others. He couldn't rely on tapping into his Travelnet files. Les deliberated, pacing the small room. There were other methods. Breaking into his apartment and installing a telephone bug. Following Arthur. Neither scheme seemed realistic. He should develop a plan independent of Arthur. He could book a car under Arthur's name, using Arthur's California driver's license number. Leaving a paper trail from motel room to motel room would certainly place Arthur in the vicinity at the time of the deaths. Though there might be some credible eyewitnesses to declare that Arthur wasn't there. It was a close call, Arthur's eyewitnesses against the man at the car rental agency, the motel manager—the witnesses that he would set up. If Arthur became sufficiently desperate, he might spill the beans, show the photos of all of them, reopen all the investigations.

Unlikely. The first two killings hadn't aroused any suspicion. Suicide was so common that it no longer warranted more than a cursory investigation.

Les walked to the dresser and palmed Paul's medal. After a few minutes he lay down and closed his eyes, the medal resting on his chest. He was tired of scheming and planning. He wanted to be done with it and get back to Truckee with its smaller scale and snow-obscured horizon. It was why he spent summers at tiny Sardine Lake rather than huge Lake Tahoe. Scale was what had gone wrong with civilization, the ultimate disease that had brought man's soul to its collective knees. Larger wasn't better. More meant imitation—heartbreaking attempts at duplication, from tract houses to shopping malls, from modern architecture to New Age music.

Scale was the disease and imitation was its pus.

The sooner he was finished, the sooner he could be free of the city. He heard the moan of the wind in the tall Sierra pines. Truckee huddled in white expectation.

With a little luck he would be finished before Christmas.

He awoke to the sound of tires on wet pavement. It was dark outside, the street damp with a heavy fog. Men huddled in doorways, smoking, chatting quietly. From his eighth-floor window the men seemed boxed in by their respective doorways, as though already dead and tilted upright for easier viewing. A landscape of failure, one that would never see the light of day.

Les turned up the thermostat, and opened his notebook. Four names. He closed his eyes and ran his index finger back and forth along the page, giving each of them equal opportunity.

He opened his eyes.

Asher Newman was next.

TWENTY-ONE

>My twin sister died last month in a car acci-
dent. I am not writing this note to elicit
sympathy, but to point out how painful the death
of a clone must be to the others.

>I get the feeling that you're trying to make
personal identity a bigger issue than family
bonding. This will make your story ring of fal-
sity and distorted values. Look into your own
heart, imagine the death of a close sibling,
then multiply it by the factor of sameness. Re-
think the plot. One death is devastating. Three
is unthinkable, unbearable.

>I am sorry to hear about your twin. My field
used to be cell biology. Under the microscope we
watched the cells being separated and said the
division was complete. But this was only a gross
generalization. Certainly there were bits of cell
that remained behind. What difference does that
make, you might ask? The DNA is all the same.
The difference is in metaphor. I believe that an
incomplete separation represents bonding at the
membrane level that defies the most clever of
technologies. This is not mere retention of frag-
ments of extraneous cytoplasm. It is the cell's
urge toward unity, or at least an attempt to

retain some shred of embedded memory of its origin. But what ultimately is left behind is the
emptiness of nostalgia and a profound sense of
loss, an incompleteness that requires the other.
Please accept my condolences.
P.S. Note to the author. Though I no longer work
in science, I confess to a continuing curiosity
that borders on an addiction. Perhaps your book
should have one clone involved in a twelve step
program like Science Anonymous that downplays
technology and emphasizes spirituality.

>Until recently, custom dictated that the male
members of the Fore tribe in the New Guinea
highlands eat the brains of their recently de-
parted elders. Unfortunately the brains carried
the agent for Kuru, a rare infectious disease
that caused progressive brain deterioration. In
seeking to consume the wisdom of the elders each
successive generation of males was destroyed.
Question: Is this a comment on family values,
the nature of falsely acquired wisdom, or tradition as infection?
A footnote: Only after scientists clearly demonstrated to the tribesmen that the disease was
transmitted through eating the brains did the
tribesmen begrudgingly give up their practice
of cannibalism. Though freed from disease, many
now suffer from depression.

>I don't get the point. We're trying to help write
a novel, not dwell on irrelevant irony. Please
stick to the topic.

>The murders are metaphors for lives not chosen.
Each of the clones represents a separate possibility of experience. When we choose one way of
life, we kill off the other ways we haven't chosen. I think depression is the recognition of
the deaths of our unchosen selves.

In the two weeks since Artie had started the discussion group there had been several hundred entries. Though many were off the wall, some were moving, perhaps accounting for his deflated mood. That and the ride back from Escalon, directly into the glaring sun and rush hour stop-and-go traffic. His head was fuzzy, he had a drawing sensation behind his eyes, the premonition of a monster headache about to descend. Even so, he cracked open an Anchor Steam beer, went to his dresser, propped up Welinda's computer-generated DMV photos. He picked them up, one at a time, held each in his hand, trying to take them in, make room for them.

Welinda wanted to smoke out the killer. But then what? Punch the *delete the killer* button on their childish game? They were ludicrous, playing real cops and robbers with toy guns and plastic bullets.

Since he'd visited Bunker he'd had no word of any further deaths. Several times he'd phoned Lippe, Newman, and Sadler, heard their voice mail messages before he'd hung up. The only one he hadn't heard was Les Robbins. He'd tried Sardine Lake; the answering machine at the rental office said to phone back in April when they'd be taking reservations again.

Welinda voted for Les, but had no hard reasoning beyond Les's unavailability. Artie's gut feeling was that Les was either the most or least likely, but couldn't make up his mind—not being accessible was so hard to interpret.

Welinda assured him that the killer was waiting for Artie to make the next move. If Artie didn't contact any more of them, perhaps the killings would stop.

If Welinda was right, the killer had set Artie up to be the prime suspect should the suspicion of murder be raised. Which put Artie in the peculiar predicament of being somewhat protected by his potential role as fall guy. The killer needed him alive, as an alibi, at least for now. A reasonable presumption, but by no means a certainty. There were no guarantees that the killer's plan was securely fastened to logic's rails.

The second beer was serving notice, a dull pain gathering behind his eye. Artie lay back on his living room couch and envisioned a family get-together, all of the clones huddled around a holiday turkey. Rather than seeing his brothers one at a time, the killer would experience them all together, comparing childhoods and passing the sweet potatoes. Artie would give a speech about misunderstanding and forgiveness; they would all shake hands, hug each other. The murderer would be anonymously pardoned and the killings would end.

Not like last Thanksgiving at the nursing home dining room, his mother staring out into the garden, Artie delivering a quiet monologue—telling her about the store, about his new CD-ROM plans and the latest books he was reading. He shivered as he remembered how he'd been embarrassed and had hoped that the other visiting families wouldn't notice how far gone she was. It wasn't necessary, he knew that, but he'd wanted to go from table to table and explain that today wasn't one of her good days, that she didn't always need the wide cotton restraining belt around her waist. He wanted to leave the others with the impression that improvement was still possible. It did not comfort him to know that many others in the room were as bad off, or worse.

He remembered wishing that she would die soon, in her sleep. That both of them would be freed of this terrible burden.

Through the beery haze came a sensation of endless falling through darkness, as if he were a space-walking astronaut suddenly disconnected from his tether. He could not shake the gathering sense of dread. He tried to recapture the image of his new brothers laughing and sharing and working their way through the turkey, but he saw only blank faces watching him. Stalking him.

The computer beeped. Artie rose and went to the study. There was a new message.

```
>Because we find the others
Deserted like ourselves and therefore brothers.
```

He stared at the monitor, then shifted files, scrolling through old saved email. He came to the passage:

```
Obsessed, bewildered

By the shipwreck
Of the singular

We have chosen the meaning
Of being numerous
```

The two belonged together, as in a poem he might once have read.

It was eleven-thirty. City Lights Bookstore would still be open. With luck Jim Bloom would be at the register. Giant Jim had worked at the store for fifteen years, and had been in charge of the poetry section for the last ten. If anyone would know, Jim would.

He printed the two messages, slipped the paper in his shirt pocket, put on a heavy wool sweater and hurried down Grant Avenue to Columbus. He was in luck. Jim was behind the front register, wearing his usual mountain-man overalls, flannel shirt and black beret, as though he had just stepped out from one of the old Beat generation photos hanging behind the counter. Artie often kidded Jim that he was nothing but a pseudo-connection with fake nostalgia, but that he appreciated the sincerity of his effort.

Jim nodded as Artie entered the shop. "You're sure a dreary sight for sad eyes."

"No need for compliments. I just wondered if you recognized these lines." Artie handed Jim the printout.

"Are you from the government? Coming in here all friendly-like but with devious intentions? Such as checking my sanity?"

"Please. I don't have all night."

"So what's the deal? I sell you a book, and a couple weeks later you come back and try to see if I can recognize the main poem. Who do you take me for, the village idiot?"

"What book?"

Jim checked his digital watch, then tapped it with his hand. "I guess it's running slow. Says November 24, but should it read April 1?"

"Cut the crap. What book?"

"Unless it was your long-lost twin. Right here, right at this very register, on this planet, you paid twelve smackers for George Oppen's *Collected Poems*. And then you said to me that 'Of Being Numerous' was your favorite." Jim dropped his smile, gave Artie a concerned look. "You do remember, don't you?"

"By any chance was that the day I was wearing my Captain Marvel jacket?"

"Purple with a yellow lightning bolt. Pretty ugly."

"Some distributor gave it to me. I normally bring it out on Halloween. Do you have another copy?"

"Sure." Jim went downstairs to the poetry section. A minute later he returned and handed Artie a used copy. "On the house. For five dollars."

"I guess I was spaced out that day. Do you remember anything else I said?"

"Only that you wanted to discuss the book with a close friend." Jim leaned over the counter, his face only inches from Artie's. "You sure everything's okay? Nothing personal, but the other day you looked a little wild-eyed, like you'd OD'd on one of your computer games."

"I always get a little messed up before the holidays. My third shrink—or was it the fourth—called it pre-seasonal affective disorder." As Artie slipped the slender book into his back pocket, he tried to smile and look nonchalant. But he felt transparently anxious. More questions, he didn't need. He nodded at Jim and quickly left the bookstore.

Next door, a video arcade was pushing telephone sex with live models. Three bucks a minute, private booths, a nude model on the other side of a glass partition. Artie wondered if he could slip inside one of those tiny booths and let out a gigantic scream. A five-dollar bellow that would leave him gasping for air and the model on the other side of the window running for cover.

A foot patrolman approached as Artie reached the corner of Columbus and Broadway. The two men looked at each other. Artie wanted to drag the officer into the nearest coffee shop and tell him everything. How relieved he'd feel to watch the policeman ask questions, take notes, and say that the department would start on the investigation right away. He yearned for the touch of the policeman's hand on his arm, a reassuring pat, the passing of a business card and a promise to phone back in the morning.

Instead Artie quickly averted his eyes, as though he were the guilty one. He felt the policeman staring, assessing him. *It's not me*, he wanted to say. *It's one of my brothers.*

Another me, but not me.

TWENTY-TWO

In the Friday morning mail was a letter from William Barrett, Sarah Woolfson's attorney. Enclosed was a check for ten thousand dollars, an announcement of a memorial service at noon on Sunday, and a brief note of apology from Sarah written in a feeble script that made Artie wince.

Barrett was discharging his legal obligation, the ten thousand to cover the costs of contacting the others, though it might end up in Tuna's chip stacks, a temporary resting place if there ever was one.

The service was held in a wooded glen in Golden Gate Park. Artie stood to one side, against a large pine tree, listening to contemporaries of Sarah and his mother try to ease Sarah gently into history. Some looked familiar, some glanced at him, trying to place him. If introduced, there would be no escape. They would troll for memories of his mother, vague recollections would be kneaded into testimonials. The momentary pleasure of hearing his mother praised, eulogized, would be followed by the bad dreams and the grief.

During the recitation of the Lord's Prayer, while the mourners' heads were bowed, he retreated, backing away through a grove of pine trees. On the main drag people were bicycling, jogging, roller skating in a mixture of Sunday laughter and needless effort. He slid behind the wheel of the Peugeot, started up the motor, eased out into traffic.

Everyone connected with his origin was dead. Neither Sarah nor his mother—once young women with long hair, hot blood, and a future overflowing with dreams—could have known that Henry Woolfson's new technique would lead to this. He avoided passing final judgment, instead concentrating on avoiding smug bikers hogging the road, steering himself toward his final meeting with the past: a two o'clock appointment with Richard and Harriet Fleischer.

His letter of introduction had said that he was a part-time reviewer for a local literary magazine, that he had come across *Failing Light* in a second hand bookstore and wanted to write a small piece introducing it to a new generation of readers. During a followup phone call, he had overcome Mrs. Fleischer's initial hesitations. Artie had considered wearing a disguise—a blond hairpiece and horn-rimmed glasses—but he reminded himself that Benjamin had died at nine, at a time when they had all been short and chunky, their hair curlier. He had seen the Fleischers' photos on several of their publications; Artie bore little resemblance. This morning he had gone over his own childhood pictures as well as the photos in Sarah's album. Without knowledge that their embryo had been partially lifted, the Fleischers would have no reason to be suspicious.

Seated in the upstairs front living room of their spacious two-story home in Noe Valley, Artie had a view of the city and the Bay. Below the window, close together on an elaborate brocaded couch, sat the Fleischers, his hand on hers.

"I hope you don't mind my husband joining us," Mrs. Fleischer said, squeezing his hand. "Sometimes I think he remembers the book better than I do." Mrs. Fleischer was in her early sixties, with a shock of thick white hair that reminded Artie of a middle-aged Einstein. She was simply dressed, and there were traces of dirt under her fingernails, as though she had been potting or working in the garden.

With his broad high forehead and wire-rimmed glasses, Mr. Fleischer exuded academia. But Artie was interested in Fleischer's long tapered fingers. Artie jammed his own hands in his jacket pockets and tried not to stare.

Mrs. Fleischer was describing the book that she had been working on for the last twenty years. It was to be set in the future, when brain tumors were curable. "It's going to be an adventure story, something along the lines of *Ben and the Lost Ark*." She smiled weakly, looked at her husband who nodded for her to continue.

"I wasn't sure that I wanted to do this interview, but Richard said that it would be good for me. Ben was a special child."

"I could come another time. Or . . ." Artie paused and cautiously glanced at Mrs. Fleischer. "But somehow I had the feeling that you might have something you'd want to add after all these years."

"Would you care for some tea?" Mrs. Fleischer said, rising from the couch. "We have herbal and regular."

"Herbal would be fine," Artie said.

"Perhaps," she said, as she stepped into the kitchen, her voice hollow in the high-ceilinged room. Artie wasn't sure if she was answering him or talking to herself.

The two men remained behind, Fleischer looking from Artie to the window, drumming his fingers on his thigh, looking toward the kitchen, then back to Artie again. He was a father about to tell his son about a serious illness, something mental in his mother. A shared secret, a tacit declaration that the remainder of the Fleischers' lives would take place in muted light, shuffled steps, abrupt silences and conversational changes of direction. Fleischer's face was lined; the dazzling eyes of old pictures were no longer there. He had gone from Nobel laureate to a guardian who warded off unwanted memories. "You liked the book?" Fleischer asked.

"It's why I still go to bookstores. To make new friends. After reading the book, I feel as if I actually know your son."

"We thought of having another, but Harriet was getting on. We decided it would be too much." Fleischer got up and went down the hallway. He reappeared a moment later with a few snapshots. He poked his head in the kitchen. Mrs. Fleischer was setting out some cookies on a plate. "Quickly," Mr. Fleischer said, handing them to Artie. "It's better if she doesn't . . ."

Artie nodded, staring at the plump little boy with curly hair and playful smile. Even chubbier than he, Artie, had been. Artie wondered if it was a medication effect; last night's Medline search had revealed that steroids were still the main treatment for brain tumors. In another photo the Fleischers were at the beach, squatting near the water's edge. Each had an arm around their toddler son. It had been an overcast day; Artie could imagine the damp wind and ocean spray.

There was the rustle of china. Mr. Fleischer took the photos back and slipped them in his jacket pocket. The motion was eerie in its similarity to what Artie might have done.

Artie looked down to realize that Mrs. Fleischer was trying to hand him his cup of tea. He took the cup with both hands, grateful to hold onto something.

"I've been thinking about your offer," Mrs. Fleischer said once she was seated, her teacup balanced on her knee. "If you have the space, I could write a couple paragraphs and mail them to you. I think I'd like that."

"You know publishing. You could be bumped by a review of the first wheelchair ascent of Mt. Everest. But I'll see what I can do."

"Yes. Publishing isn't exactly lawn tennis anymore. Or so I read. It's been a while since I've submitted anything." She ran the rim of her cup along her lower lip. She had a sudden change of expression. "So how can we help you?" Mrs. Fleischer said, her voice now courteous but distant.

"If you could tell me how you worked on the book, your writing habits, whether you used a word processor or a quill pen, that kind of thing."

Mrs. Fleischer waved her hand. "Mechanics. Like wanting to know how someone killed himself. Hardly matters, especially when you're dead."

"Harriet," Fleischer said quietly. "It helps the readers to know the author. It's a pretty standard question."

Mrs. Fleischer drew herself up straight. "I sat and cried until the tears turned to sentences." She shook her head as though chastising herself. "Sorry. I used a Smith-Corona my mother gave me in college." She turned to her husband. "And a red ribbon. Do you remember that, dear?"

"How could I forget?" He nodded at Artie. "Perhaps you'd like to see the original manuscript."

"If it wouldn't be too much trouble."

Fleischer was up and out of the room, moving down the corridor. As soon as his footsteps had faded, Mrs. Fleischer excused herself. A minute later she was back, with the same photos that Artie had seen.

"You take them; it'll help you to understand. I can trust you to send them back?"

"Absolutely. You have my word."

As she held them up for Artie, the sleeve of her blouse fell back. On her upper arm was a row of fading bruises the size and shape of fingerprints. Mrs. Fleischer saw Artie staring. "Take them," she said abruptly. "Before he finds out." Her cheeks red, her eyes averted, she shoved them at Artie, then dropped her arm and held it tight against her side.

Artie wanted to ask, but didn't want to know. Gentle Mr. Fleischer?

"Would you prefer that I didn't do the article?" Artie said after a considerable silence, surprised at the shakiness in his voice and what he was thinking. He could almost see the overlapping scans of the Fleischers—it would be his scan.

Before Mrs. Fleischer could answer, her husband appeared, carrying a large manila envelope. "Found it," he said. He took the manuscript out of the envelope and handed it to Artie.

"I'll just take a peek." Artie looked at the top page, the title in red capital letters. "Did you type all your manuscripts in red?"

"Just this one. It seemed appropriate." She gave Artie a look that hinted of thinly veiled madness. Artie worried that Mrs. Fleischer might come unglued at any moment.

"I should be going. I saw the meter maid carrying a shotgun. Which would give a new meaning to the word *expired*." Artie forced a laugh, handed back the manuscript. Mrs. Fleischer took it and disappeared down the hall.

"It's not all Benjamin. But then it never is. Life is a series of explanations gone awry," Fleischer blurted out, leaning forward in his seat as though there were more, and as though he had already said too much.

Mrs. Fleischer returned, walked to the front door, opening it. "You have to leave so soon?" she asked, her face clouded over, sullen, feelings welling up. Mr. Fleischer looked down at his feet, cleared his throat.

Artie stood at the open door. Outside, traffic made ordinary patterns in the street, comings and goings of no particular consequence. *I am your son,* he could say. But he was shaking hands, muttering, "I'll be in touch."

He put the photos on one side of the mantel, between his mother and the shot of Dr. Samson and Hank Woolfson in the laboratory. At the other end were Sarah's photo album, the snapshot of Sarah and his mother in Sproul Plaza, and the DMV three-by-fives of the others. He stood motionless, staring at the Fleischer beach scene until the figures swam in front of his eyes. He had played second-string varsity basketball in high school, and could hear the coach yelling *Get in there, Singleton.* But that was basketball, not life. For the Fleischers the game was over; it was not a matter of last-minute substitutions.

Their resentment, rage, depression—all were explicable without Janine's scans. Though Artie knew what the scans would show.

The others deserved to know about the Fleischers, though he had no idea how he'd explain Mrs. Fleischer's moods and her bruises. But he wouldn't be phoning, not if Welinda was right, that the killings would stop if he stopped the visits. It had been nearly three weeks without any death announcements on the computer or cryptic entries on the discussion group.

No sooner had he decided against any further contacts than he felt pangs of loneliness. Artie picked up the phone, just to hear their voices. He wouldn't say anything. Bernard Sadler's machine answered and said, "I'll be away for a few days, at a clown convention in the city. God be with you." Lippe was also out. His message said, "Speak up or fuck off." Good for you, Artie thought as he clicked off and dialed Asher Newman.

"Please direct any inquiries to the County Coroner's office," said the recorded message. Artie slumped in his chair. Minutes later, he had verification of number four. Final report to follow.

Artie checked his computer; there were no new messages. The killer had broken loose, was operating without him.

He should warn the others, but couldn't without tipping off the killer.

He should buy a gun, change the locks.

He should leave town, change his name. Relocate.

Artie was frantic.

It was only a matter of minutes before he broke down and phoned Welinda.

It was nearly two-thirty when Welinda arrived from her gig at Moose's. She reeked of cigarettes and red wine, her speech was slightly boozy, yet her eyes danced when she heard of number four. It was what she had always dreamed of, real life as a game to be solved.

"It's time to stop acting half-assed. Hunch players are the first ones busted. If you were writing the program for the game of your life, you'd realize that a succession of suicides isn't an adequate narrative driving force. Neither is a suicidal genetic flaw. But serial murders . . .

"If the story is about differences in motivation, there's one killer. If it's about a murderous gene, any combination of murderer and victim would work."

"We're down to four. Three, not counting Tuna. We do some background checks . . ."

"I wasn't finished," Welinda interrupted. "Game theory is a closer approximation to life than something as arcane as trying to unravel motivation. For the purposes of problem-solving it's preferable to see yourself as a character in someone else's story. And, if you pardon my bluntness, your story is basically the redo of *The Bad Seed*." Welinda gave Artie a hard, steady look.

"I've always thought of clowns as spooky. I vote for Sadler."

"More so than a man without a steady address?"

"Sadler, the clown murderer. What could be a more perfect disguise?"

Welinda waved her hand. "Please. The author must know that you are particularly self-absorbed, that you can't step outside your personal narrow-minded view of yourself. Maybe that's part of the plot. Did you ever think of that? That your egomania is put in to prevent you from solving the problem?" Welinda poured herself a glass of red wine from a bottle she'd brought with her.

"Welinda. It's late. I thought you might be able to help."

"You have it here?"

Artie nodded. A minute later he was standing over Welinda, looking over her shoulder as she considered Artie's scan. "Which is which?"

Artie pointed out the single defect in the frontal lobe and the symmetrical temporal lobe abnormalities. "Suicide's up front, violence is between the ears."

Welinda wasn't listening. She was running her finger between the two defects, then tapping her finger on the scan.

"Of course. Right here." She was jabbing her finger at Artie's frontal lobes. "It's been right in front of our eyes." She turned and handed the scan back to Artie. She stood and punched Artie lightly in the abdomen. "You get a good night's sleep. I'll work out the details. This should be a snap." Welinda was beaming as she started toward the door.

"Don't forget your bottle," Artie said, suddenly exhausted.

TWENTY-THREE

Les dropped off the rental car at the Budget lot at San Francisco International Airport—it was an automated check-in, with no attendant in sight. He took the Airporter bus to the main terminal at Taylor and O'Farrell; from there it was a short walk back to his hotel room—three blocks of Asian grocery stores, empty lots, a theater that had been converted into a plasma donation center, boarded-up strip joints, video arcades. The sidewalks were dotted with the homeless, a variety of pushers, peddlers, and potential troublemakers, people who wouldn't remember him, or, if they did, wouldn't be considered reliable witnesses.

He was exhausted from the six hundred miles of driving, two days in Santa Barbara and two in Monterey, four nearly sleepless motel room nights.

Les had preferred Asher Newman. A cabinetmaker living halfway between Monterey and Big Sur, Asher possessed a quiet dignity not shared by Jefferson Lippe, a software designer who lived in a two-bedroom condo in Montecito, an upscale Santa Barbara suburb. Jefferson had converted one bedroom into a "state-of-the-art entertainment experience," with a floor-to-spackled-ceiling TV screen, mega-surround sound, and dual virtual reality headsets. "Women are always skeptical, so I start with an art demo first. Have them walk through the sculpture section of the Louvre. You know they're ready when you catch them trying to cop a feel on the Greek statues." Jefferson's laugh had been like fingernails against a blackboard.

Asher Newman was more troublesome. He was soft-spoken, thoughtful. His home reflected an old-world craftsmanship. They had stood on his deck, looking out over the tree line to the ocean, silently sharing the moment. Les had considered abandoning his plan. If Asher were his brother, they'd be close. They'd go backpacking together, scuba diving. They would be able to sit and not feel the need to talk, talk, talk.

Just past dusk, the sky a cobalt blue, scattered sounds of small animals, Asher had said the area was filled with mountain lions, the occasional bobcat, foxes, coyotes. It had been more than fifty feet from the deck to the sloping forest floor below. Last night face down in some nameless motel, the pillow tight over his ears, Les had continued to hear the echo of snapping boughs, but strain as he did, he could not hear a final thud.

Disappearing without a sound was nature's way, certainly more than harvesting embryos for a world already bursting at the seams.

If only he could find the original clinic, blow it and its amoral high-tech doctors sky-high. On the Internet he'd read the Unabomber manifesto. He agreed with almost the whole thing, except stooping to the scientists' level. He wanted transcendence, not retaliation, though he had to admit that it had been weeks since he'd meditated or taken a long, quiet walk.

He climbed the eight flights of stairs to his rented room, double-locked the door behind him, and, bone-weary, dropped onto the bed. His head cradled in his hands, he tried to visualize Sardine Lake with its pristine water, white shores, and miles of fresh snow without footprints or history.

Outside there was shouting, some muffled sounds that might have been gunfire, followed by approaching sirens. More heated conversation. By the time the street noises returned to ordinary, Les was frazzled. His hands tingled as though every nerve ending had been filed to a fine point. A patch of reddish-orange neon was ablaze on the closet door. He pulled the curtains tight together, the light from the street now an angry, fiery slit, the door bleeding hot neon.

In a far corner of the room, in the near darkness, he imagined he saw Asher Newman standing at his deck, his arm outstretched, pointing to a red-winged hawk. This image alternated with a view of the deck unoccupied, empty, its owner away. In the cabin would be Asher's things, what he had gathered together into the materials of his life—his carpentry tools, architectural books and journals, a telescope.

Les had been afraid to linger. He'd grabbed only a pair of Asher's underpants and a heavy cotton turtleneck shirt. They were in his travel bag, along with a pair of Jefferson Lippe's blue-and-red argyle socks. He shouldn't have taken them—he'd had no clear reason, his arms were on fire, he should try to get some sleep. But now he was standing beside his bed, undressing. Naked, he unzipped the travel bag and pulled out his new possessions.

He smelled Asher's neatly folded jockeys, pleased with the faint fragrance of laundry soap and the softness against his cheeks. He slipped them on, watching his legs step into them, his hands draw them up over his calves, then his thighs, his thumbs making the final adjustment of the elastic waistband.

Jefferson's socks were rolled in a tight ball. Les bounced them in his hand, weighing the motion against some internal standard that could apply to either of them. *Yes, this is what Jefferson would have felt.*

He pulled on the argyle socks and the turtleneck sweater, started toward the bathroom to look at himself in the mirror. *Not necessary. You don't need to see what you already know.*

The socks made his feet hot and tingly, in contrast to his legs, which were like ice. It was unclear where the chill ended; Les thought he could feel it creeping up into his chest. He went to the closet, pulled out the Captain Marvel jacket, put it on over the turtleneck. As he turned to close the door, he caught sight of himself in a full-length closet mirror that he hadn't noticed before.

Backlit by the reddish-orange light, he was a frightening imposter, a pathetic imitation, a court jester, a madman. Jerkily he pulled off the jacket and turtleneck, then the socks. For a moment he lingered in the underpants, which were identical to his own. These were no different except that they were Newman's. No difference and all the difference. *Have respect*, he said to himself, taking off the underpants, refolding them the way that he had found them and putting them back in his travel bag. The socks and turtleneck went on a shelf in the closet, the jacket back on its hanger.

In the mirror, the flames continued to backlight his head. He closed the door behind him, slid into bed, under the covers, the neon now only an innocuous patch of city sleaziness to be side-stepped. He looked away to the ceiling. In the distance he heard the sound of a bough breaking. Les dismissed it as street noise.

When he woke up, it was noon. He was groggy from sleeping late, stiff from the cold room, the lumpy mattress and lack of exercise. Today's plan was to track down Mark Caputo. Perhaps there was someone in records over at city hall. A few bucks to grease the database. But first he phoned Bernard Sadler in Bakersfield. Not to talk with him. He just wanted to hear his voice, make sure Bernard was home, wasn't up to anything. Would be available.

Bernard's answering machine told him of the clown convention in the city. City? LA or SF? Bakersfield was closer to LA. He phoned the *Los Angeles Times* current events desk. No, there wasn't any clown convention. He tried the *Chronicle*; yes, there was a parade starting at noon in front of city hall.

Had he known this at some telepathic level? Was Sadler broadcasting over their special clone frequency? Was this why he was already on the way to city hall? To find Mark and Bernard?

Outside, he walked quickly toward Polk Street, not sure whether to breathe deeply for the exercise, or to hold his breath and save his lungs. Though it was a brisk, windy day, he could smell stale cigarettes, alcohol, urine, traces of vomit and excrement. He told himself that it wasn't possible, but the smells persisted, grew stronger as he approached the park in front of city hall.

To his right, adjacent to the entranceway of an underground parking lot, a group of homeless men gathered around their shopping carts. "Hey, brother," one of them called out to him, holding out his hand. Les slowed, gave the man two dollars, then hurried around the garage entrance corner before others could converge.

He nearly bumped into a group of seventy-five to a hundred men in clown outfits. Les looked through the park to city hall. Polk Street was cordoned off. There were a dozen mounted policemen, hundreds of excited children playing and waiting behind sidewalk barricades. Throughout the park, clowns were making final adjustments to their costumes, stretching, practicing their juggling, baton-twirling, and pratfalls.

Several were still dressing. One, standing with one leg balanced on a park bench near the street barricades, was applying his whiteface with one hand while holding a hand mirror with the other. He was having trouble maintaining the mirror's proper angle; he did not notice Les staring, then retreating to the corner of the garage entrance where he could see without being seen.

It had to be Sadler. There was no doubt; as the man completed his makeup job and attached a large purple nose, Les saw himself slide beneath the greasepaint and disappear from view.

His heart was pounding.

The clowns were closing ranks, they began marching five abreast through the central plaza and out onto Polk Street. Les tagged along at a distance, in an opening between the clowns and a group of drum majorettes. A policeman motioned for him to move aside. He nodded, turning his head away and stepping quickly to the sidewalk. He ran on ahead, behind the barricades, stationed himself at the corner of Market and Polk. Next to him a little girl was tugging at her father's hand. "Here come the clowns," she squealed, jumping up and down. The sound of children's laughter rippled down the street.

Les panicked. Several clowns were his size and had bright purple noses. A tall man in a greasy overcoat had stepped in front of him, blocking his view. Les pushed past the man and hollered, "Hey, Sadler, over here!" No one turned. The father pulled his daughter closer to him, away from Les.

"Hey, Sadler!"

A clown in the middle of the group looked out at the crowd. Les waved. "Wait up!" he yelled, hopping over the barricade and out into the parade.

A mounted policeman was coming down the street, clearing a path between the barricade and the parade participants. He motioned to Les with a baton. Les hopped back over the barricade and faded into the crowd.

He waited until the mounted policeman passed by, then again pushed forward to the barricade. To Les's surprise, the clown had dropped back and was making his way toward him.

"We should talk," Les said when they met at the barricade. He was grateful for a trio of unicycle-riding jugglers that had the crowd's attention. No one would notice the two of them working their way back in a direction opposite the parade's.

"Five minutes and you can catch up with the others," Les said when they reached the corner of Polk and Grove. He was barely audible over a blast of amplified rap music echoing in the street.

Bernard Sadler stared at Les. "You're Arthur Singleton, the one who sent the letter? Pretty good job, recognizing me under all this makeup."

"Let's grab some coffee and I'll explain."

Bernard hesitated, sizing Les up. "I thought it was a crank letter, some mail scam. That's why I didn't phone back."

"Come on," Les said. "From what I saw, it'll be fifteen, maybe twenty minutes before the police clear the traffic on Market Street. Give me five minutes. You'll have plenty of time to catch up with them."

They ducked into a sandwich shop with windows filled with hams and turkeys basting under infrared lighting. Les was reminded of the neon in his room and the curious notion that the lights made raw meat presentable. They picked up two cups of coffee at the end of the cafeteria line. Les paid for both, then led Bernard to an empty booth at the rear of the nearly deserted restaurant.

Les proceeded as he had with the others, introducing himself as a twin given up for adoption at birth and that he'd learned this only as a recent deathbed revelation from his mother. He talked slowly, frequently pausing to sip his coffee, taking his time. He wondered about the large plain wooden cross hanging from Sadler's neck. A cross on a clown outfit?

"You live near here?" Bernard asked. "We could meet after the parade."

"I did, but I've moved to Truckee. I'm just down for the day to pick up some last things. I read in the *Chronicle* about the parade and took a chance."

"You knew that I was a clown?"

"Your phone message."

Bernard nodded. "We're really twins? No, let me rephrase that. We're really twins. Wow. And we're going to be living nearby."

"How's that?"

"I've landed a full-time gig at a new casino in Reno. The casino's giving me two half-days a week to do my ministry work at Children's Hospital and at Truckee Memorial. I guess they think it's good PR. Anyway, that'll make it easy for us to get together, spend some time getting to know each other. Besides, I've heard that Truckee is a great place to live, an easy commute to Reno. What do you think?"

"Ministry?"

"Sure. You haven't heard of the clown ministry?"

Les shook his head.

"It started as Pentecostal—can you imagine? A thousand clowns singing and speaking in tongues. That was way back when, in Louisiana. Now it's an international organization, strictly ecumenical. We spend most of our time with young children—in hospitals, inner cities, and juvenile halls. Religion without fear and trembling, that's our motto." With his right hand Bernard reached into a slit-like opening in his Bozo outfit. With his left he mimed a series of exaggerated gestures as though his right hand were that of a marionette controlled by the left. At the same time he raised his garishly painted red eyebrows.

The effect was unnerving, even frightening. Les's hands felt weak, as though they were no longer in charge of themselves, as though Bernard's imaginary marionette strings somehow controlled *his* hands. This was beyond coincidence—Paul Lafora and

Bernard independently being drawn into the clergy. *It could happen*, Les tried to reassure himself, but he knew the odds were low.

With another series of elaborate gestures, Bernard pulled out a business card, handed it to Les. *Bernie, The Clown Minister*. It listed a Bakersfield address, crossed out. Below was neatly printed: *c/o The Silver Legacy Casino, Reno, Nevada*. Bernard gulped down the rest of his coffee, being careful not to smear the bright red greasepaint outlining his lips. "Give me your Truckee address. I'll phone you as soon as I get into town."

"I don't have a permanent place yet. I'll get in touch with you at the casino."

Bernard was shifting in his seat, getting ready to leave.

Les had to do something now, or their next encounter would be on the streets of Truckee, with Bernard introducing himself to everyone as Les's long-lost brother. He looked around the restaurant. Two old women were sharing a turkey sandwich at an adjacent table. They were deep in conversation and had scarcely looked up from their food. A single server at the front of the restaurant stood with his back to them while he cleaned the steam table, wiped the drippings from the metal counter and the glass partition in front of the meats.

He could use the stun gun and the car-fentanyl—several quick sprays should be fatal. He could holler "911," run out of the restaurant, and be forgotten in the commotion.

But he couldn't be sure.

Bernard stood up. "This is an important parade. I'd better get going, right after I hit the head. That coffee's already percolated." He started toward the men's room at the rear of the restaurant.

Les followed. "By the way, you're not going to Reno to gamble, are you?" he asked.

"I've been known to, on occasion." Bernard gave Les a big clown smile. "I've got a foolproof system. Just make the sign of the cross on a Keno card. If you win, you win. If you lose, you still win."

The restroom was small—one urinal and one stall. Les hurried toward the urinal, leaving the stall for Bernard. He reached into his pocket, grasped the stun gun, trying not to compare Bernard with Harold Weinstein.

It took only seconds. The stun gun discharged one hundred and fifty thousand volts. One pop to the back of the neck dropped Bernard to his knees, his body falling forward against the toilet bowl, his face flush with the seat. Les reached around, grabbed Sadler by the chin and pulled his head back far enough to spray him several times in the face. Bernard was heavier than he'd expected; Les eased him down, Bernard's head slumping forward onto his chest. Bracing him with one arm, Les turned and reached back, pulled the stall door closed, and bolted it.

He moved his free hand up and down Bernard's neck, checking for a pulse. His own heart was pounding wildly; he could not be certain whose pulse he was feeling. He stayed in this position for some time, until there was no movement of Bernard's chest, and no pulse.

The door to the men's room opened. Les heard feet on tile, someone urinating. The door opened and closed again.

If only he had a plastic bag, he could fake a suicide. He wanted to go through the trashcan for something suitable, but he couldn't risk being seen. Making it look like suicide was out of the question. So be it, he thought, turning Bernard on his side, and finding the zipper to the clown outfit.

Les took several minutes struggling to pull the outfit over Bernard's arms, and another to slip into it. The clown shoes fit perfectly. Once dressed, the outfit tight against his own clothing, Les lifted Bernard up on the toilet, this time leaning his head against the back wall of the stall. He stopped and took a deep breath, his arms shaky from the effort. Les could see a hint of mottling beginning through the whiteface on the lower part of Bernard's face and chin.

From his front pocket Les drew out a small penknife and, with the dull edge, began to scrape some of the grease paint from Bernard's cheek. He was careful not to nick Bernard. With his index finger he wiped the greasepaint from his knife and applied it to himself, rubbing it over his cheeks, forehead and chin. Next came the red eyebrows, with Les removing enough to cover his lips and circle his eyes, enough to give himself a watered-down clown appearance and be able to leave the restaurant unnoticed. After he was out of sight, his appearance would be irrelevant—he would be one clown among many.

He went through Bernard's pants, removed his wallet, his ministry calling cards and several scraps of paper. Bernard would be John Doe, a robbery victim.

The nose was fastened by a thin elastic band that wrapped around Bernard's head. As he pulled it off, he was aware of Bernard's head in his hands, much as Paul Lafora's had been. He looked down at Bernard, at his greasepaint-streaked face, the red and white blurred at his mouth and eyes, as though he had been weeping. Or bleeding.

Gently he closed Bernard's eyes, his fingers lingering on each lid. Squatting in front of the toilet, holding Bernard's head in his hands, he was surprised to recall that time, long ago, when he'd shot the trapped deer, then dismembered it. He shook his head rapidly, driving away any further sentiment. He pulled off Bernard's red wig, slipped it on. It was warm.

Perhaps he could show up for Bernard's volunteer assignments at the hospitals, carry on in Bernard's shoes. The idea pleased him, as if Bernard's spirit might be continued by ... no. Bernard was his own man. That was what this was all about.

The cross came last. Les put it in his pocket. Later it would go with his other things—things of the others.

He listened carefully, bent down and took a peek. The restroom was empty. Quickly he crawled out from under the stall, leaving it locked. He straightened himself out in the mirror, adjusted the wig, smoothed out some lumps of greasepaint around his eyes. He tucked his own shoes under his arm, under the outfit, slipped on his aviator glasses. Moments later he was passing through the restaurant, out into the street, moving quickly toward Van Ness Avenue.

Twenty minutes later he was back in his hotel room.

TWENTY-FOUR

After missing their dinner at the restaurant, Artie had sent Janine flowers, apologies, and had in return received a two-week cold shoulder, followed by a "Let's try it again, and you be on your best behavior." And Janine laughing. "Anyway, with your scan, I guess I won't have to worry about a long-term relationship." More laughter, from Janine.

They'd clicked.

For the first time in recent memory Artie felt safe, somehow protected from trouble. Extraordinarily lucky. He wanted to wake up Janine, pull back the light blanket covering her and take her in, head to foot. Instead he propped himself up on one elbow and listened to her breathing fill his bedroom darkness.

He went back and forth over the last hour, rubbing and rerubbing into polished memories her look of pleasure when he'd entered her, as though it were her first time, as though she had always been waiting for him. The smile that became a laugh, then a moan. The grip of her hands at the back of his neck. Afterwards, her hands holding his face as she kissed him. Her feet rubbing against his. More laughter. Janine saying, "I'm going to hate myself in the morning, but it's not morning yet."

Artie couldn't remember ever feeling this good.

The phone rang. He grabbed the portable phone and eased himself out of bed, careful not to awaken Janine. He padded to the far end of the small living room before saying anything.

It was Welinda. "Thank god you're okay. It's been on all the stations. Murder at the sandwich shop."

Artie looked back through the open bedroom door. Janine hadn't budged. "What?" he whispered.

"Some clown that had Artie written all over him. I'm over at the Washbag, noodling 'Melancholy Baby' for some tourist from Whitesocksville, when I glance up at the TV over the bar and see you being carried out of some toilet stall."

Artie flipped on the TV and muted the sound—the only news program on was showing clouds gathering over the Midwest.

"He's here in town," she continued. "Trust Welinda. There's no question about it."

The clouds passed over Arkansas; the TV shifted to preparation of lasagna for six.

"I'll phone you right back," Artie said. He hung up, closed the bedroom door, dialed Las Vegas. "We've got problems," he said when the Glass Slipper operator finally connected him with Tuna. After Artie told Tuna about the latest death, the two men speculated on Lippe versus Robbins. But their tone was desultory, as though both recognized that their efforts at identification were diversionary from their real concern. They were both targets. "You stay in the casino, no wandering out back for a Danish or whatever," Artie said.

"I was on my way back to the motel."

"Forget the motel. You get a room at the Glass Slipper, under some phony name, and double-bolt the door. If you think I'm kidding, buy a copy of tomorrow morning's *Chronicle*."

"We made the papers?"

"Not exactly we. You don't say a word, not to anyone. This isn't the time to drum up some cheap publicity stunt."

"Rooms here are *tres chèr*. It'll cost extra."

"The check's in the mail."

"It's not nice to con your own family. And don't worry. There're security guards every ten inches, like maybe someone might steal one of the plastic jackpot buckets or a gross of swizzle sticks. But you . . ." Tuna's voice was softer, the bravado gone. "Is there something I should be doing? Could be doing?"

"I'll let you know later today," Artie said into the din of slot machines. Louder still was Tuna's uncharacteristic silence. "Be careful," Artie added, before hanging up.

Lippe was out, as usual. Artie disconnected without leaving a message. He wanted to warn Lippe, but the odds were fifty-fifty that Lippe was the killer.

The only voice he'd never heard was Les Robbins's. Artie tried to imagine how it might differ. All the others had the same pitch and tone; it was only in the phrasing that Artie could hear differences in personality—presumed differences, which Artie had to concede might be entirely superficial, no more than different presentations of the same underlying urges.

Robbins's tone of voice would prove nothing.

The phrase *looks are deceiving* was never truer.

Artie needed protection, but buying a gun could make matters worse. With their high-powered computers, the police could scan his photo and trace him to the others. Using his plane flights and car rentals, he could be placed at the other death scenes.

Calling the cops was out of the question.

He phoned Welinda back. She had been unable to find a more recent address or telephone for Les Robbins or another unlisted number for Lippe.

"Any new email or messages on your newsgroup?"

"None since yesterday afternoon."

"Good," Welinda said. "You phone me if you hear anything. In the meantime you stay put and double-locked."

"Just in case, I'd prefer being cremated."

"I can't imagine him doing anything more until he lets you know about the latest. You're his audience."

"That's comforting."

"Trust me." Talking rapidly, Welinda began outlining her plan. Artie listened, agreeing with Welinda's logic, but uncertain whether or not it would work. His brain scan as a way out of the nightmare?

"I don't know," Artie said when Welinda finished. "We're taking a real chance. Rather, I'm taking a real chance."

"You have a better suggestion?"

"No."

The computer beeped. Artie checked his bedside digital clock; it was three AM. Naked, he stumbled into his study, wiping his eyes. He'd had perhaps a half hour of sleep. Not enough time for dreaming, just enough time to feel disoriented.

```
>Find me
So that I will exist, find my navel
So that it will exist, find my nipples
So that they will exist, find every hair
Of my belly, I am good (or I am bad),
Find me.
```

To his relief, there was no mention of any other deaths. Artie pulled out his volume of collected poems of George Oppen. Sure enough, the quote on his email was from "Of Being Numerous."

He'd heard stories of murderers reaching out, asking, pleading, later blaming those who hadn't come forward to help. Or was this a sly attempt to implicate him further, to pass the blame to him?

He logged onto his discussion group. There were some new messages.

>Why men? Why not women? You should rethink the gender and the nature of the urge to murder.

>You wouldn't have a story if you used women. They kill out of love gone wrong, not because someone else has on the same dress.

>Forget gender. Why do the clones have to kill each other? What's wrong with a quiet story about family values?

>A good book needs big emotions, a sense of vindication and retribution, not pleasant small talk, smiles and prayers over a stupid turkey.

>We wouldn't need so many murder mysteries if we felt better about each other.

>And ourselves.

>Not ourselves. Myself. Feel better about myself.

>Being without family is like being born again. A new man.

>You show me a new man, I'll show you the ultimate conceit.

>You show me a new man, I'll show you a dead man.

The video monitor's glow seemed otherworldly, dangerous; every cell in his body was on alert. He dialed Lippe's number.

No one answered.

He had the urge to phone Newman, though he knew that Newman was already dead.

Artie put down his portable phone, walked out into the living room. Through his window he could see darkened North Beach. He wanted to stick his head out the window, feel the fresh air, but he didn't. Instead he double-checked the window latch and the bolt on the door.

If Welinda's plan didn't work ...?

He heard Janine stirring. He cleared the computer screen, then went to the bathroom. He sat quietly on the toilet, waiting until she was asleep again. Until he could convince himself that the killer, either Lippe or Robbins—probably Robbins; yes, he'd bet on Robbins—wouldn't hurt her. It was strictly a family matter.

At five AM he once again checked his computer. Finding no new messages on the newsgroup, he checked his email.

```
>Lippe, too. But you already knew that, didn't
you?
```

From the bathroom he phoned the Santa Barbara Coroner's Office. Still closed. The *Santa Barbara Register* had no listing of an obituary. The Monterey County Coroner's office was also closed and would not be open until nine AM. In four hours he would know for sure—but he had already guessed.

When he came back from the bathroom, Janine was sitting up in bed. "You told me you were an early riser. I guess I wasn't expecting this early." She leaned forward and lightly rested her cheek against his thigh. She stroked him once, then stood up, her arms draped across his shoulders. Despite his racing mind, Artie began to grow excited.

"A man of your word," Janine said, pulling Artie with her as she fell backwards onto the bed. "But no dallying. I've got to be at the lab at eight sharp. We need to finish up the numbers for the New York conference Friday."

"My friends've warned me about professional women. Priorities. Schedules." Normal chatter suggested normal times.

"Ssssh." Janine put her finger to his lips. "It's already us against the morning commute."

Five minutes of bliss, then the terror returned. Artie kissed Janine good morning, hoping that she didn't notice his change in mood. As soon as she left the apartment, he worried that he should have told her that she should be careful, that someone was after him. But the direction of that conversation was off-limits. He ran to the front window; the street was empty. After watching Janine climb into her old Fiat convertible and drive away, he hurriedly dressed, gathered his things, left the apartment. If Welinda was right, today might well be the day.

He took a combination of side streets and alleyways, walking quickly, ready to break into a run, at the same time inexplicably anxious to meet Les Robbins. He could anticipate a combination of tortured psyche and scrambled metaphysics, but then what? With the unsuspecting others, Les wouldn't have had to be violent. He could have snuck up behind them or shoved the spray in their faces. A split second, a whiff of the spray, and curtains. With him Les would be on guard, prepared.

Artie ran through his options—take the initiative and belt Robbins, knock him down and use the spray on him, run away at full tilt? All reasonable possibilities, but not what he would do. They needed to talk. He needed to understand, to know that Les wasn't just an alternative self, what *he* might have become had he not snapped out of those bad times when *he'd* needed help.

Their differences had to be based on more than mere luck, a random act of kindness of some therapist or orderly, a mother's nod, a tip of some passerby's cap at just the right moment.

According to Welinda, the murders were about trimming away unwanted options until Les's life appeared to be deliberately unique, not merely one path among many.

Yes, Les would want to talk with him, get to know him, know which alternative he was getting rid of. He wouldn't just rush up to him in the street and kill him.

He recalled the first meeting with Sarah Woolfson and the ride to Cloverdale. The short-order cook had said that he'd kill the others. Artie had understood. If he hadn't been subdued with grieving for his own mother, he might have been truly pissed. Once ignited, his unstable biology fired up, the defects on his scan might activate a neural meltdown, rage could easily become self-consuming. Not his scan, he reminded himself. *Their* scan.

Reaching his store, he glanced up and down the block before unlocking the front door, slipping inside and relocking it behind him. In the early morning gray the rows of comics leered at him, a rogue's gallery of stylized villains. He heard a knock, jerked his head. It was Welinda.

"You bring everything with you?" Welinda asked after she stepped inside and Artie rebolted the door. She held two Styrofoam cups of coffee and a sack of bagels. She handed one coffee to Artie, who put it on the front counter, next to a reissue of *Plastic Man.*

"Everything." Artie pulled out a large manila folder he'd tucked beneath his shirt and gave it to Welinda. He took two bagels from the bag and put them next to his coffee.

"You stay behind the counter, but keep the lights off. I'll be back as soon as I can," Welinda said.

Though Welinda's plan smacked of madness and desperation, it was reassuring to see her scurrying away, full of good intention and enthusiasm, as though she'd stepped through some philosophical barrier and had delivered herself directly into the game of life. It just might work, Artie told himself as he retreated to the rear of the store.

He took his bagels and coffee, ducked behind the waist-high counter, and crouched down so that he could not be seen from the front of the store. As a little boy his favorite game had been to crawl inside a kitchen cupboard and pretend that he was invisible. It had worked; he had never been discovered. While in college, he had often taken the train to New York—to walk the streets knowing that he would not be recognized.

The recollections of his trips remained vague—rather he remembered the delicious sensation of the freedom of invisibility and irrelevancy. What he felt Ligott and Lafora had been seeking. And Les Robbins? Perhaps the murders were a different means to the same end.

He could sit down with Robbins, explain that the concept of *family* was arbitrary, that uniqueness was absurdity's handmaiden. Robbins would be able to understand; the two would agree, shake hands, and disappear from each other's lives. Terribly civilized.

Exhausted from his lack of sleep, momentarily comforted by the neatness of his logic and thoughts of Janine, Artie lay back on the linoleum, his head resting on a pillow of unopened comics. He fell asleep, dreaming of himself as a solitary soldier behind enemy lines, deep in his foxhole, out of sight, invisible, easily overlooked. He curled up in a fetal position and waited for outside forces to settle the score, end the war. Meanwhile he was safe in his tight little ball.

He woke to the sound of pounding at the door. It was Welinda returning. "Not exactly the liberating army," Artie said as he opened the door, ushered Welinda inside, and closed it again.

"One last thing," Welinda said. "Have you made any progress on *Clothesline*?"

"You must be kidding. This hasn't exactly been leisure time. Why? Do you think I've become an expert on victims' attire?"

"I was wondering what kind of clothing you think Les Robbins will be wearing."

"No steady address or job, Cal Tech dropout, a desire to be inconspicuous. I'd guess worn brown corduroys, flannel shirt, and hiking shoes."

"Not something from your closet?"

"He could be wearing my dreadful Captain Marvel jacket."

"That would be too obvious," Welinda said, putting down her notebook and opening the Oppen book she'd brought with her. She started to read, then stopped. "Loner, personal identity crisis, need for solidarity. That much is clear. But is he emotional, does he have a heart? Do you think part of him is grieving?"

"It depends on whether he's on automatic pilot. Probably."

"Is that how you'd see it?"

"With my mom, it was like someone had rolled up your favorite season and was carting it away. With the others . . ." Artie paused, shook his head. "Let's just say that I've got some sorting out to do."

"Right. You'll need two sets of matching brown corduroys, flannel shirts and hiking boots."

"You sure this is going to work?"

Welinda was again thumbing through the book of poems. "We need to choose an appropriate stanza or two. How about this ?

> He wants to say
> His life is real,
> No one can say why

That should get the message across."

Artie took the book from Welinda. "Try these.

> I cannot even now
> Altogether disengage myself
> From those men

Or:

> They made small objects
> of wood and the bones of fish
> And of stone. They talked,
> Families talked,

They gathered in council
And spoke, carrying objects.
They were credulous,
Their things shone in the forest.

They were patient
With the world.
This will never return, never
Unless having reached their limits

They will begin over, that is
Over and over . . .

They carry nativeness
To a conclusion
In suicide.

That's more to the point," Artie said. "We post the first stanza now, the next later this evening or tomorrow."

"Good choices, but let's wait until this evening. I think by then it'll have more impact."

Artie phoned Las Vegas, explained to Tuna what he had to do. Tuna was subdued, agreeing without argument. "We're all set," Artie said, hanging up the phone.

Welinda handed him the key to her apartment. "You stay at my place. We don't need your presence to be an extra variable."

"And if this doesn't work?"

"You can sue me." Welinda gave Artie a broad smile and a pat on the shoulder.

"I'll leave that for my estate," Artie said as he opened the door and walked out into the morning fog.

TWENTY-FIVE

F or some time after returning to his room Les sat on the edge of his bed, still in Sadler's clown outfit. Though the cloth was heavy and constricting, particularly at the shoulders and hips, he was reluctant to take the suit off. Sadler had worn the outfit to hospital wards, had played with children with leukemia, brain tumors, paraplegia, blindness, retardation. The worst that god could dish up, Bernard had tried to undo, if not in fact, at least in spirit. He had mocked disease, stuck out his tongue at fate, stared it down and made silly faces.

In Les's pants pocket, underneath the clown suit, was Paul Lafora's medal—for helping inner city kids.

And he, Les Robbins, the man who wanted nothing but liberation from a society gone mad, had killed them to preserve his own sanity.

He was nauseous. There were dense knots behind his throat and in the pit of his stomach. Out on the street he had attributed his queasiness to the bad coffee at the sandwich shop, to the smells around Civic Center, to the sight of so many government buildings. But the feeling was more intense now.

If he'd spent more time thinking it through, he might have found another solution, some easier way out. Knowing that he was not alone, that none of Arthur's newsgroup had come up with any alternative suggestion, didn't make him feel better. He lay down, his pillow pushing the red wig down low on his brow, until it was resting on his eyebrows. The warmth was comforting. Les left the wig at this jaunty angle.

Through the thin wall he could hear the tinny sound of a cheap TV set; his neighbor was watching the news. It had been over two years since Les had sworn off TV, and the sound, although muffled, was alien, a popular song in a language he no longer understood. He could not make out the words, though he could identify, by their volume and shrillness, the frequent commercial interruptions.

Bernard's death might be on the news right now. Or not. It would make no difference if he did not listen. From the pocket of the clown suit he pulled out Bernard's cross, rested it on his chest. It was the plain wood of an earlier time, a time of monasteries and monks and silent penitence, a time when all men wore the presumption of guilt. Sin was the norm; it was in the offering up of your soul through prayer that you conceded man's nature.

Les gripped the cross with his right hand, rested his left, palm up, on his forehead, as though he might be able to generate a religious current that would clear his head. All he heard was the babble leaking through the walls, honking rising up from the street, the loud beating of his own heart.

In the morning, following a night of fragmented sleep and disturbing, unremembered dreams, he left the hotel, walked to a nearby theater supply shop, and purchased several tubes of greasepaint. Back in his room, he freshened up until his face was thickly covered in white, with red lips and eyebrows, and a cluster of black freckles on each cheek. With his purple nose, red wig, and aviator glasses in place, he barely recognized himself.

Though the knots of nausea were gone, there remained a generalized sense of imbalance, of body parts misaligned. Being outside did not help. Several drunks pointed and laughed. Les didn't want to create a scene that might later be remembered, so he hurried, head down, trying to imitate walking in a storm, looking up as little as possible, until he arrived at Shazam.

He checked his reflection in the store window—there was no reason to fear that he would be recognized. They would chat briefly, he would hear Arthur's voice, then he would make his plans. He would have to be quick; the city was already clotting his blood stream. He could feel the clunks and bangs of civilization coursing through his arteries. Soon they would block off the blood flow to his head. He would be reduced to street noise and TV commercials.

The store was empty, except for a tall, slender woman with red hair, nearly as red as his wig, standing at a computer in the center aisle. Les entered and looked around.

"Could I help you?" the woman asked.

"Just looking. I'm particularly interested in any original copies of *Bozo the Clown*. I believe they were put out by Dell Publishing." Earlier this morning Les had looked up the information on the Internet. "If I'm correct, it was 1950 to 1963."

Welinda smiled as she thumbed through the plastic-covered collection of clown comics. She'd had a private wager with herself that Robbins would show up between ten-fifteen and ten-thirty AM. Not right at opening time, but as soon after as possible without appearing to be impatient. Though Welinda had to admit that she hadn't anticipated the clown outfit.

She tried not to stare; she'd seen pictures of the others, but this was the first, other than Caputo—who didn't count, not with those dead eyes, medication-coarsened skin, and blank expression. This time it was the real thing.

"We've got a couple raggedy *Bozo*s, but nothing of quality. Try again in a couple days."

"How's that?" Les asked.

"The boss is on his way to a private meeting at the Anaheim Hilton to scout out a new collection. Some old guy who wants to chuck his childhood. Happens all the time; they save everything for fifty years, then, on a whim, want to clean everything out, like they're getting ready to go and want to travel light. The boss makes the deal, we'll be in comic book heaven."

"He's already gone?" Les asked.

"The noon flight. He'll be back tomorrow evening. If you're interested we can give you a call. Or if you want to leave your name, we can put you on the mailing list."

"That won't be necessary. I'll drop by tomorrow evening."

So far, so good, Welinda thought as Les walked out of the store.

Les took a cab to the airport. Once inside, he checked at central information; the only noon flight to Anaheim was on United, gate 86. Les made his way to the check-in counter. Sure enough, Arthur was standing at the window, his back to the main aisle, watching the planes take off. Les stepped back, out of line of sight, and waited until he saw Arthur board the plane.

He had to remind himself that Arthur surely knew about him and that it could be a trick. But the plane was taking off with Arthur on board. Later in the day he would phone the Hilton to see if Arthur had checked in.

A little boy was pulling at his sleeve. Les flashed a smile, held up both hands, palms outward, did a clumsy imitation of a tap dancer, and finished by falling face forward. The boy laughed; his mother offered Les a dollar. He took it and gave it to the little boy. All three of them laughed; then the mother took her son to an adjacent check-in counter, the boy looking over his shoulder, waving at Les.

When this was over, he'd volunteer at Tahoe Memorial. It would be the least he could do, Les thought, his back sore from his clumsy nosedive. But first he would work on his pratfalls.

After returning to the hotel and changing his clothes, Les spent the day in Golden Gate Park. He had a cup of green tea in the Japanese Tea Garden. If he were terribly nearsighted, it would have been beautiful. But Les saw beyond the raked sand paths and bonsaied trees to the herd of tourists milling about. He lasted through half the cup of tea, then left the garden. He wandered aimlessly, trying to stay off the concrete, out of sight of cars and packs of joggers and bicyclists in their spandex and brightly colored helmets.

At dusk, from the pay phones in front of the aquarium, he dialed the Anaheim Hilton.

"Yes, Mr. Singleton is here. Would you like me to ring his room?"

"That won't be necessary. He's expecting me later in the evening," Les said.

He would walk; it would probably take an hour. By then it would be dark. He had plenty of time—all night if he needed it.

At Arthur's door, Les wasn't surprised that his key didn't work. He'd expected Arthur to change his lock. If necessary, Les would get the manager to open it, but only as the last resort. He walked down the several flights of stairs and out the front door. Most old San Francisco apartments had fire escapes; Arthur's building was no exception, with its fire escape opening onto a back alley. It was a wintry night, dark and cold. The alley was poorly lit by a single street lamp and a dim patchwork of lights from apartment rear windows. With a running jump, Les was able to grab the bottom rung and pull himself up. The ladder was old and rusty, and made a squeaking noise as Les climbed to the first landing.

He looked around. There were no new lights on, or heads peering out. He reached Arthur's window, gave a gentle tug. The window opened without much effort. Could this be a trap? Arthur was smart and into games. He would be cautious.

Les took the halogen penlight from his pocket and ran the beam over Arthur's bedroom, careful to cup the light with his hand so that it would not be visible from the alley or adjacent apartments. Cautiously he went from room to room, satisfying himself that the apartment was empty and that there were no obvious traps. In Arthur's studio the computer was on; several email messages were waiting. One said that the meeting was set for four PM at the Anaheim Hilton. Another confirmed his return flight tomorrow evening. Two inquiries from other comic book store owners, but nothing else of interest.

He walked back to Arthur's bedroom closet, pulled out a pair of khaki pants, a plain blue chambray shirt, and a pair of moccasins. In case someone should barge in—perhaps a friend checking on Arthur's plants—he told himself as he slipped out of his own clothes and into Arthur's. That done, his own clothes in a neat pile on top of Arthur's dresser, he turned on the bedroom lights, then the lights in the other rooms.

He had been here before; the smells were his as though he had marked the territory himself. His and yet not his—it was Arthur's address, Arthur's home, he felt compelled to remind himself, to ward off the strong undercurrent of familiarity. The boundaries between the two of them should have been obvious, but the more freely he moved in Arthur's space, the more he needed to press on.

Les had a sinking thought: What if he were to return to Truckee, to his room, and find Arthur in his bed, reading his books, or downstairs in the lobby hitting on Ann Fritz? What would he say? *Move aside, you're not me.* And would Arthur ignore him? Turn and say *Prove it*? The word *interchangeable* reverberated in his mind, as it had from the time he'd first received the news.

Bernard had been planning to move to Reno. Bernard could have become a local figure, a Main Street clown, and he, Les—

would he have become a mere sibling shadow, the other brother, Bernard's twin? And if Bernard had come to the hotel, would he, too, be drawn to Ann? The question was rhetorical; its answer was biological. Soon, like moths to light, they would all arrive, convene in the lobby, converting it into a hall of mirrors. They would be stumbling and crawling over each other, like maggots. Not that he had any rights to Ann Fritz. It wasn't a matter of rights. It was a matter of priorities, of territory claimed—he had spent the last three winters in Truckee, in the Star Hotel—certainly that should count for something.

But in this farce of duplication there was no homesteading or precedent. Les realized that he was standing at Arthur's mantel and was holding a large sheet of cardboard backing. On it were mounted nine Xeroxed photographs, three to a row, nine identicals in all but hair style and the presence or absence of beards, moustaches, or long sideburns. Some smiled, others stared without expression. But they could have changed places, number four breaking into number two's smile.

Les started to read the labels, but knowing that there were still two others left, plus one unaccounted for, enraged him. He wanted to rip up the pictures. If only it were that simple, Les thought as he put the collection of photos back, repositioning them as he had found them.

There were other photos on the mantel: a middle-aged couple, a woman of about sixty with her arm around a young Arthur; a man in a full beard standing in a medical laboratory; an elderly woman standing at a window. Names weren't necessary. It was enough to know that these were people who would miss Arthur. Les turned quickly away, hoping they hadn't noticed him, as he would try to forget them.

A quick search of the living room produced only a loose quarter stuck in a crease of the couch. The bathroom was spotless, nothing but shaving cream, toothpaste, some disposable razors, a small vial of Tylenol, a few odds and ends. It could have been a generic motel bathroom.

Arthur's study was last. The room was filled with the computer's phosphorescence. Running through the open files, Les found nothing of interest. He pulled Arthur's password from his wallet and typed it in. The directory was empty. Arthur had changed the password or erased the files, as Les had anticipated.

He pried open the bottom desk drawer. The letter from Sarah was gone; there was nothing but a stack of paid gas and electricity bills. He knew that the other drawers would reveal nothing of importance, but he went through the motions anyway, prying each open, working his way through comic book invoices, health insurance claim forms, other minutiae.

Perhaps he was keeping Mark Caputo's address at the store. Les cringed at the thought—the store was secured with a burglar alarm system. He had seen the security company decal on the front door and the video camera monitoring the aisles. Breaking in and risking the police was out of the question.

He wandered into Arthur's bedroom and lay down on his bed. If he were Arthur, he wouldn't leave his private matters in the store. There were other employees, the possibility of a break-in. No, he'd keep everything at home. But where? In an old shoebox in the closet? In the bottom of a garment bag?

In ten minutes Les had gone through every item in the closet, but had found nothing. Arthur was clever; he'd anticipated Les's return. For an instant Les felt the keen pleasure of knowing that Arthur was no fool. Curiously, the unyielding apartment was a compliment, a reflection of two smart brothers trapped in a circumstance not of their choosing. Les lay back on the bed.

If the information was on the computer, he had no idea how to access it. Arthur wouldn't have an obvious password, not after going to the trouble of sanitizing his apartment.

Les felt close to the edge, an inner vertigo like the swirling of dead leaves inside his head. Bits of city debris scraping against his inner skull, small crackling sounds, the breaking of his spirit. Lying flat in bed, Arthur's bed, his head in the indentation Arthur had left in his pillow, the sinking feeling returned. He stretched out and tried to clear his mind. Instead he was aware of assuming Arthur's position, of taking Arthur's place, maybe of having Arthur's thoughts.

Suddenly Les knew where to look.

He bolted off the bed, looked under it. Nothing but a few dust balls and a torn empty condom packet. He pulled back the blanket, slid his hand under the mattress, between it and the box spring. He started at the head of the bed, was nearly to the foot of the bed when he felt what seemed to be a corner of an envelope. He tried to work it out from under the mattress, but couldn't get a grip.

With a single giant heave he pulled the mattress halfway off the bed. On top of the box spring was a Federal Express overnight mail bag. Les balanced the envelope lightly on his fingertips, weighing its contents. Debating. Instead of immediately opening it, he put it on an end table and slowly remade Arthur's bed, carefully tucking in the blanket as he had found it. He then went through the entire apartment, double-checking to be certain that everything was as it had been.

He knew he was stalling. Perhaps he and Arthur could negotiate domains, each to his own territory.

No, that wasn't it. He was dreadfully afraid that the envelope might be the start of another chapter. Perhaps there were photographs, family pictures, or letters from the others. To see the others' lives would open the door to a lifetime of bad dreams, regrets, remorse, guilt. He had intentionally tried to minimize contact, to see them solely as a problem to be solved.

Not true, not true at all. Right now he was wearing their socks and underwear; in fact, everything he had on was theirs. Why? If he'd wanted to be rid of them, he would have kept nothing. He remembered a soft, concerned voice saying: "I think it's in your best interest to spend a little time in the hospital. Until we can get a few things sorted out." The resident had looked him straight in the eye, kindly suggesting that this could happen to anyone.

It wasn't too late. He could take off Newman's jockeys, Lippe's socks, Arthur's pants and shoes. It was no big deal. And he did. The apartment was unheated; the skin on his arms bumped up. That he could stand naked was proof that he didn't need them. He could manage. Having demonstrated this to himself, he could see no reason to stand here freezing. He slipped back into their clothing which, he had to admit, was good protection against the cold.

It was time. He sat down on the edge of the bed, picked up the envelope, opened it. There was a video cassette, several letters, and—

It's not possible. Not possible! Les looked at his face on each of the fifteen Department of Motor Vehicle printouts. Larry Morton. Charles Anderson. Manuel Sanchez. There were a dozen more, but Les couldn't bear to read the names. He dropped the photos on the bed and picked up a letter from someone named William Barrett.

Dear Mr. Arthur Singleton,

Enclosed is a deathbed statement from Sarah Woolfson. She insisted that you have it. Please arrange with my office for the additional money necessary to contact the others.

Sincerely yours,
William Barrett, Esq.

Les turned to the next page, a feebly handwritten letter.

Dear Arthur,

Please forgive me for having withheld these names. I knew that ten would be shock enough.
I will miss you.
Can you ever find it in your heart to forgive me?

Your friend,
Sarah Woolfson

On the next sheet of paper were the fifteen names.

Les held the letter up to the light. It was on perfumed stationery; the handwriting was shaky and indistinct, that of someone elderly or sick. He put down Sarah's letter, picked up one of the DMV printouts. The embossed official State of California stamp was clearly visible in the photocopy. As far as he could tell, it was the real thing.

Fifteen more? Les shook his head, the floor moving in waves beneath him. What if Sarah Woolfson was going to deliver the bad news in bits and pieces? Ten here, fifteen there, then maybe a hundred more, once she got rolling.

Les opened an envelope sent by a Mr. Darryl Mintz to Arthur. Inside were two letters and a scan from the University of California at Berkeley Neuroscience Laboratory. The first read

Dear Mr. Mintz,

Enclosed are the photocopied results of the most recent Positron Emission Scans on you and your brother. As I explained over the phone, they are essentially identical, which is to be expected. We have presented your case to several of the consulting neurologists at the University. They concur with our preliminary conclusion that the defects noted are correlated with an increased incidence of both suicide and violent behavior. However, I wish to emphasize that these represent tendencies, not inevitabilities, and that we do not yet have supporting long-term data.

I would suggest that you and your brother come to the center for counseling, as well as further follow-up testing.

By the way, you mentioned that you have several other brothers. We would be glad to test them, free of charge.

Yours truly,
Janine Richards, M.D.
Associate Chief, Division of Neuroscanning
Department of Neuroscience
University of California

The second letter, from Mintz to Arthur, suggested that Arthur also be tested. "We need to know," Mintz concluded.

Les looked from the letter to the enclosed scan reproduction. The defects in the temporal lobes and in the frontal lobe would have been obvious even if they hadn't been circled in red. He gazed out over Arthur's bed. Sitting side by side were the DMV printouts of William and Darryl Mintz.

It was duplication reduplicated, clones twinned, cells proliferating like cancer. Les picked up the phone and dialed Berkeley information. "Yes, there is a listing for a William Mintz." Les dialed. A sleepy voice answered. It was his own voice on both ends of the receiver. Les hung up.

He tried to remember how he'd felt at Sardine Lake before he'd received the news, how personal harmony and transcendence had seemed such a beautiful goal, a spiritual liberation from the ugliness of daily life.

But the scan showed the truth, the barely contained rage that had fueled his need to distance himself from others, from something he could not control or accept. Look how easily he had slipped into the role of self-righteous killer. It hadn't required any coercion; it was as though he had always been waiting, his anger on alert, poised and ready to fire if given the proper justification. His meditations were nothing more than violence redirected.

The time that he had been hospitalized, he had considered ending it, ending himself. How melodramatic, his family at his bedside, pleading. At the time he had felt in control, even in his lack of control. In the perversity of his moods he was in charge, the captain of a sinking ship.

He looked at the scan again. How peculiar that a man can come to believe that he is other than biology. If there was any doubt, if he really believed that he was master of his destiny, he need only look at the red-circled holes in the scan. Anger and self-destruction—he had it, they had it, the whole lot of them. He might kill them all, yet he would be no more than they were.

The videotape remained. What more could he possibly learn? He took the unlabeled tape, walked to the living room, and slipped it into the vcr.

The tape ran less than a minute. It was a close-up of one of them, but with a blank expressionless face and unfocused eyes. Which one was this? And what was wrong with him? Disease? A failed suicide with brain damage? What was he looking at? Why did Arthur have the video? He watched the brief tape several times, then turned it off. Though he did not know what he was watching, the tape seemed personally directed, full of implication, maybe a veiled threat.

As he was putting the tape back in the envelope, there was a beep from the computer.

```
>We need to meet. Tomorrow morning at nine sharp
at Mel's Drive-In on Lombard. By the way, we
received this bit of poem on our email today.

They will begin over, that is
Over and over. . .

They carry nativeness
To a conclusion
In suicide.
```

```
If this was from you, we don't think it's funny.
Please be prompt. We hate waiting.
W and D Mintz
```

William and Darryl Mintz. Bill. Darryl. He ran through the names on his new list. Manuel—would that be Manny, in a familiar tone, or would it be Manuel, full and dignified? And Phillip Reagan. Would that be Phil, or Phillip, the name wrapped in a nice silk ascot, or would it be a cute, midtown Philly? Peter Warchik. Good old Petey, or was it Pete, short and curt, barely a name?

With Paul Lafora, he'd had the sense that he was embarking upon a journey, a pilgrimage toward consolidation. He had assumed that ten was the magic total, the grand sum. Now he knew that he would never know. Sarah Woolfson was not to be trusted—her feeble script could hide further deceits or failures of memory. The end was no longer in sight. The final number would remain indeterminate.

It was late. Outside sounds had died away—there was only the hum of an occasional passing car, a muffled cough or sneeze arising from an adjacent apartment. Les stared at the poetry on the computer monitor. He had considered mailing this stanza to Arthur, to explain Roger. But he hadn't; he had waited until after Lafora, and had chosen another passage from Oppen's poem.

He still felt that stanza's particular resonance. As did Arthur the comic book salesman, picking out these very lines. Was nothing sacred?

The poem mocked him. Les wanted to punch his hand through the screen and rip it out, line by line. Instead he snapped off the monitor, the computer still on, its disc spinning endlessly, bereft of speech as though its tongue had been torn out. *There*, he thought. *You can't talk to me and I don't have to listen.*

Les walked back to the bedroom and lay down again in Arthur's indentation—correction, *their* indentation. If only this were a matter of garbage, of civilization's debris that he could pick up from the shores of his lake. If only there were an off-season, a time to regroup. He kicked off Arthur's moccasins, took off his pants and shirt, Bunker's argyle socks, Newman's underpants, and curled up on the bed. He imagined the cool night air coming through the open bedroom window was fresh from the mountains, free of soot and pollution.

Soon he would be home again.

TWENTY-SIX

A t eight AM the Department of Motor Vehicles' main office on Fell Street opened for business. Les was there at seven, preferring an hour's wait in the street to the after-opening queues of the discontented. First come, first served, normally a source of some cheap pleasure, couldn't cheer him this morning. He walked up to the first available clerk, introduced himself as William Mintz and said that he'd lost his license and needed a duplicate. The clerk, a short, expressionless woman with thick glasses and slow, precise movements, punched up his name and gave him a once-over, comparing him to the photo on the video display. "Five dollars," she said, looking somewhere over Les's head, in what Les took to be a demonstration of bureaucratic verification, ontology at the clerical level.

Les walked out, around the block, then back again, going to the far end of the counter and waiting for another clerk. "Darryl Mintz," he told this clerk.

And a third time, as Manuel Sanchez.

No doubt about it. They were all real people, not some clever Arthur Singleton trick.

It took an hour to walk to Mel's Drive-In on Lombard, the day cool, crisp, the Bay bright silver in the morning sun. Three hundred years ago the hills would have been covered with trees and grass, not concrete and steel. The Bay would have been pristine, full of fish, seals, maybe even whales. Instead a huge cargo ship was passing under the Golden Gate Bridge, full of containers labeled in Chinese.

When would it all end? Sometime soon. The signs were all in place.

Contemplating the end of the world, he was not prepared for William and Darryl. Though he had no reason to expect them to be huddled at the rear of the restaurant, out of sight in some deep dark booth, he was startled to see them at the front of the restaurant, at an open table. They were engaged in animated talk, oblivious to his staring at them.

Both were wearing identical checkered flannel shirts, faded brown corduroy pants and thick-soled high-top walking shoes—outfits similar to his own. Both had their hair neatly parted on the left, falling across their foreheads at the same angle.

One of them looked up and waved at him. So did the other, their gestures synchronized as though choreographed. Both motioned for him to come in and take a seat.

"William," one said, pointing to the other.

"Darryl," said the other, pointing to his brother.

"Again," Les said, taking a seat. He tried to ignore the dizziness behind his eyes.

"I'm Darryl," said the man to his left. "He's William." The two men nodded, simultaneously extending their hands. "Glad to meet you, Artie," both said.

The restaurant grew silent; several of the diners at adjacent tables were openly staring. "Do you think we could talk somewhere else, somewhere a little more private?" Les whispered.

"The place has great chicken-fried steak and garlic mashed potatoes. We've just ordered," Darryl said.

"We're being watched," Les said, his hand over his chin and lower cheek.

"Let them stare. When we get all fifteen of us together, they'll be able to say they saw us in person," William said.

"Today's stares will be tomorrow's acknowledgment," Darryl said.

"You don't find this all a little . . . weird?"

Both men shook their heads, tiny side-to-side movements that might once have been covert signals between them—the private language of two twins in a crib.

"That's why we wanted to get together with you today. We've figured out that the initial get-together should be somewhere private where we can get to know each other without intrusion. There will be time enough to go public."

"Someplace with adequate facilities."

"Secluded, but within an hour or two of an airport."

Darryl pulled out a map of California and Nevada. "Reno is centrally located."

"We drew a hundred-mile radius from Reno International," William said. His finger hovered over the northern Sierras, then zoomed down to Sardine Lake. Les watched in horror.

Two orders of fried steak and mashed potatoes arrived. The two men put their plates in identical positions in front of them, the map between them. William and Darryl both motioned to the waiter, who asked if Les would also like an order.

"No thanks," Les said, trying not to gag. He covered his mouth with his napkin. "Getting over the flu," he added, holding the napkin to his face until he adjusted to the greasy odor.

"A friend of mine in Berkeley raves about it. We phoned their reservation office—we've got all fifteen cabins booked for opening week in late April."

"At Sardine Lake?" Les asked.

They nodded in unison. Darryl said, "Our friend's a whiz at picking out undiscovered places. It's supposed to be beautiful, not at all crowded."

"Pristine," William said when Darryl finished. "Still off the tourist route," he added with an air of smugness. "We thought that you could help contact the others. The three of us could work together."

"In return for helping with the phoning, you could have first pick of the cabins, the one nearest the lake."

"Until then, we can start our own private chat room. We've checked with AOL; if we all chip in, it'd only be a few dollars a month to stay in touch around the clock."

"I've been to Sardine Lake," Les said. "It's really very small and out of the way. There's almost nothing to do. How about meeting here, where there's something for everyone?"

"We've already made the down payment. Besides, my friend's shown us pictures. It's perfect, the kind of place we could come back to, year after year. It's a natural for a reunion site."

"So, you'll help us?" William asked, his finger now directly on the middle of the lake. Les imagined the fish swimming away; even at this distance, William was poisoning the water.

"I'd prefer San Francisco. I'm sure you could get back your deposit. No, San Francisco would be central and more fun."

Both men shook their heads. Darryl added, "Trust us. Besides, we think it would be better to be inconspicuous until we get to know each other. Remember, we've booked the whole lake."

"Let me check my schedule and get back to you." Les rose from his seat.

"We'd love to have you onboard," both said at the same time.

"We think it's wonderful that there are others. As though we've been singled out," Darryl said.

"Not singled out; that's a contradiction in terms," William corrected Darryl.

"Always the stickler for accuracy," Darryl said. "Sometimes I wonder how we can be twins and be *so* different."

"Me, too," William said, winking at his brother.

Les made a point of looking at his watch. "I've got to be going. I'll call you next week."

"It's been great meeting you at last," the two men said, looking at each other before simultaneously offering their hands.

Les made it to the corner before he started gagging and retching, dry heaving at the curbside on Lombard and Steiner. He stood up, wiped his mouth, walked a few feet, overcome with nausea.

He held onto a waste receptacle, his legs pressed up against the metal container, his hands clammy, a rapid vibration in the pit of his stomach. He could feel the pressure of the stun gun against his thigh. The gun had served him well, but now the problem exceeded the solution.

Perhaps he could just kill Arthur, to show him that he couldn't get away with this. If Arthur hadn't started this get-together crusade, he wouldn't be standing here with the dry heaves and an empty future. But Arthur wasn't due back until this evening. Les doubted that he could cope with the city that long.

It's a toss-up. Retribution versus escape. He started back downtown, taking side streets, hoping that he wouldn't run into any of the witnesses from the diner. "There's one of them!" they would shout and point. There would be no place to hide. Les found himself checking his watch again, calculating how many hours before darkness descended, whether he could catch the afternoon Amtrak back to Truckee.

He broke into a slow jog. It was three miles back to his hotel. He could make the train. If not, Arthur would be his consolation prize.

Back in his room, Les packed, swept his hand along each of the dresser drawers, beneath the bed to be certain that he hadn't left anything behind, and dropped the room key in the day clerk's hand. Les interpreted the clerk's lack of eye contact as practiced, a studied indifference requisite for city life. No smile, no goodbye, no nod of the head. He was room 35 checking out, a bit of day's end accounting. Not like Ann Fritz, who would smile, serve tea, chat. But being invisible wasn't all bad; the clerk wouldn't be able to tell the police anything more than Les's height and hair color, if that.

The afternoon train to Truckee left at three. Not enough time to grab the connecting bus at the Ferry Building. From the hotel doorway Les hailed a cab to the Amtrak station in Oakland.

The cab driver had a thick neck, swarthy complexion, dark unkempt hair that curled over the back of the grease-ringed collar of his blue windbreaker, and the hint of an Eastern European accent. At the intersection of Market and Jones, the driver turned to Les and asked whether he wanted scenic or economic.

"What scenery? Stick with the straight shot, and make it quick."

"Whatever you say, boss." The driver started across Market, heading for the freeway. At Tenth Street, traffic was bumper to bumper, creeping around a half-dozen double-parked trucks with drivers unloading furniture and appliances, including a row of one-eyed washing machines that seemed to be passing judgment on the traffic. The cab sat, the light changed from green to red to green, the driver drumming his fingers on the wheel. Les leaned forward, halfway into the front seat, and asked whether there wasn't a back-alley way around the traffic.

The driver shook his head, honked several times, as though demonstrating solidarity with Les. But he was entirely too relaxed, his fingers tapping to the combined rhythms of the ticking meter and some old rock and roll leaking out of his boom box on the passenger seat.

The clerk hadn't looked at him, the driver didn't care if the traffic moved or not, as long as the meter was running, and the men unloading the trucks and vans were completely indifferent to the growing line of cars trying to squeeze by. If he didn't make the afternoon train, he'd be back at the hotel tonight when Arthur returned. Was that what the traffic was all about? Was he somehow destined to stay in town in order to meet up with Arthur?

Back at the store? Back at his apartment? "No," he thought he said to himself, but actually said aloud. "You can't just kill him without a plan." A plan that included some public humiliation, some message to the others to stay away, keep separate, leave him alone.

"Problems?" the driver asked, turning to look at Les.

Les nodded, not sure whether or not he had spoken aloud, and whether or not the driver had heard him. Or was reading his mind. He waved his hand, indicating that he didn't want to talk about it.

"Something you need done?"

Les acted as if he didn't hear him.

"Just a guess. Not the thing you normally talk about with strangers." The driver looked straight ahead. "It's up to you." The cab inched forward, then again came to a stop.

Why this cab, this driver, this traffic jam, Arthur's scheduled return? Telling the cabbie was dangerous; even a vague allusion could be disastrous. But why had he asked? It was as though the driver already knew what he was trying not to think about.

"It's nothing," Les said cautiously. "Just some guy that looks like me and is trying to extort money. I'd go to the police, but it's all been by phone, nothing in writing that I can show them."

"You want to get him off your back?"

"Something like that."

"I've got a friend, works out of LA. You want, you can talk to him. First class, satisfied clients, completely confidential. I don't know a thing, everything is between the two of you. You talk, you don't agree, there's no cost. You come to terms, I get ten percent."

"What can he do?"

The driver shrugged. "Some traffic. You sure you still want to make the train?"

"Are we on the same wavelength?" Les asked.

"I'm just making a suggestion, a business contact. What you arrange is between the two of you." The driver pulled a card out from a stack of cards clipped to his visor. He jotted down a name and phone number. "Be sure to say Frank R. sent you."

"How do you know that I'm not police, or FBI, or whatever?"

"There's no law against making honest business referrals." The driver rubbed his hands together, as though washing them. "Besides, if you're undercover, then I'm Mother Teresa, or whoever that broad is."

Suddenly the traffic thinned and they were heading toward the onramp to the Bay Bridge. "Hold it," Les said, putting his hand on the back of the driver's shoulder. "We'll never make it in time. Why don't you drop me back at the hotel?"

"My brother used him once. Neat as a pin, clean as a whistle, no sweat, nothing unexpected afterwards, nothing. Like the whole problem evaporated."

"What did your friend do for your brother?"

"Intervened. Yes, that's what my brother told me. That my friend intervened."

"Thanks," Les said, stuffing the card into his shirt pocket. Moments later he was out of the cab and inside the hotel lobby, registering for a room. The clerk acted as if he'd never seen Les before. Perfect.

That afternoon Artie went back to Welinda's apartment and stretched out on his cheap sleeping bag. He figured he'd slept two to three hours the last two nights, if you counted awake but down time, forty-five minutes if you calculated only amnesia.

If he and Les had some special telepathy, he might know where Les was, what he was planning. But he didn't.

He phoned the store to check with Welinda, knowing that there was nothing to check on. He hoped the sound of Welinda's voice would be reassuring.

"So far, so good," she said. "The next twenty-four hours are key. If he doesn't come by the store tonight or tomorrow, you should be in good shape. Don't get careless. Keep your head down, your ear to the wall, your eye to the window, your neural network to the modem."

Artie clicked off, again tried to sleep, couldn't, and with a sigh of resignation, got up, went to the folding card table and his laptop. He plugged it into the telephone line, logged on. Finding no new email, he connected with his discussion group.

There were new entries.

```
>You need to have more information on the par-
ents. We need to know antecedents, early childhood
influences. And, later, how the parents feel
about the death of their child. You can't just
have ten men drop in from nowhere and expect
empathy from the reader.

>Family would slow down the story. With fiction,
pace is everything. Besides, familial influence
is vastly overrated. In monkey experiments they've
shown that peer pressure is equally important.
See Harry Harlowe et al.

>Bear down on sibling influence. You hate your
parents, you take it out on your brother or
sister. Psych 101. Kick the weak, spare the meal
ticket. Siblings are how we transmit feelings
toward our parents to the next generation.

>Have the plot revolve around pathological jeal-
ousies in the killer and your protagonist. The
killer feels that the others are sapping his
strength, intruding on his uniqueness. The pro-
```

robert a. burton

tagonist is jealous of the killer being able to act on his feelings. We've all dreamed of killing our brothers or sisters. It's the reason behind moving to the suburbs, so each of the kids can be safe in his separate bedroom. Getting in touch with those feelings will help strengthen the killer's character.

>If you, the author, expect to have control over the narrator, you better have a clear understanding of how you feel about your own sibs.

>And how they feel about you writing this book.

>Excuse me for butting in, but I thought the story was about DNA and inexorability, not about pop psychology. The central purpose of evolution is the survival, not of any species or individual, but of DNA itself. Let me quote from Richard Dawkins' book on evolutionary Darwinism. "The universe we observe has precisely the properties we should expect if there is, at bottom, no design, no purpose, no evil and no good, nothing but blind, pitiless indifference."

>We're talking story, not meaning. We can't feel evolution, but we can feel slighted, hurt, wounded, betrayed, cheated.

>Give the killer a sense of remorse and suffering. After all, metaphysically speaking, each of his murders is a bit of suicide. Try to capture the rage and the guilt. Perhaps show the killer visiting the grave of his parents after one of the murders. That's usually pretty effective in a novel.

>Have him befriend a child, or have a pet, perhaps a cat that accompanies him to each murder, but stays in the car.

```
>No. Less is better. Make the killer stark and
determined. No family, no remorse. Just the urge
to get back to unique as quickly and efficiently
as possible. The killer could be a metaphor for
the successful American businessman. As in, he
made a killing.

>Winner take all. Including the lives of his
brothers.
```

Artie doubted that any came from Les, though he could not be certain. At least there was no poem, no entry on email, no reference to Bernard Sadler. He paced the tiny apartment, working his way between the piano bench and Welinda's unmade hideaway bed. The room had the dimensions of a holding cell; Artie had the distinct sensation of being a prisoner trapped in an indefinite sentence.

Or awaiting execution.

An hour later a message came over Artie's email:

```
>You are the last
Who will know him . . .

Not know him . . .

You are the last
Who will see him
Or touch him . . .
```

As usual, the site of origin of the message was anonymous. Les could be anywhere. Artie was angry at the ambiguity of poetry. And encouraged. Maybe Welinda was right.

TWENTY-SEVEN

Artie stayed in Welinda's apartment for three days, the weather stormy, Welinda bringing in deli food. On the fourth day, overcome by cabin fever, Artie left the apartment, his sleeping bag and overnight bag under his arm. The sky was bright, the streets washed clean by the storm. Approaching his block, he looked in every alley, glanced at each parked car and the few coming and going. He encountered some laughing kids playing hopscotch outside the apartment building.

Artie checked with the manager—no one had asked for him. He unlocked his apartment door, threw the door open, expecting anything.

No need. The apartment was empty. He checked the rear window; it had been opened, but he already knew that without seeing the loose piece of Scotch tape Welinda had fastened at the junction of the window and the sill.

The Federal Express envelope was tucked between the mattress and the box spring, opened and resealed. He dropped it in the top drawer of his dresser.

The email from William and Darryl Mintz was on the computer screen. Fifteen more? Right now having a huge family seemed like a pretty good proposition, an opportunity that he would not squander.

On his answering machine was a message from Janine in New York; after her neurology conference she was going to spend a few days in West Virginia with her family. Artie replayed the message three times, savoring the *miss you*, then worrying that there was some distance in her voice. *Long distance, not her distance*, he told himself, trying to settle back into his apartment.

For the next two days he heard nothing. No new entries on the newsgroup. His email was mainly comic book orders and the occasional request for a new CD-ROM.

Welinda finally blew the all-clear whistle. "He's probably gone back to Truckee."

Artie wasn't entirely convinced, but he was tired of bolted doors, locked windows, and perpetual vigilance. Returning to work, everything was as before, yet nothing was the same. Artie couldn't relax, his eye glued to the front door. Welinda resumed her center-aisle mornings at *Autobiography*. She said little. Artie saw through her feigned nonchalance.

Violence and suicide, Welinda had mused, looking at the scan and outlining her plan. But which one? And how would they know?

That evening Artie received a letter from Mrs. Fleischer.

> *Dear Mr. Singleton,*
>
> *I have decided against going ahead with the article on Benjamin. I'd prefer to leave his memory as is. I'm sure that you'd understand if you had known him. He was truly one of a kind.*
>
> *Sincerely yours,*
> *Harriet Fleischer*
>
> *P.S. Could you mail back the photographs? Richard was terribly upset that I gave them to you. You know how possessive men can be.*
>
> *Please know that he means well.*

Artie folded the letter and shoved it into the manila folder in the top drawer. He fought back the thought that Mrs. Fleischer was his real mother, quickly closing the drawer and flipping on the TV. No, his real mother was somewhere in the Pacific, freed of an empty mind and frameless days.

He would not visit the Fleischers again, he promised himself, standing in front of the TV, idly cruising the channels, not really interested in watching, simply glad to have the distracting noise and color.

In the eighties the phrase *dysfunctional family* had become popular, before it became generally accepted that *dysfunctional* was redundant. What would the media drum up to describe this turn of events? All Artie knew was that no word or phrase, no matter how many qualifiers, would approximate what he was feeling.

A computer beep announced new email: a note from a Pete Bonetti, who introduced himself as a comic book collector from Kansas City. Bonetti indicated that he'd be in town tomorrow, and that he was having a private showing at three PM at the Hyatt Regency. Included would be a dozen first editions of *Plastic Man* and an original, mint condition *Spider Man*. If Artie was interested, he could have an advance showing. The message concluded by inviting Artie for coffee at noon at Humphrey Yogurt, across from the Hyatt.

Artie did not recognize Bonetti by name, but that wasn't surprising. With the skyrocketing prices of comics, everyone with a basement full of old magazines was a "collector." Such finds often became Artie's best high-ticket items.

He was scheduled to meet Tuna for lunch; they were going to say goodbye before Tuna left for Las Vegas. He could break for a few minutes to see Bonetti's collection. Artie phoned the Hyatt; Bonetti was expected in the morning. Artie left word on the hotel voice mail that they'd meet at noon and that he'd be wearing a brown leather jacket.

Artie overslept past Shazam's opening time. He slipped on a pair of jeans and a blue cotton sweater and hurried out into the brilliant morning light. A day for sunglasses and a baseball cap. He was vaguely aware of having forgotten something, but whatever it was, it could wait. He could hear Welinda: "Here comes the late Mr. Singleton." He didn't need her lip. Not this morning. He had to go over the last week's receipts, cover some new inventory, open the mail, get over to the Hyatt.

After reclaiming room 35, Les stayed put, seldom going out, mainly eating takeout from a nearby deli, spending most of his time on his bed, staring at the ceiling, at the letters from Suzanne to Roger, at Paul's medal, at his own collection of CD-ROMs. He had discs on American and European literature, evolution, cosmology, and simulations of consciousness. He even had a recent CD on the interrelationship of John Van Neumann's game theories and famous battles like Agincourt and Iwo Jima. All fascinating for brief periods, but never truly engaging. Les inevitably returned to ponder the few things he'd gathered from the others.

He spent the greater part of one afternoon flat on his back, his shirt off, Paul's medal directly over his heart. He had an urge to take his penknife, make an incision, insert the medal under his skin. Perhaps if it lay directly upon his heart, if he kept it there long enough . . . a scary thought. If he opened his chest, he might find nothing but ice and stone.

Later, while pacing the room, he fastened the medal to his chest with two strips of inch-wide adhesive tape in the shape of a cross. He stood at the mirror, his hands clasped at his chest. He contemplated having feelings for someone else.

Several times he returned to the photos of Suzanne, running his fingers over her face, stopping to caress her cheeks, to trace the outline of her lips. There was love in her eyes. It could have been for him.

He dreamed of being finished, then awakened to the nightmare that he was no longer in control. Getting rid of fifteen more was impossible. Artie would have to do for all of them, a public demonstration that would scare the others into retreat. Then he could work on the lessons of Paul's medal and Suzanne's photos. It was not too late to learn, to change.

Let the others know without implicating himself. He would be an innocent bystander, establish proof that it wasn't his doing. Artie would go down alone.

The cabbie's friend, who referred to himself as Mr. Sharp, preferred not to meet Les face to face. The preliminary contacts were made over the phone, via public telephone booths. The final arrangements were made via email, each of them using anonymous addresses in public cafés. Les scanned Artie's dmv photo into the café computer; Mr. Sharp downloaded it and printed it at another location. The cab driver had been right; Mr. Sharp was reasonable, so negotiations were pleasantly brief. Les arranged for a drop-off at the Hyatt. Mr. Sharp would check in under an assumed name. Les's going-away money from his family would be waiting in an envelope at the concierge's desk.

Artie met Tuna in front of the fountain at Justin Hermann Plaza at five til noon. They walked over to the yogurt shop and took two free seats at the counter. Tuna scoffed as he looked at the menu. "You got chili con carne?" he asked the waitress, a young woman with a shaved head.

"Just what you see," she answered.

"Whatever happened to fat? They should rename this place Slim Pickins," Tuna said as the woman retreated. Several of the customers turned and stared. Though Tuna was in his casino cowboy attire, and Artie was dressed in his blue cotton sweater, they clearly were identical twins.

The waitress returned to take their orders. "Two coffees," Artie said at the same time as Tuna stood to leave.

"You gentlemen seem undecided," the waitress said. "Two peas not in the same pod?" She turned and smiled at the others at the counter.

"I'll have a decaf and a shot of amphetamines," Tuna said.

"One decaf, one regular?"

"Two French roast, black as my heart," Tuna said. "Make it dissolve the cup."

"Two coffees would be fine," Artie said, shrugging in apology to those still staring.

"By the way, I've kept the room at the Glass Slipper and at the Day's End. I didn't think you'd mind."

"Two rooms? You could have moved out and back in."

"A sunny southern exposure isn't always available. Certainly you're not going to quibble over a few bucks, not after what we've been through."

"How much are we talking?"

"No need to calculate. Next week you bring some *dinero* down to Vegas, I enter the first annual Glass Slipper poker tournament, win some serious number, cut you in on the take, and you won't even remember the question."

"How much, Tuna?"

"Twenty-five hundred for the tournament. First prize will be over two hundred grand. Enough to buff up your store to a high gloss, maybe burn a little money on a cruise, some new threads. You don't want to get pulled over for living too slowly."

"Tuna."

"Maybe another grand or two."

"And when exactly is this tournament?"

"Monday. You come on down, bring Welinda. I think she deserves a piece of the action after what she's done."

"It's not over yet," Artie said. "You've got to stay alert."

"I'm at the top of my game. Body language, intuition, eyes in the back of my head, my mojo working."

"I feel better already," Artie said.

The waitress brought the two cups of coffee. Artie said thanks. Tuna grabbed the sugar dispenser, poured five or six teaspoons' worth. "Men have been killed for less," the waitress said, sliding the sugar dispenser back against the salt shaker, tidying up her station.

Tuna ignored her. "You think we're really done with him?" he asked softly, looking into his coffee.

Artie started to stir his coffee before realizing that it wasn't necessary. "I don't know. Welinda says it's time for a victory celebration. But Welinda thinks that games and life are the same."

"They aren't?" Tuna quickly downed his cup and motioned to the waitress for a refill. He helped himself to another long pour of sugar. "No, they aren't," he said, answering himself. "If you ask me, this cat's got nine lives. We haven't heard the last of him."

"Welinda's been right on so far."

"I don't know. We're supposed to be the same, I mean down in the engine room or wherever the wiring is. But what's that got to do with being able to predict? Take me. I sit down at the poker table telling myself that the operative word for the session is *discipline*. Fold the bad hands, wait for the primo cards to show up. For a while it works. Then the wheel rolls off. Maybe it's something someone says, the sight of some idiot raking in the chips. Some little irritation that rocks the circuits. If that's what we mean by *predictable*, knowing that each of us can shoot off in any direction, then Welinda's right. But that kind of being right don't mean diddly."

"It's been over a week; other than that bit of poem, there hasn't been a peep."

"Bad feeling." Tuna looked at his watch. "It's twelve on the button and I don't see any anxious collector hovering, trying to push his goods. All I see is high noon and the two of us waiting at this counter like sitting ducks." Tuna got up from the stool. "You stay right here. No matter what, you don't leave, OK?"

"Where're you going?"

"To the dumpster. I do my best thinking with my elbows on my knees."

Mr. Sharp stood at a twelfth-story Hyatt hotel room window, scanning the plaza with binoculars, listening to the traffic news on his Walkman headset. Due to road repaving, I-5 was down to two lanes near Coalinga—Caltrans apologized for any delays. Mr. Sharp hated complications. At eight o'clock Jimmy, his oldest son, was starting in his first junior varsity basketball game. San Francisco to LA was six hours plus pit stops. Now he had to factor in the probability of stop-and-go in the valley. If he wasn't on the road by twelve forty-five, one at the latest, he'd miss the opening tip-off. The mere possibility put Mr. Sharp in a foul mood; he knew from his own childhood that not being there was a sign of not caring. And since he'd have his rifle and equipment in his trunk, he couldn't make up time; he'd have to keep his speed down, let all the other cars whiz by, honking and sneering at him like he was some simple-minded old fart.

The room was warm, and his cheap woolen business suit made him prickly all over. He hated the suit, but felt it was more businesslike. He was a professional. He would change as soon as he was out of town.

Deep breaths, in and out. Visualize the seashore. No point in getting angry. Five grand for a few minutes' work plus travel time was easy money. Before he'd parlayed his high blood pressure into a lifetime total disability stress claim, he'd been the LAPD SWAT squad's best marksman. With a high-power scope he could knock the head off a match at one hundred yards. Today's job was a snap, and would soothe some inner apprehension that he might be losing his touch. Shooting a man in a crowd from this distance would be a clear testimonial to his steady hand.

Mr. Sharp wondered what this particular job was all about. A telephone call from someone who wants to knock off a look-alike, claiming extortion. He knew that wasn't the real story, particularly when the caller was vague about all personal details except that the target was the owner of a comic book store, as though that single fact should condemn a man to death.

He and Joe (Mr. Sharp referred to each of his employers by the same name—this way they would be collectively stored in memory as former employers, nothing more) had talked earlier this morning, Mr. Sharp using the lobby pay phone. He'd told Joe of Singleton's call and that he'd be wearing a brown leather jacket. "That's fitting," Joe had said with a nervous laugh.

Joe was a flake, which meant extra precautions, including not meeting in person and being paid entirely in advance. The cash was in his jacket pocket, atop his suitcase.

Mr. Sharp stretched, took off his pigskin gloves. He put an eight-by-eleven blow-up of the DMV photo on the sill, then, with his elbow, opened the window as far as it would go, which was only a few inches, enough to stick a muzzle through, but not enough to jump out. Mr. Sharp chuckled; he could see some ridiculous management conference where a bunch of suits decided how many inches the window should be allowed to open.

He hoped his kid would be high scorer and shake his foul mood.

The plaza was filling up with the lunchtime crowd, a rock band was setting up on a portable stage. Mr. Sharp stared, patiently waiting.

Shortly he saw his man simultaneously approaching the fountain from the east and from the west. Neither was wearing a leather jacket. He looked at the blow-up, then at each of them through his powerful binoculars. Joe had been right; they were lookalikes.

They were shaking hands. Mr. Sharp watched for hidden gestures, but the two men seemed pleased to see each other. They walked across the plaza, into Humphrey Yogurt. During the few seconds the men were face to face, Mr. Sharp sensed something was wrong. But Joe had hired a killer, not a therapist.

Though sometimes he saw his job in a therapist's light. If you can't talk away the childhood bruise or the insult that hits the mark, then cut it out; blow it away. Zap the pain and its messenger.

Mr. Sharp checked his watch. Twelve on the button.

Tuna was one hundred percent intuition, his entire life powered by hunches. Artie looked around the restaurant, at all the lunch hour feeders, then back again at his cup of coffee. He shifted on his stool, but couldn't find a comfortable position. His feet tapped on the floor, his shoulders were contracted with tension. He wasn't sure if it was Bonetti's being late, that this might be some kind of a setup by Les, or if he was disappointed that he didn't feel what Tuna felt. Where was this magical twin telepathy, communication flowing effortlessly, soul to soul?

It was a tough call, knowing whether or not he wanted his mind opened up to the outside, someone else with the password to his unspoken thoughts. It would be like hooking his mind up to the Internet, like the patient Janine's psychologist friend had mentioned. Yet real friendship thrived on the uncompleted sentence, the knowing nod or wink, the lack of need for explanation.

Maybe that was it, his increasing anxiety being Tuna's, shared over their private airwaves. He turned abruptly to see his likeness moving toward him, wearing a checkered shirt like they'd worn at Mel's Drive-In. He gave a downward motion of his hand and turned away, intentionally ignoring him, addressing his coffee cup. "Very funny. You and your bad feelings. Well, go spook someone else."

"I didn't mean to scare you, but we need to talk. I know that you know all about me, but there's no need to worry. I just wanted to meet you before I move away."

"Please," Artie said, staring straight ahead.

"It won't take but a few minutes. I want to explain."

The voice had the same pitch, but the inflection was different. He turned and saw the eyes. They were Tuna's eyes, all of their eyes, but there was something additional, or maybe missing.

"Les Robbins?" Artie said in astonishment.

Their one ace in the hole was Les's belief that there were another fifteen waiting in the wings. If Les saw Tuna, he might suspect that the two of them had been William and Darryl. If it occurred to him that the other fifteen were trumped up, Les could return to his original plan. Artie was in a hurry to leave the restaurant.

Les had both hands opened, palms up. The Captain Marvel jacket was tucked under Les's arm. "It's not what you think. I'm not here for you, not that way. I just want a few minutes to explain. Pay for your coffee while I make a phone call. Then we can take a stroll around the plaza."

Artie looked skeptical.

"Come on. If you think I have some plan in mind, do you think I'd choose a plaza with hundreds of people milling around? Come on. I'll be back in a second."

By the time that Artie had caught the waitress's attention Les had already returned, his expression a bit less cocky, as though the call hadn't gone well. Now he was carrying the jacket in his hand. Artie debated mentioning it, decided not to. He glanced over his shoulder to see if Tuna was coming, or watching, but saw only the crowded restaurant. Artie couldn't figure it out. Was Tuna pulling some counterplan? Where was telepathy when you needed it most? Artie wondered as he dropped five dollars on the counter and led the way out of the restaurant.

The restrooms were tucked away in an alcove at the rear of the shop, near the pay phone. From this vantage point, Tuna could see the majority of the restaurant and the front door, but not the counter.

He'd had the feeling before, usually the moment before being dealt the hand that busted him. Long ago he'd concluded that when he got the feeling, he should quit immediately. Of course he rarely did. After going broke, he'd swear that next time he would pay attention, act on it.

Five after twelve.

He dropped a quarter in the phone, dialed the Hyatt. "Mr. Bonetti, please," he said, not knowing what he would do next.

"Yeah," a gruff voice answered. "I already seen you two, but he ain't in any leather jacket."

Tuna pulled a pack of cigarettes from his shirt pocket, crumpled the cellophane into the speaker. "I can barely hear you. Hang up. I'll phone you right back."

As Tuna put down the receiver, Les walked through the door, said something to the hostess, who motioned to the counter. At Mel's Drive-In Les had been cool, not giving away anything. Now his eyes were narrowed, on fire, like someone on major-league tilt, someone who had lost his rent money, his wife, his children, everything. A man who had nothing left to lose.

In one hand, rolled into a ball, was a crumpled wad of shiny purple.

Tuna was about to rush over, but reconsidered. The restaurant was nearly filled, with only a few empty tables near the kitchen. At least twenty customers were watching Les approach Artie, shaking their heads, pointing, talking to each other. One looked back in his direction; Tuna ducked back into the alcove, waited, then looked again.

Les was standing alongside Artie, his hand reaching out. "Not here," Tuna whispered aloud, partly as conclusion, partly as prayer. Not in front of all these people. Les's hand was empty. Unless he had something in his balled-up jacket, there was no weapon.

A bomb? Did he plan on blowing up the place—a murder and a suicide as a final statement?

Put yourself in his mind; see it his way. The other murders had occurred in private, all but Sadler's staged to look like suicides. Not this one. Les had chosen the plaza at noontime precisely because it was crowded and there would be plenty of onlookers.

He wandered around inside Les's thoughts, trying to gather them together, make them his. Les was the kind of player who lulled his opponents into a sense of false security, then blindsided them. A sandbagger with an alibi.

Not Les. The gruff voice at the Hyatt. Someone who needed to know what Artie was wearing. Someone who had been watching the two of them at the fountain before they walked to the restaurant.

Tuna picked up the phone.

"Mr. Bonetti's line is busy. Please hold."

Tuna wanted to check on Artie, but Les was facing his way. Tuna moved further into the alcove, his back to the restaurant, tapping his fist against the wall in time to a faraway busy signal. The operator's voice came on again, said, "Please continue to hold." Tuna asked her to interrupt the call, but he was drowned out by the beeps, then weepy violins abusing "My Funny Valentine."

An automated voice came on. "The room you are dialing is presently unavailable. Please stay on the line and you will be connected with voice mail."

"He's in a checkered red flannel shirt," Tuna said, not sure where his voice was going, whether it was being recorded, or if Bonetti would check the recording before . . . He might already be on his way.

Tuna took another peek. Les was coming his way. Tuna slipped into the bathroom, into one of the stalls. He locked the door and tried to think what he would do, what Bernie Sadler had thought. The restroom door did not open. Tuna waited, pulling himself up, peering over the stall door. The restroom was empty. He snuck back into the alcove, looked out over the restaurant.

Artie and Les were gone. He ran out the front door, past a corridor of staring eyes. Ahead, beyond several rows of outdoor tables, the two men were moving toward the far end of the plaza, away from the rock band long on decibels, short on talent.

Think. Artie's no fool. He must have some plan of his own, though Tuna couldn't imagine what it was. Tuna walked briskly, trying to be inconspicuous. He was slowly gaining on them, keeping to the noon shadows cast by the row of office buildings along the western edge of the plaza, when he heard the sound.

"I don't get it," Artie said to Les as they worked their way through the crowded plaza to the fountain. "Your own flesh and blood."

"You've never hated yourself?"

"Not that much. Not that way."

The two men were side by side, not more than a foot apart. To Artie, their casual proximity and the immediate intimacy of their conversation was both soothing and alarming. He was on alert, watching Les's every move, yet he was not frightened in the way that he had expected. Apprehensive, cautious, but also curious.

"Too many," Les said. "But that's behind us now. I just wanted to meet you, tell you that I'm finished."

"There's still me and Weinstein."

"Three is tolerable. Triplets, even quadruplets are within the ordinary realm of possible."

"If there were more?" Artie saw Welinda's plan backfiring.

"You're just making a for instance, right?"

"Yes. Hypothetically."

"There aren't, are there?"

The two men stopped walking and looked at each other. Was Les's plan to smoke him out? Was this to be their personal endgame, the two of them the final pieces moving across a board of Les's choosing? Where was Tuna? Had Les seen him? Was Tuna to be part of Les's plan for the day? Stick with the fifteen no matter what, Welinda had said.

Artie shrugged, flashed an enigmatic, taunting smile. "It shouldn't matter. Say, speaking hypothetically, that there were another fifteen. So what? You don't think I'd tell you so you could go around knocking them off, do you?"

"I told you that I was through."

"If we're down to three."

"So, which is it, a trick or the truth?"

"I'm not my brother's keeper," Artie said, his smile gone, his jaw set. "You're on your own, just like you wanted."

Several passersby were smiling at them, nodding in the way that often addresses twins as a unit. The two men ignored them, resumed walking toward the fountain.

"It's not important, not anymore," Les said, looking down at the textured concrete of the plaza. "Besides, Roger killed himself. I found him that way." Les shook his head as though rearranging some distant memory.

"You're not trying to tell me that these were all suicides."

"You must know. If you don't, I can't explain. If you do, there's no point." Les looked to the western end of the plaza, toward the Hyatt. His pace slowed; he appeared to be gathering his thoughts. A gust of wind kicked up some dust. Les rubbed at his eye; so did Artie. In so doing, he saw himself.

Murder had been his first reaction, before he had told himself that the others were family. It's what the cook in Cloverdale said that he would have done. The difference wasn't in the urge, it was in the act, perhaps only a difference of degree. Les was staring at him again, his eyes dark pinpoints, devoid of the safeguards of ambiguity and complexity. Artie looked away, frightened far beyond mere personal safety.

Years ago, the morning after his episode in Copley Square, he had stood at the mirror in the Harvard infirmary, wondering through the haze of tranquilizers who the man from the night before was, where he had come from, where he had gone. *It wasn't you*, he remembered saying to himself. Yet it had been. It would be there in his college health records, a detailed clinical description of his mini-breakdown.

"I could kill you," Artie said, the words popping out before he knew they were there. "With my bare hands."

Les nodded. "A fight to the death, right here in the plaza, in front of hundreds of onlookers. I suppose that would be fitting. A real winner-take-all. Except for Weinstein. And Caputo. We'd need them too."

"With my bare hands," Artie repeated. "Doesn't that mean anything to you?"

"I knew you'd understand."

"We've talked long enough," Artie said.

"Yes," Les said. "One last thing, before you go." Les shook out the Captain Marvel jacket that he had been holding in his left hand. He unfurled it like a flag, then slipped it on. "Look at me. Is this how we want to be?" He pulled the jacket tightly around him, zipped it up, slipped both thumbs under the collar and held it away from his neck. "You call this special?"

"Keep the jacket," Artie said. "It fits you perfectly." With his bare hands he would kill him. He could feel Les's neck snap beneath his fingers.

"No, this is you," Les said, followed by the clang of metal against metal. Les spun around, facing the Hyatt. He shook his head, waved his arm, pointed frantically at Artie. "He's the one," he shouted, before his face disappeared in a red mist.

Mr. Sharp's scalp itched, the traffic was piling up at Coalinga. Every ten minutes the cars grew thicker, like a metal pudding clotting the road. If he wasn't on the road in fifteen minutes, he could kiss his son's love goodbye.

In the corner of the room the message light on the telephone blinked unnoticed. Mr. Sharp was focused on the two men moving slowly across the plaza. "I'll be wearing a brown leather jacket." Bullshit. Next time check the weather report. It was one of the two, but which one? And why? Sibling rivalry was one thing, but plugging your brother? He'd done a bunch of husbands and wives—that was understandable, par for the marital course— but brothers, this was a first.

Mr. Sharp had never had anyone. No brothers, sisters, cousins, aunts, uncles. No one. Not unless you count a drop-in father, the smell of stale alcohol thicker than love, and a mother who was present in body, gone in the mind.

Through the scope he could see the two men stop, their conversation suddenly heated. Each looked capable of killing the other. Two murderous look-alikes. But getting mad meant that they cared. Much worse was indifference, the long cold nights alone with peanut butter sandwiches and a black-and-white TV that didn't get cable. He hoped they would make up before he shot one of them.

Did it make a difference which one he plugged? If he killed the one he was hired to kill, he was doing a professional job. If he killed the other, he was saving a life. It was a win-win situation, he had the money in his pocket, there was no additional bonus one way or the other.

There was a three-car pile-up, more cars stalled while the CHP tried to clear the right lane.

They were identical. There was no point in trying to choose. Mr. Sharp spread his legs apart, balanced himself on the balls of his feet. He moved the rifle back and forth, looking for clues in facial expression, body language. It was a toss-up, both men grim and determined. He recognized the look, knew it in himself.

It would be a matter of the cleanest shot.

There was a flash of purple. One of the men was putting on a jacket. As he turned to the other, Mr. Sharp could clearly read the words through the scope. Goodbye, Mr. Comic Book Man, he said under his breath, pulling the trigger.

Nothing. The man spun around and was waving at him. A shot right through the heart and he was still standing? Mr. Sharp wondered if the bullet was defective. The man was pointing at the other. How cool can you be, this was real cleverness under fire. He aimed higher and fired a second round.

After a close look through the scope, there was no point in lingering. Mr. Sharp quickly dismantled the rifle, packed everything up inside his travel bag. As he was leaving, he noticed the message light blinking.

"He's in a checkered red flannel shirt," said the first caller.

"He's in a blue cotton sweater," said the second—or was it the first calling back? The voices were the same.

Mr. Sharp deleted both messages.

Normally he felt good after a job. Not this time. He felt that he'd been had, some trick between the brothers, a double-cross, a triple-cross, a mind game where there should have been love.

Whatever, Mr. Sharp muttered as he double-checked the room and stepped out into the hall, quietly closing the door behind him. After checking out at the front desk, he walked downstairs to the garage. An ambulance passed going in the other direction, toward the Hyatt. No point in hurrying, he wanted to say to the driver. It's hard to save a man without a head.

The front of the Captain Marvel jacket was ripped open, a hole directly through the zipper; many of its teeth were missing, the others pointed in all directions. The checkered shirt was also torn, exposing Les's bare chest and the thick bronze medallion taped to it. Artie would always remember the words: Portland Inner City Man of the Year. The medallion was scored and dented.

Lafora had shown him the medal.

He wondered if Tuna had done it, though he couldn't imagine how. Tuna didn't have a gun with him, let alone a rifle. It would be a nice touch if it were true.

An act of god, a divine intervention—that was how he felt, why he stood motionless in the middle of the rapidly emptying plaza. He felt no fear, only a sense of relief and a profound sadness, tears forming and running down his cheeks. At first he brushed them away, then he didn't bother.

At a distance a crowd formed, gathering in a circle. People looked at him staring at the body, judging their safety by Artie's calm presence. Gradually they came forward, some to gawk, others to take a quick look. There were voices, the sound of gagging and crying, but Artie heard nothing except his own heart beating wildly, and Les's last words: "He's the one."

Though the image would remain with him forever, it was necessary. He forced himself to look.

Les's face was gone, reduced to shreds of red tissue, bits of white and pink bone. Les was beyond identification. A pool of blood and a hideous emptiness marked where Les had been.

One day it will be me, Artie thought, staring at a lifeless version of himself. He felt the urge to pray, for Les, for all the others, for himself. A part of him wanted to pull the shattered Les to his chest, hold him tight, let him know that he wasn't alone, didn't die alone. Maybe that wasn't what Les would have wanted, but it was what he would want. But he didn't; the sight was too repulsive. He lightly trailed his finger along one satiny sleeve of his old jacket, thinking *goodbye*, but saying nothing.

Tuna was tugging at his elbow. In the distance the police were arriving with flashing lights and screaming sirens. Artie nodded, took a last look.

It wasn't until they were across the plaza, slipping into the shadows between two large office buildings, that Tuna told him about Bonetti.

"Saved your fucking life," Tuna said, clapping Artie on the shoulder.

"Forever indebted," Artie said. "But then I already was." Artie gave a smile, then a huge grin. Tuna *had* saved his fucking life.

A life that felt smaller without Les. He expected more self-congratulation from Tuna, but Tuna was silent, didn't seem anxious to cash in, claim his reward. They walked through the Embarcadero, out onto a large grassy enclosure in front of one of the buildings. In the distance was the Ferry Building and the Bay Bridge. Traffic was flowing smoothly, ships were passing on their way to Oakland.

"You see his face?" Tuna said after they took two seats on a concrete bench. He was running his fingers along his own cheeks. "There was nothing left. Nothing." He continued to rub his face, as though documenting its presence.

"In Vegas you get a bad beat, you think it's the end of the world. But the worst beat doesn't mean squat compared to this." Tuna reached down, pulled out a blade of grass, began sucking on it. "You think he could have been helped. I mean, seen someone professionally." Tuna didn't wait for a response. He shook his head. "Nah, that's a pipe dream. We are what we are." He looked at Artie and laughed. "And what's that, you ask? Well, don't ask me. Because, in this case, *we* are what *we* are."

"'He's the one.' That's what he said. "Not 'I'm the one.' Do you think he was trying to signal Bonetti? Is that why he slipped on the Captain Marvel jacket?"

"You mean as in suicide?"

"A minute earlier he told me that he found Roger dead."

"Roger did himself?" Tuna looked up at Artie. "You're okay, right? I mean, your feet are on solid ground? No funny ideas?"

Artie laughed. "I don't think so. But then, I'm always the last to know." He thought of Copley Square and how he hadn't known there was anything wrong until afterwards.

"And these scans? Do they mean that I want to lose? That I'm programmed to give my money away?"

"Correction. Our money. And no, I don't think so. Like today. You played your hunch like a true champion."

"Yeah?" Tuna shifted to an aw-shucks tone of voice.

"Sorry I mentioned it," Artie said.

"You think so, but you're not sure. It's something you need to test out, right?"

"Tuna."

"I figured out expenses and subtracted them from the ten thousand that Sarah Woolfson left, including hotel and living costs, through today. There's still three thousand, enough for the entrance fee for the tournament plus roundtrip tickets and hotel rooms for you and Welinda. We'll divide the tournament winnings three ways, you and me for being brothers, and Welinda for playing the game that saved our lives." Tuna stood up. "Time to go. See you next week. Bring your lucky charms, shamrocks, four leaf clovers, rabbits' feet. It'll be them versus the genes. Don't you worry. I've got a feeling. . . ."

Artie stood up. The two men hugged, their cheeks tight against each other, Artie imagining Les's empty face and wondering if Tuna was, too.

TWENTY-EIGHT

A rtie took Welinda to dinner at the US Café. "On me, whatever you want," Artie had said, aware that no gift was suitable for the occasion. It should have been a time for rejoicing, but they were both subdued. Artie was exhausted; Welinda kept circling back to her plan, wondering how it might have been improved. She had been so sure that Les would have opted for suicide, but his last-minute signaling with the Captain Marvel jacket could have been intentional or accidental. Not knowing was bad enough; conceding to the possibility of blind luck was a real pisser.

She toyed with her food.

"You took the names off the DMV computer?" Artie asked.

"Tomorrow all fifteen will be ancient history. Pretty shrewd," Welinda said, brightening up, tapping at her temple. "Digital scanning, upscale color photocopying, left-handed letter-writing, telephone numbers and call-forwarding for each of your new brothers." Her expression clouded over. "It's funny. I thought that Les would have checked more of them."

"Disappointed?"

"Only in the money wasted. I hate to see the final bills. I'll bet we'll end up blowing Tuna's tournament buy-in."

"It'd have been money down the drain," Artie said.

"Not down the drain. He's asked me to coach him in tournament play."

"You help him? You don't play cards."

"I've already worked it out. The problem with Tuna's game is neurological."

Artie held up his hand. "Enough already."

"A matter of refocusing on the temporal areas. Controlled aggression, attack and destroy. It's analogous to converting garbage into energy. Silk purse from a sow's ear. Psychiatric alchemy. Janine called the areas on the scan defects. Wrong. Assets. Tuna's programmed, ready to go. We just shift his mental cursor from frontal to temporal."

"Fake out the circuitry? You've been reading too many self-help manuals," Artie said. It was tortured logic, a ridiculous bluff, trying to make your mind believe that it was in control of your brain.

On the other hand, if Tuna could win, anything was possible.

"I can't wait," Welinda said. "We're a shoo-in."

Artie smiled, Welinda's excitement contagious. The tournament would be the ultimate contest—Tuna versus reason. And, as Tuna had told him earlier in the day, "as long as you have a chip and a chair, you're still in the game."

After walking Welinda home, Artie took a late-night stroll around the neighborhood, thinking. If Les had met Tuna first, seen that Tuna was no threat to anyone else's sense of individuality, the others might not have died. But he'd gotten to Ligott first, because Artie had chosen Ligott first, because he was the furthest away, because, he, too, didn't want . . .

If Sarah'd sent the letter to Tuna, they'd have megabuck contracts with the National Institutes of Health, *People* magazine, and *Entertainment Tonight*.

If the letter had gone to Mark Caputo, no one would know, each of them would think that he had the world to himself.

If Les hadn't put on the Captain Marvel jacket.

The following morning Artie woke late. He had only a few minutes before he was to meet Welinda and fly to Las Vegas. He threw
some things in his suitcase, and, despite his hurry, checked his
computer for recent messages on his newsgroup.

```
>Be sure not to include the Narcissus myth in
your story. Don't have the remaining brothers
stare into each other's eyes. It's too corny.

>But that's what they'd do. You've seen them on
the streets, with that sappy self-absorption,
as if no one else in the world existed or mat-
tered.

>More reason not to include it. You'll turn off
your readers.

>Don't try to sum up nature versus nurture. Un-
derscore ambiguity. The very existence of the
controversy provides a social loophole, allows
for hope. DNA speaks for inherent good and evil,
immutability of character. No, we need to be-
lieve in the possibility of change, of moral
enlightenments, epiphanies of the spirit. That's
what we look for in great literature, that's what
we hold out as a goal for ourselves.

>Wrong. If there was definite proof one way or
the other, I'd want to know. The goal of fiction
is to reveal a greater truth.

>Not so. Fiction should provide a sense of moral
worth. In case of conflict, throw out truth.
```

Artie smiled. There was no truth, any more than there were
similarities or differences between them. Innocuous traits or
murderous instincts; he could not say, others should not decide.

Traits weren't facts, weren't specifics. They were gathering devices, attempts to categorize, to satisfy some physiological need for ordering.

There was no point in trying to decide what was unique, what was programmed, what was what.

The computer beeped. Artie checked his email.

```
>Having a blast with the family, relatives up
the wazoo. Enough love to drive you crazy, but
not that kind of love.

I hope you're getting plenty of rest and quiet,
time to get the batteries charged.

2:00 A.M. Thursday. United #2214. Show me you
can be on time.

Janine
```

Artie downloaded Janine's message, went back to his discussion group. His would be the last word.

```
>Thank you for all your input. However, I've
found ten clones to be unmanageable and have
decided to abandon the novel.
```

Before he could turn off the machine, another message appeared.

```
>Hey. We want to know what happened, what's going
to happen. You can't just quit us like that. We
demand an ending.
```

He would have to hurry if he was to catch the flight to Vegas. Artie turned off his machine.

Made in the USA
Lexington, KY
31 October 2012